No Deals,
Mr President

William Gretton

Elabrio

Published by Elabrio Limited

This paperback edition first published in 2022

The author can be found at: williamgretton.author@gmail.com

No Deals, Mr President is a work of fiction. Where named individuals, including actual historical characters, appear in the story, their words and actions are imaginary, and are not intended to represent their personal qualities, attitudes or views. Except where actual historical events are being described, all situations in this narrative are fictitious.

ISBN 978-1-3999-1856-5

For Eleanor

CONTENTS

	Prologue	1
1	Fangy	4
2	Home Truths	12
3	Nancy	18
4	Tom and Edith	27
5	The Big Idea	31
6	John and George	38
7	Fleet Street Calling	45
8	Pincher	49
9	*The Trip*	59
10	The Call	63
11	Miriam	67
12	Running Scared	77
13	Malcolm and Gail	85
14	Gallimore	93
15	Bluffing	98

16	Ted and Nicola	105
17	*Royal Children*	113
18	The Hideaway	121
19	Wallace	129
20	America Beckons	138
21	Simon	145
22	Misadventure	154
23	Kurt	162
24	Brian and Sally	170
25	Newspapers and News	179
26	Warburton	184
27	Consequences	194
28	Elaine	197
29	Confrontation and Conciliation	202

PROLOGUE

Wednesday, 5th September 1962

Reckless oaf wasn't a term Bobby normally applied to foreign statesmen, but then, 'statesman' wasn't a word that readily came to mind when he contemplated Chairman Khrushchev. Nor was authorising the destruction of a Soviet ship the kind of thing Bobby's brother did every day, but this was no ordinary day – not, at least, in the minds of thousands of American city-dwellers, or why the frenzied rush to get away? Never mind the official advice to stay put, 'Cities give better protection from radiation'. No, 'Just cram the kids into the back of the car, honey, and let's get the hell out of here!'

Similar scenes were being enacted across the urban centres of Canada and much of western Europe: frightened citizens jamming the highways in a desperate bid to survive at all costs, even though instant incineration might well be preferable to a lingering death from radiation sickness.

For Bobby Kennedy, the strain of the previous two weeks was all too evident. It was hard to believe that fate had brought him to this moment, this knife-edge confrontation between the superpowers, in which he seemed destined to play a key role. As well as being the President's brother, Bobby was also the Attorney General, and it was he who had summoned the Soviet ambassador to the Justice Department in Washington, to confront him with photographic evidence gathered by US spy planes. Evidence of what Dobrynin's masters in Moscow had been denying for several weeks, that Soviet military engineers and technicians were installing nuclear missiles in Cuba, a mere ninety miles from the American coast – weapons that would threaten every city in the south-eastern United States with destruction. It was in response to this imminent danger that the president had declared a quarantine zone around the island, with orders that no vessel from the communist bloc be permitted to approach Cuba without verification that its cargo was innocuous.

Thus were sown the seeds of a deadly confrontation – and now the day of reckoning had arrived. Earlier that afternoon the president had authorised the navy to intercept a Russian ship that had been about to enter the forbidden zone. As the marines attempted to board the vessel they had been met by a squad of Soviet special forces, resulting in a shoot-out, with fatalities on both sides. Meanwhile the ship had continued on its course toward Cuba, inevitably drawing the wrath of the big guns. An hour later it was lying on the ocean bed, a victim of fire from a US destroyer.

This skirmish, the most serious clash between the superpowers since the start of the Cold War, was on the brink of escalating out of control. Early warning radar stations from the Arctic southwards were scanning the horizon for signs of the approach of Soviet bombers or intercontinental missiles. Thus far, nothing.

Bobby rose to his feet and began pacing the floor of the president's office.

'Remember your own impression when you met Khrushchev face to face?' he said. 'You suggested that a nuclear exchange would kill seventy million in the first ten minutes, and the reckless oaf didn't seem to give a damn.'

He knew that his brother's desire had been to avoid, at almost all costs, a war that would be catastrophic for mankind. In dealing with the Soviet leader the president's policy had always been to leave the door open to a dignified climbdown that could be represented as honourable rather than needlessly humiliating. He'd been careful to avoid backing his opponent into a corner where the only face-saving option would be to resort to the ultimate act of violent madness, and even at this late stage neither of the brothers wanted to believe that Khrushchev was a fool.

'And now we've sunk one of their ships, for God's sake!' Bobby continued – but even as he spoke, the ticker-tape machine chattered into action again with a message that raised the tension yet further.

ONE OF OUR DESTROYERS ATTACKED.

ON FIRE AND LISTING. PLANES FROM THE
ESSEX SCRAMBLED. WILL BE OVER STRICKEN
VESSEL IN 15 MINUTES.

Bobby hardly had time to digest this new information before he heard
footsteps. It was the Defence Secretary, Robert McNamara, entering
the office with further news from the nearby Cabinet Room, where a
select group representing the upper echelons of American power were
monitoring all available sources of tactical intelligence. They included
the Secretary of State, the Director of the CIA, the Joint Chiefs of
Staff, and last – and probably least – Vice President Lyndon B
Johnson. A grim picture was beginning to emerge, and it fell to the
Defence Secretary to inform the Commander-in-Chief.

'We have convincing evidence that a Russian submarine has been
shadowing the supply convoy and was the likely source of the
torpedo. Planes from the *Essex* have located the sub, and it's still close
enough to the surface to be destroyed.'

'Another step nearer to full-scale war,' Bobby muttered.

'May I suggest that the time has come to abandon this place?'
There was no mistaking the tension in McNamara's voice. 'The
helicopters are standing by, Mr President. I urge you to give the order
to evacuate.'

Bobby caught his brother's eye.

'Time to get out, Jack,' he said.

'Very well. Let's go.'

Bobby looked down on the capital. It was late afternoon, and a gentle
breeze was playing on a thousand sunlit trees. Soon the White House
would be lost from sight. A few citizens were still scurrying along the
streets, some glancing up at the helicopter, perhaps guessing what its
mission signified.

As the pilot accelerated away, an image of ground zero at
Hiroshima intruded into Bobby's consciousness. Devastation caused
by a mere squib compared with today's weapons. Is this how
civilisation ends – the scorching flash, the mushroom cloud, the
deadly radiation? Surely there was still a chance to avert the ultimate
catastrophe. Or had that point already been passed?

3

CHAPTER 1: Fangy

Nothing that morning could have been more shocking than the sight of my own face. Even before I glimpsed it in the mirror, I'd sensed that something was amiss. That uneasy feeling began before I was fully awake. There was something odd about the light. In my room the window was to the right of the bed, but with eyelids barely half-open I was aware of a glow – undeniably daylight – filtering in from my left. Had I been so restless in the night as to completely turn around? No, I was lying normally between the sheets, with my head on the pillow. The problem was the room itself. Not only was the window in the wrong place, it was a different shape: a wide bay, in contrast to my own tiny window. Even the bed was different – single, rather than the double bed into which I'd collapsed a few hours earlier. Had some prankster moved me to another room while I slept? Surely not! Not without drugging me first.

Wide-eyed at last, I was confronted with a baffling scene. This was a place I thought I recognised. I'd been here before, long ago. Unless I was profoundly mistaken, this was the bedroom I'd occupied as a teenager half a century earlier – my own room in a bungalow on the outskirts of Nottingham, looking as though it had hardly changed since the 1960s. The objects surrounding me were simultaneously strange yet hauntingly familiar. Tired pieces of furniture dating from before the Second World War: a bookcase that had seen better days, a stool that had once been a chair, a wardrobe that wouldn't have looked out of place on the Ark; and in the window, a dressing table with three tall mirrors, the outer ones hinged in such a way that a curious child could discover a mysterious tunnel of reflections. Was it conceivable that someone had preserved that room in its precise state for almost fifty years? Or could it have been recreated as part of a cunning hoax? And if so, how had I ended up here?

Still fresh in my mind were the events of the previous evening. It had been a reasonably enjoyable occasion, saying a final goodbye to colleagues from the chemical works. And not a week too soon! I would have quit the job years ago if the pension had been half-decent, but I'd waited until the eve of my birthday in 2010 to make the final break. Admittedly, I'd let Eric Mayfield from Payroll ply me with a little too much alcohol, but he'd made sure I was safely in the taxi – that much I could remember – and once home I'd fallen asleep as soon as my head met the pillow, in that dubiously blissful state that comes from being sixty-six and newly retired. But now, what was I to make of this place where I'd awoken, this room stuffed with relics of a long-forgotten age?

My eyes focused on the nearest object, only inches away on the bedside table, an almost perfect replica of the short-wave radio my uncle had given me after it had 'fallen off a lorry' when I was twelve. Back then, in the late 1950s, I'd spent many an hour scanning the world's stations: *Radio Moscow, Radio Free Europe, Voice of America* – the whole cacophony of the airwaves – but now, as I stared at the yellow dial, the thing seemed to glare back at me with more than a hint of menace.

What the hell was I doing here? I slapped my cheek. Then again, harder, hoping to wake from this ridiculous dream, but to no avail. Leaving the comfort of the bedclothes, I reached over and cautiously parted the thin curtains. Was this room in the original house, or had it been rebuilt somewhere else – in a museum, perhaps? I peered out in disbelief. I *was* in my old home, and to my astonishment the road outside appeared exactly as it would have been in the late fifties or early sixties. I could see cars belonging to that era: a Ford Consul, an Austin A30, a Renault Dauphine, and most incredibly of all, a Morris Oxford Estate, of exactly the type my father once drove, parked on the driveway. Instinctively I let the curtain fall from my hand and moved smartly back from the window, as if fearing someone out there might see me. Turning to get back into bed, I caught sight of myself in one of those old mirrors. Only a fleeting glimpse, it nevertheless had the punch of a high voltage electric shock. Thrown off-balance I landed on the bed, where slowly I summoned up the courage to take a second, longer look. I hadn't been mistaken. To my utter horror I was staring at my own *teenage* face. No moment of my existence before or since has been more traumatic. The image was definitely mine, but where had the wrinkles gone? My complexion was suddenly more youthful, my eyes brighter, the mousey-brown hair thick and abundant in contrast to my familiar silky baldness. What had begun minutes earlier as mild puzzlement was rapidly turning to terror. My whole frame stiffened, as if frozen in fear, and when at length I persuaded my body to move, the flexing of muscles revealed another devastating detail. Not only did I look like a teenager, I *felt* like one. My body was lighter, movement easier, and to complete the illusion – if that's what it was – my vision was clearer than it had been for decades. It didn't matter that I couldn't find my spectacles; I didn't need them any more.

A fearful cry began to form in my throat, but I strangled the thing before it could escape. Panic was barely a breath away. What would I find if I opened the door into the hallway? Would the rest of the house appear just as it had been in the 1960s? And, heaven forbid, if I crept over to my parents' room, would I find them there, younger than I was now? Impossible!

Heart pounding, I peered around the curtain again. Nothing out there was moving. The roads and pavements were deserted. Could it be that I was the sole inhabitant of this strange world? Had I died in the night and entered the afterlife? If so, this was hardly heaven. Retreating from the window once more, I reached for something to steady myself, and felt my hand come to rest on the polished wooden cabinet of the radio. Suppose I was to turn it on, would I hear anything? If I could pick up broadcasts at all, it would at least prove that I wasn't alone in the world. So, with the volume control turned to minimum, I switched on, waited half a minute for the beast to warm up, then cautiously increased the sound. As luck would have it the receiver, with its array of glowing valves, was tuned to the BBC Overseas Service, where a man's voice was announcing '*06:00 hours Greenwich Mean Time*'. With summer time in force, that would make it 7 a.m. in England. Then, '*Here is the news for today, Sunday the third of June*'. But which year? He didn't say.

A feeling of urgency seized me. I had a horror of some malevolent torturer bursting into the room at any moment to inflict dire torment on an innocent victim. Or even my mother or father peering around the door! Of course, I knew they couldn't be there.

6

For one thing, my father had been dead for over forty years. But just in case, through some weird distortion of reality, they or their ghosts actually were in the house, I had to make myself scarce. On the stool was an untidy heap of clothes, such as those a teenage boy might discard last thing at night. A quaint assortment: a white vest, a creased but formal-looking shirt, trousers that were a little too tight, a woollen necktie and a hand-knitted cardigan. It would be the most contemptible gear I'd worn in decades, but it was all I had at that moment, so I began to get dressed. The finishing touch was to pull on some slightly smelly socks and slip my feet into a pair of grubby leather shoes.

Hardly daring to breathe, I opened the bedroom door and tiptoed the few feet across the silent hallway to the kitchen, where I encountered yet another scene of eerie familiarity. The square wooden table in the middle of the tiled floor, the stainless steel sink under the window, the coal stove in the left-hand corner – and on the opposite side of the room, my target, the back door.

Inching forward, I happened to glance to my left and spotted something on the wall. A calendar! A *1962* calendar, open at the month of June. So I now had a precise, if implausible, date: Sunday, the third of June, 1962, which would have been my eighteenth birthday. But what was I doing here? And where had 2010 gone? The urge to flee the place was overwhelming. I unlocked the back door and slipped out into the fresh air, which was chilly despite the sunshine. Could this really be June, in England? Wrapping my arms around me to ward off the cold, I tiptoed down the steep concrete driveway and onto the pavement below. The bungalow was in a smart but modest residential area, on a short through-road with other properties disappearing up the gentle slope to my right. There was still no one to be seen. The world was empty.

I could have headed either way, but chose to turn right, toward open country. Furtive glances over my shoulder revealed no twitch of curtains at any of the windows, and with my quickening pace the bungalow was soon out of sight, lost among countless other properties. I was an interloper in a strange but almost familiar world, a fugitive from reality, terrified yet intrigued by the ease with which my rejuvenated legs propelled me to the brow of the hill, from which I could see ahead to the row of small shops at the next junction, and the green fields beyond. I began to formulate a plan. I would head up into those fields and find somewhere to hide away and think. It was a plan that lasted all of ten seconds before colliding with a new reality. Although thus far I hadn't seen a soul, passing the last few houses I came face to face with a young chap emerging from one of the driveways.

'Hi, Roger! What brings you out at this hour on a Sunday?'

What? He knows my name!

'You look scared witless. Seen a ghost or something?'

'Er…'

I should know this guy, I thought. He must have been one of my classmates at school. Could I remember his name? Just about.

'Hi, Fangy,' I spluttered. A slight but perceptible grimace betrayed his feelings about the use of that epithet. 'At this hour? I could ask you the same.'

He swung his shoulder bag into full view. *Guardian Journal* proclaimed the large black letters.

'Eighteen, and still doing a paper round?'

'Why not?' he said. 'I only do it at weekends, and it rakes in a few extra bob to spend on football tickets. Anyway, this morning's round was an unusually short one, so I'm heading back to the shop. Want to come with me?'

No, I didn't. I wanted to be alone. To think. But I found myself tagging along behind him. Before we left the newsagent's he grabbed a couple of Crunchie bars.

'Here, have this. You look as though you need it.' Then, 'Okay, Roger, you still haven't told me what you're doing.'

'I needed to get away from—'

'Are you in trouble with your dad?'

'Why do you ask?'

'Man, it's obvious you're a nervous wreck. How about coming back to my place?'

'Thanks, but I'd rather head up the fields for a while.'

'Okay, I'll come with you.'

I wanted to say, 'Get lost!' but the words wouldn't come out, and a minute later we were bounding up the path behind the shops, eventually stopping at a fence that marked the boundary of British

Railways' land, from where we stared down at the shiny rails emerging from the tunnel to our right.

'Remember when we were eleven or twelve?' Fangy said. 'A gang of us used to meet up here to watch the trains go by. They were all steam locos in those days, but now they're mainly diesels. Hardly worth the effort! Remember how you would hop over the fence and put an ear to the rail? You could hear a train coming from half a mile away.'

'No! Well…perhaps…I'm not sure. I certainly wouldn't put my head on a railway line now.'

'Ah, but back then,' he enthused, 'we were experimenters. We'd put things on the line and watch them get flattened under the train wheels. Pennies would end up wafer-thin, like chocolate wrappers. Someone – I think it was you, Roger – even dared to put a six-inch nail on the track. It came out looking like a fish knife. You can't have forgotten, it was only six or seven years ago.'

Had I really done things like that? Maybe. But then, as he was speaking, Fangy's real name came back to me. It was Paul Barton. Poor lad, he couldn't help growing up with protruding teeth, and kids of eleven can be cruel when it comes to nicknames. But now, at least, a dental brace was slowly putting things right. Unfortunately it wasn't doing anything for his rounded shoulders.

'Anyway, Paul, it may be seven years to you, but to me it feels more like fifty.'

'Good grief! You are in a state. What's the word for it? Insomnia?'

'I think you mean amnesia.'

'If you say so, but how can you not tell the difference between seven years and fifty?'

'I'm not sure. Life's become very confusing all of a sudden. I hardly know where I am this morning.'

'Sounds like a bad hangover to me. How much did you have to drink last night?'

'*Last night?*' I said, '…last night feels like a different world.'

'Join the club! That's exactly how I felt when I got thoroughly sloshed for the first time. No wonder your dad threw you out this morning!'

I wanted to scream. None of this was helping, and what he said next only made things worse.

'So, Roger, if you've sobered up by eleven, how about joining me and the other lads for a game of footy in the park? It might help to clear your head.'

I kicked the fence. 'But it's Sunday, Paul. My parents will be expecting me to go to church.'

'Well for once, matey, sod the church and come out for a game. I know you're not much of a footballer, but we could use you on the right wing.'

'I'll see what I can do, but I warn you, it could be World War Three at home if I don't go with them.'

'Hey, man, lighten up. Remember what fun times we had back then, before we left school and the cares of the world landed on our shoulders?'

I wanted to tell him I'd just retired, and hence those cares had already been lifted from *my* shoulders, but was interrupted by the sound of a three-unit diesel train emerging from the tunnel. Automatically we turned to wave at the passengers as it sped by.

'That's it, Roger! Just like old times – except for the lack of steam. Remember how we used to perch on the fence and wave to the men in the cab, imagining that one day we'd be engine drivers, too?'

'I don't know about you, but I reckon by the time I was eleven I'd grown out of wanting to be a train driver.'

'So, what are you into now? Have you got a girlfriend?'

'I don't think so. Why do you ask?'

'You don't think so? Surely you must know if you've got one!'

'As I said, I'm a bit confused this morning. And in any case, what time is it?'

He glanced at his watch. 'Half past eight.'

'Crikey, Paul! My parents will be up by now. They'll be frantic. I need to leg it home right away.'

Running down the field as fast as my legs would propel me – and it did seem remarkably fast – I could hear his voice yelling after me.

'Don't forget, Roger. Eleven o'clock!'

Did I really believe what I'd just said? That my mum and dad might actually be around? After my encounter with Paul – the real flesh-and-blood Fangy – I had to face up to the possibility that I might soon be meeting them. How would that go? A sixty-six year-old man encountering his fifty year-old parents? No way! Yet it seemed that I had only two options. To remain terrified out of my wits, or try to go along with the illusion, and merge into this world of '62 as best I could. Assuming that a teenager, presumably identical to me, had gone to bed in that bungalow the previous evening, and I'd awoken to replace him, what might the consequences be? For starters, an old mind was now inhabiting this young body. Wouldn't it be blindingly obvious that I'd changed?

If my parents really were down there in the bungalow, they'd be up and about by now. My dad would have discovered the unlocked door on his trip to the back yard to get coal for the stove, and would have searched the house and garden, baffled by my absence. *My* absence? Someone's absence. If this truly was 1962, might there be another Roger Parnham lurking in the neighbourhood? Might I even come face-to-face with myself?

For a brief moment I was tempted to make a run for it. Flee to some distant place where I could assume a new identity until this mess had sorted itself out. But no, it was as if an invisible hand was drawing me back toward that bungalow. I would have to face whatever – whoever – was there. Try to be myself. But which self?

CHAPTER 2: Home Truths

I would hardly call my childhood normal. My parents didn't do 'normal'. They were devoutly – some would say, fanatically – religious. A whole spectrum of activities was frowned upon as *worldly*. Going to the cinema was worldly, dancing was worldly, alcoholic beverages were worldly. All were strictly forbidden. Even higher standards were set for avoiding worldliness on Sundays. On the Sabbath they wouldn't permit the TV or the 'wireless' to be turned on – not even for broadcasts that most people would have regarded as essential, such as Neville Chamberlain's declaration of war in 1939, or news of the Great Storm of 1953, when the North Sea breached coastal defences and surged inland, drowning hundreds of people on that January night. My parents owned a caravan on the Lincolnshire coast, and the whole camp was destroyed, but because it happened on a Saturday evening they knew nothing about it until the Monday morning. News bulletins were too worldly to be allowed to fall on saintly ears on the Sabbath. As for slinking off to a football match on a Sunday, that would be tantamount to supporting the devil's squad.

Plenty of people were up and about as I hurried back along the road. An old guy weeding his garden looked up and waved as if he knew me. I returned the gesture, but kept running until I was at the bottom of the concrete drive. Then it was up to the back door, which I pushed open just widely enough to see into the kitchen beyond.

'Where in heaven's name have you been?'

Sitting at the square table in the middle of the room was a woman wearing a cream cardigan over a summer dress, tea cup in hand. Her permed auburn hair glinted in the sunlight reflecting off the stainless sink. Even though she had her back to me, I knew who she was. The prospect of seeing her face was almost too terrifying, too bizarre to contemplate. I wanted to turn and run, but something seemed to be anchoring my feet to the floor. In a nightmarish moment she turned to look at me.

'Your dad is out searching for you. I can't imagine what he'll say when he gets back!'

For a few seconds I was struck dumb, which had the effect of making me appear guilty. Of what, I wasn't sure.

'Well, what have you got to say for yourself?'

Still panting from the homeward sprint, I forced myself to speak, in a strained sort of way.

'Sorry...Mum...I needed some fresh air. It...it's a brilliant morning.'

'Huh, that's a first. And fancy leaving the back door open! Anyone could have walked in.'

Again I was speechless. What do you say when you encounter your mother and realise she's sixteen years younger than you are?

'You were meeting someone, weren't you?'

'No.' There was an awkward pause. She didn't believe me.

'Was it that girl from the florist's? I told you she was up to no good.'

'No, Mum, I wasn't meeting anyone.' She still didn't believe me.

'Well, actually, I did meet Fangy, but that was purely by accident.'

'Who?'

'Fangy. You remember Fangy. He was always round at our place a few years ago.'

'Ah, you mean that lad Paul,' she said. 'And why was *he* up so early, if it wasn't to meet you?'

'He was doing his paper round.'

'Another bad influence! Why was he working on the Sabbath?'

'Because people want their papers delivered.'

'Why do they need newspapers on a Sunday? We don't have one.'

I was about to say, 'No, but you do have one on a Monday, and that's only possible because there are people working on Sunday to produce it,' but was interrupted by the sound of footsteps behind me. My father was back. Slowly I turned to look at him, instinctively avoiding eye contact, which would have been unbearable.

'So, there you are!' he said. 'Is this your idea of a joke?'

He was far too close for comfort, so I backed off, almost stumbling over the final step into the kitchen. Encountering him was even more surreal than meeting my mother, for he'd died suddenly when I was twenty, meaning that he had just two more years to live. Maybe I ought to warn him.

'You're lucky I didn't call the police.'

Finding my voice again, I summoned up a sliver of self-confidence. 'Come off it, Dad. An eighteen-year-old going for a stroll on a summer morning is hardly likely to be treated as a case of child abduction.'

I was struck afresh by his good looks. He was only five-foot-seven, and had lost most of his hair, but he still had a handsome face, much more symmetrical than mine.

'Don't try to be clever with me,' he said. 'What were you doing out there?'

'Nothing, apart from walking.'

'Who were you meeting?'

'Mum's just asked me that! Nobody.'

The stress of interrogation was beginning to get to me, and sensing a sneeze coming on, I reached for my handkerchief. Unfortunately the Crunchie bar wrapper came out of my pocket at the same time and fluttered awkwardly to the floor. My father seized on it as evidence of wrongdoing.

'Have you been to the shop – on a *Sunday?*'

Fearing the row might get out of hand, Mum intervened.

'Anyway, son, happy birthday! I've put your cards on the mantelpiece in the lounge. Now, sit down and have some breakfast. What would you like? Some toast? A cuppa?'

My dad took his customary seat and glared at me across the table. 'You may be eighteen,' he said, 'but don't forget you're still under my wing until you're twenty-one.'

Mum opened the stove door and held a slice of bread on a toasting fork in front of the glowing coals. 'It's not just that you wandered off without telling us. There's something different about you. You sound – how shall I put it – *posh?*'

Posh? Me? That was a laugh! Then it dawned. The source of her bafflement was indeed the language thing. Back in 1962 my mates and I had spoken in more-or-less broad Nottingham accents, but over the years, as I'd moved up the social and professional ladder, I'd amended my speech, almost unconsciously, to sound more refined – one might even say, *erudite*, but that would be a slight exaggeration. So, even if I'd appeared normal in every other respect, the way I was speaking would betray the fact that something odd had happened. My speech was suddenly more precise, my accent more standardised, than that of a typical Nottingham youngster.

'Er...' I stumbled, 'I've thought for some time that I ought to improve my diction, and I've decided now is the time to start.'

'Then you must have been having secret lessons,' Mum insisted. 'Changes like that don't happen overnight.'

Actually, overnight was precisely when it had happened.

'Well...I'm self-taught...yes, that's it. I've taken note of how the radio announcers speak and I'm trying to imitate them.'

Did that sound convincing? I didn't suppose so, but it was the best I could come up with at short notice. BBC English was the gold standard in 1962.

By now I'd reached the point of daring to make eye-contact with both of them, but wasn't yet comfortable to linger in their presence, so after a quick breakfast I excused myself under the pretext of 'going to tidy my room', which brought a flicker of a smile to my mother's otherwise troubled face. In solitude once more, I reflected on how, considering the circumstances – the utterly outrageous circumstances – I was remarkably calm, calmer than I had any right to be. Perhaps that's the effect that fresh toast has on people, but by now I was beginning to think that I might be able to survive this crazy situation, provided it didn't last too long.

But what if I was stuck here all week? Or even longer? There could be countless pitfalls ahead. What commitments might my former self have made? Perhaps I had a vital appointment, with the dentist, say, or a driving lesson, or a job interview – or something even worse. Tricky situations could be lurking around every corner. If only I could find a diary – 'my' diary!

With the time fast approaching ten o'clock, I could anticipate what would happen next, and sure enough, it did. My mother put her head around the door.

'You'd better get ready. We'll be leaving for church in a few minutes.'

I took a deep breath, uttered my prepared response, and awaited the inevitable reaction.

'I'm not going to church today.'

'What?'

I could imagine her shock. Never before had I resisted the imperative to fulfil this religious duty. Illness alone was a valid excuse for non-attendance. Now, at age eighteen, here was the first evidence that I might have a mind of my own. It was more than my mother could cope with alone, so she called on my dad for support.

'Roger says he's not coming to church.'

He joined her in the doorway. 'Come on,' he insisted, 'we're going!'

But I was in the business of treating him to a new experience: having to take 'no' for an answer. He tried to reason with me for five more minutes, building up to threats of hell and damnation, not to mention the devil and all his works.

'Dad, I'm eighteen today. You'll have to let me take responsibility for my actions.'

'Alright,' Mum said, 'have it your own way. We'll be back at twelve. The roast is in the oven.'

'Ah, wait,' I said. 'There's something else you need to know. Paul has invited me round to his place for lunch.' I was lying, of course, but I could hardly tell them I was going to play football.

'Just the sort of thing I feared,' said my father. 'Associating with *worldlings* on the Sabbath. They'll lead you even further astray!' And with that he stormed out, my mother following and tut-tutting in his wake.

Once they'd gone my priority was to find a half-decent set of clothes to replace the ones that had been cast off the night before. Rifling through the drawers I discovered a reasonably cool tee-shirt and what looked like a brand-new sweater. Then it was into the wardrobe for some trousers, but lying there in the bottom I spotted something of greater significance: a crash helmet. Of course! I'd had my own motorbike in 1962. Why not use it to get to the park? A quick game of football would be an opportunity to test out my new, youthful fitness. And hanging in the wardrobe was the motorcyclist's other essential, a leather jacket. I'd soon be on my way! Yet I couldn't help noticing one more oddity about the room. As I rummaged through the furniture I kept sensing a strange sweet taste, even though there was not so much as a grain of sugar to be seen anywhere. What could that be?

By the time I'd tried on at least four pairs of trousers, and still couldn't decide which would suit me best, it was almost eleven o'clock. Fangy would be waiting. I knew where to find the bike: it was kept in the back of the garage. I'd need to get the hang of riding the thing again after almost five decades behind the wheel of a car, but it was only a small machine, a 150cc James Cadet, so I'd give it my best shot. The next problem was to find the blasted keys. If I couldn't start it up, I'd be stuck. After five minutes of frantic searching, I remembered. The bike had no key to the ignition. In fact, it had no security features whatsoever. Anyone could release the stand, kick-start the engine, and ride it away. Who, I thought, would have bought a machine like that in 2010? Even the petrol tank wasn't secure. The filler cap was a mere plastic plug that could be removed with a simple pull. Yet, in the three years I'd owned the bike in the sixties, it had never once been stolen or vandalised.

The engine roared into life at the first kick, and I was soon gliding down the driveway and onto the road below – only to jump off and run back to the house, having overlooked the main purpose of my excursion. Dashing inside I grabbed some football gear, and by the time I set off again it was well after eleven. Fangy would have given up on me.

CHAPTER 3: Nancy

'The buggers haven't turned up!'

Fangy cut a forlorn figure, leaning against one of the goal posts. Now in football shirt and shorts, he looked even skinnier than he had when wrapped up against the 7 a.m. chill.

'Are you sure you've come to the right park?'

'Of course I am,' he said. 'They're taking the mickey. Sometimes I can sense them laughing behind my back.'

The optimism of early morning had deserted him. I wasn't altogether surprised, for like me he lacked the physique to be a footballer. In fact, neither of us was built for contact sports, although I would take strong exception to being called a weed. As for Fangy, he was more daisy than dandelion, but that didn't seem to stop him fancying himself as an Arsenal centre-forward.

'You could try again next Sunday.'

'*Next* Sunday? The only important match next Sunday will be England versus Brazil in the World Cup!'

'What, is it the final?'

'Don't pretend you don't know, Roger. It's the quarter-final.'

'And let me guess, Brazil are favourites to knock us out.'

'Unfortunately, yes.'

'Well, if it's any consolation, I can tell you now that England will actually win the Cup in four years' time.'

'Whaaat?'

'You heard. England will win the World Cup in 1966.'

'That's the daftest thing I've heard in ages. If you don't mind me saying so, Roger, you're behaving very strangely today. It's got to be more than just a hangover. How can you pretend to know the outcome of the *next* World Cup?'

'Hmm…it's complicated. I know this sounds bonkers, but it's as if I've already seen the future; or perhaps, already *lived in* it.'

'Really? You can't have lived in the future, because the future hasn't happened yet.'

What came out of my mouth next was as surprising to me as it was to him.

'But…what if there's a parallel universe…where the future has already happened?'

He flung his arms into the air. 'What's that sound I hear, Roger? It's the men in white coats coming to take you away!'

I wasn't amused. 'Listen, Paul. I used to regard you as my best friend, so you could try to be a bit more sympathetic.'

'Sympathy? Is that what you want? Alright, mate, I'll give you a chance. You reckon you've seen the future, so let's test it out. Tell me what's going to happen tomorrow.'

'I can't remember every single day! Can you? But I tell you what, I'll make a prediction about next winter. It's going to be the most severe in living memory, the coldest in Britain for two hundred years. Much of the country will be brought to a standstill by arctic conditions.'

'But we'll have to wait at least six months to check that one out. Can't you predict something nearer than that?'

'Sorry, that's the best I can do.'

I paused and looked down at my feet. 'But there is something that's bothering me. My dad is going to die in two years' time, and there doesn't seem to be anything I can do about it.'

'Die? Of what?'

'A heart attack.'

'Oh dear, Roger, do you really believe that?'

'I'm afraid so.'

'Look, mate, it's doing you no good, this obsessing about the future. You'll drive yourself mad. I mean, what possible sense does it make?'

'Sense?' I said, propping up the other goal post. 'I don't know. Hang on a moment while I try to figure it out.'

He looked at me with the sort of sympathy he might have had for a junky who couldn't quite decide to kick the habit.

'Okay, I'll give you two minutes.'

I thought hard for thirty seconds. 'Right, here goes. Here's my best hunch. Are you ready?'

Fangy was rolling his eyes.

'It seems to me that the universe split into two identical copies on the third of June, 1962 – that's this morning, in case you've forgotten. One of the copies is the one we're living in now, while in the other I lived on into the future – until 2010, to be precise – when I would have been sixty-six. But then, for some reason I haven't yet fathomed, my consciousness got transferred to *this* universe in such a way that I can still remember my life in the other one.'

'Blimey, Roger, you must be off your head! You expect me to believe that crap?'

'Not really. Why should you? I admit, it's totally weird. But I'll tell you something else that's almost as strange. After the initial shock of waking, I seem to be unreasonably calm about the whole thing. Something very odd must be happening in my brain. I've started to think it's quite nice being eighteen again instead of sixty-six. I can do so many things that old age robbed me of. There are adventures to be had, money to be made, girls to be chased…but there *is* something urgent that's bothering me. What will I do tomorrow?'

'Tomorrow? Go to work as usual, of course. You did have a job, didn't you? See, you've got *me* talking bunkum now! You *have got* a job, *haven't* you?'

'Yes, but where?'

'Well – if you don't mind me playing along with your little fantasy – can't you remember where you worked in 1962?'

'In general, yes. I was an apprentice at a chemical firm.'

'Then it's simple. Go there!'

'It's not as straightforward as that. We apprentices were moved around to different departments every few months, and those places are scattered all over Nottingham. I could be at any one of them.'

'Can't help you there, Roger. If you don't remember where you were on Friday – just two days ago – what hope have you got?' He reached for his kitbag. 'Anyway, I'm not hanging around here any longer. I'm getting hungry. Let's go to the pub.'

'Eek, Paul! If my dad finds out I've been anywhere near a public house, he'll go ballistic! Any association with the demon drink will only confirm what he already suspects, that the devil has kidnapped my soul.'

Fangy was grinning.

'Oh, is that expression around in 1962? *Go ballistic?*'

'I've never heard it,' he said, 'but come on, there's a nice pub just half a mile down the road, where the landlord turns a blind eye to teenagers drinking. How about giving me a lift on your pillion?'

'But you haven't got a helmet. What if the police see us?'

'You worry too much, mate. Come on, start the engine.'

At the pub we both tucked into pie and chips, for which, despite intense feelings of guilt, I was, in the words of the grace that my father said before every meal, *truly thankful* – having had only one slice of toast and a Crunchie bar for breakfast. As Fangy sipped his beer, I my cider, our conversation got round to a profoundly philosophical issue. Girls.

'Remember this morning you asked if I had a girlfriend?'

'Sure,' he said. 'So, are you about to confess to something?'

'Not exactly, but let me put it this way. Can you remember the first girl you fell in love with?'

'Me? I've fancied plenty of girls, but wouldn't say I've actually ever been "in love". Have you?'

'Oh, yes. Desperately.'

He smirked. 'Go on, tell me about it.'

'Well – if you don't mind listening to a tale of woe – there's this church where my parents go, and I, of course, have to go with them. I was taken there before I could even walk. By the time I was eleven they let me to go to a kids' games evening every Thursday in the church hall. It was my first taste of freedom, and I relished it, but nature had set a cruel trap for me. After totally ignoring the opposite sex for years, I was at an age when they were just beginning to register on my hormonal radar, and there was this girl, Nancy, only four months younger than me, who grabbed my imagination like no other. Soon I was obsessing over her as "the most beautiful girl in the world". She was good looking, but to me it had gone beyond mere looks. I would call it being *in love* – and there was I, no older than twelve.'

'Soppy you, Roger.' He grinned behind his drink. 'And how did it turn out?'

'Abysmally. I was far too shy to tell her how I felt. I didn't know how I could possibly approach her with words like, "I love you", but Thursday evenings had now become the highlight of my existence, each week hoping that Nancy would notice me. Yet nothing ever seemed to happen. After a year of this torment I plucked up enough courage to disclose my feelings to her friend, Rose, who promised to pass them on to Nancy. There followed a week of suspense until the next games evening. What would Nancy's response be?'

'Was it what you were hoping for?'

'Not exactly. Immediately on seeing me she spat out the word "pig!" in my direction.'

'You poor sod! I guess that was the end of it.'

'It should have been, but hope died a slow death. Those longings hung around for several more years, but I knew deep down it was a lost cause. Eventually, when we were fifteen, Nancy drifted away and I never saw her again. With the benefit of hindsight I know I was on to a loser from the start. Girls of twelve are normally attracted to lads two or three years older than themselves. And look at me: I've always been a skinny youth. There would be plenty of meatier hunks around to attract Nancy when she was ready for romance. Then there were my parents. You're not going to believe this, Paul, but they're so fanatical about religion, anything normal teenagers might do, like going to the flicks, or the theatre or – heaven forbid – dancing, are banned. I stood no chance with a *normal* girl.'

'Why are you telling me this?'

'Well, I've started thinking about Nancy again. Suddenly I'm back in 1962, when she'd be seventeen-coming-on-eighteen. There's a reasonable chance she's still living locally, barely three miles from here.'

'You're not hankering after her again, are you, after all you've told me?'

'Sort of. She was such a big thing in my life in the fifties, it's only natural to—'

'Get stung again?'

'No. I'm just curious. It would be interesting to see her once more after all these years.'

'All these years? To bring you back to reality, Roger, you mean after *three* years. This talk of having lived into the next century is for the birds, isn't it?'

'No! Can't you see the evidence? Even you have to admit that something has changed. We were at the local secondary modern together until I moved up to technical school when I was thirteen, but we never lost touch completely. We'd sometimes bump into each other around the local streets, and at least once a season happen to meet at a Forest match, and share a bag of crisps at half-time. Yet now, all-of-a-sudden, I sound different, don't I? How do you account for that?'

'It's simple. You went to a posher school, and that's why you talk posh. It doesn't prove anything about time-travel.'

He polished off the last of his chips and pushed the plate to one side. 'Anyway, it's obvious what your problem is. You've never got over being rejected by that girl. Be honest: that's what's behind all this fantasising about the future, isn't it? You've invented an imaginary world because you can't cope with the real one.'

'Thanks, Paul. You really know how to make a guy feel great.'

'I'm only trying to help you, mate. Just face the facts. You've absolutely no hope of getting anywhere with her now.'

'I'm not intending to "get anywhere". I'm just curious to see what it was that captivated me as a kid.'

'I don't believe you. You still fancy her, don't you?'

'I wouldn't say that – but I would like to set eyes on her again, for one more time. In fact, that's precisely what I'm going to do right now: ride over to where she lived.'

'With what aim?'

'To find out if she's still there. Nothing more.'

'Then someone ought to warn her there's a nutter on his way.'

'Huh, very funny.'

I got up from the table and grabbed my helmet.

'Just leave it to me. I know how to handle women. I've had fifty years' more experience than you.'

He laughed. 'There you go again. Mad as someone who thinks

England can win the World Cup in four years' time!'

He put his feet up on the chair I'd just vacated. 'Anyway, good luck with the old love-life, Roger! Let me know how you get on…'

I think I heard the word 'sucker', uttered under his breath.

The ride from the pub to the suburb where Nancy lived took less than ten minutes, and it was just before two o'clock when I got my first glimpse, in fifty years, of the street where she'd lived with her parents and younger sister. I was sure the house was on the right-hand side, but it could have been any one of a dozen or more properties. Knocking on doors on the off-chance was out of the question. The best I could do would be to hover for a while in the hope of catching sight of her, so I selected a spot where I could maintain a low profile between parked cars, and still astride the Cadet, I waited. What were the chances of Nancy turning up just when I happened to be there? And if she did appear, would I dare to approach her? Would I be able to impress her in a way that I'd failed to do before? I reckoned it was worth one try.

After a fruitless half-hour I decided this was no way to spend a Sunday afternoon, and began to move off in the direction of home; but, passing one of the houses, I glimpsed someone coming out of the front door – a young woman if I wasn't mistaken. I braked hard and skidded to a halt. Glancing over my shoulder I could see she was now on the pavement, heading away from me, but something about her profile made me feel sure that this was indeed Nancy. I turned around and accelerated toward her, this time braking more gently as I drew level.

'Hello, Nancy!'

She didn't recognise me. I was in motorcycling gear, and she hadn't seen me for three years. She eyed me warily as I turned off the engine and began to remove my helmet.

'Hi! It's me…Roger.'

A few awkward seconds passed before her puzzled look dissolved.

'Blimey! I've haven't seen you for ages,' she said. 'What are you doing here?'

I looked her up and down. She was now nearer eighteen than fifteen, and with a mature figure was more alluring than ever. And her face? With the benefit of an extra fifty years' experience, I'd no longer rate her as 'the prettiest girl in the world' – yet she was still as magnetic to me as she'd been when we were both twelve.

'I was looking for you.'

'Really? What for?'

This was the difficult bit. What could I say? 'Would you reconsider going out with me?' Lord, no!

'I'd like a chat.'

'About what?'

'Oh, you know, things.'

'No, I don't know, and I'm not sure I want to—'

'But Nancy, you'd be amazed at some of the things I could tell you.'

'I've no time to talk now. I'm on my way to my boyfriend's place.'

Why did that not surprise me?

'Could we arrange some other time? Just a few minutes to chat. Please, Nancy.'

'I'm sorry, but you've picked a bad moment. You can see I'm in a hurry.'

She turned to walk away. I decided to have one more try.

'What about' – I thought quickly – 'tomorrow evening?'

'I don't see the point.'

'You wouldn't regret it. I mean – *seriously*.'

'Oh, alright, if you insist. Come round about half-past seven. My parents will be out, but Debbie should be around.'

'Thanks, Nancy. I'll see you tomorrow, then.'

'Just for a quick chat, though. Nothing more.'

I nodded. 'That's all I want.'

Riding away, I reflected on how my new identity as a teenager – hormones and all – was taking over my mind as well as my body. It had to be more than mere curiosity, or even nostalgia, that was driving my desire to get involved with Nancy. Now that I'd set eyes on her again a kind of restlessness was brewing, and I wasn't sure whether to be exhilarated or ashamed. Perhaps I was stoking up unnecessary trouble for myself, but having started, I had to see my obsession through to its logical conclusion. It was Nancy or nothing.

Yet I had to be realistic. How likely was it that she'd give up her boyfriend for me? And even if she did, what sort of life could I expect? It was one thing to fall for a pretty face when you're a kid, quite another to get on with someone in adult life. Perhaps I needed to pursue her one more time, if only to get her out of my system, so at our next meeting I would pull out all the stops to impress her. I was a skinny youth with not much going for me in the looks department, but I now had the sophistication of an older man. Surely, I could turn on the charm with a seventeen-year-old. And if all else failed, I could bowl her over with my superhuman knowledge!

But for now, however reluctantly, it was back home to my parents.

CHAPTER 4: Tom and Edith

A curious scene greeted me when I arrived at the bungalow. My parents were pacing around the car and gesticulating wildly as I chugged up the driveway. Some sort of panic was in full swing.

'Don't you know it's quarter to four!' yelled my mother. 'Where have you been all this time? We've been waiting for you. We'll be late.'

I looked at her blankly as I shut off the motorcycle engine and wheeled the machine toward the garage.

'And don't look so gormless! We told you about it yesterday. Your dad is preaching at Bottom Chapel tonight. Put that bike away and get into the car. Quickly now!'

I scrambled into the rear seat of the Morris Oxford and my father drove off at speed, while Mum continued the dressing-down.

'Tom and Edith are looking forward to meeting you, so they've invited us for tea. They always have it at four o'clock sharp. It'll be nearly half past when we get there. What will they be thinking?'

I barely knew what she was talking about. 'Why is it called Bottom Chapel?'

'Because it's at the bottom end of the village, of course. Weren't you listening yesterday?'

'How long will the service last?'

'No more than an hour.'

'And let me guess the average age of the congregation. Fifty or sixty?'

'More like seventy or eighty.'

'Huh! Even worse than I thought. I can picture it now. Dead boring, with some old biddy playing the harmonium at the tempo of a funeral dirge on a wet Wednesday afternoon—'

My father reacted angrily. 'That's very disrespectful, lad. I don't know what's come over you today.'

Mum intervened in her usual conciliatory way. 'Actually, Roger, you don't have to go to the service. You could stay in the cottage and keep Tom company.'

'Why? Isn't he going, this Tom?'

'No, he's disabled, mentally as well as physically. He came back from the Great War with shell-shock. He suffered horribly in the trenches, and for over forty years he's been unable to work. His mind is shattered. He just tends his garden and does simple tasks around the house.'

So, a reasonable deal was on offer. Dodge the service to keep the old geezer entertained.

'Alright, I'll stay with Tom. If I'd known about this in advance, I'd have brought my tape recorder with me to provide some amusement. I bet he hasn't heard his own voice before.'

'That wouldn't be any good,' my father said. 'The cottage doesn't have electricity.'

'What, no electric power? How far is this place from Nottingham?'

'Ten miles, give or take.'

'A house as close to the city as that, and it has no electricity? In 1962? You're kidding.'

'No. There's a whole row of cottages near the chapel that have never been connected.'

'That's astonishing! What happens when it gets dark?'

'There's an oil lamp hanging over the living room table. They lower it on a chain, light it, then hoist it up again.'

'So, that's the living room. What about the rest of the house?'

'They use candles.'

'This I must see! It sounds positively Dickensian. More like 1862!'

We were soon there. Near the far end of the village the car turned off the main road into a bumpy lane, with a row of old cottages on the left, and their gardens on the right behind a low brick wall. Tom and Edith's front door opened directly into the living room, which also served as the kitchen, with a stone sink under the small front window. Cooking had to be done on the iron fireplace to the right of the small circular table, and even on a warm afternoon there was a coal fire burning in the grate, presumably to provide hot water and boil the kettle. Our hosts must have been in their late seventies. He sat by the fire and made limited conversation while his wife, pockmark-faced with neck sinews that stood out like tree roots on a street corner, busied herself serving our tea, coping stoically with the thirty-minute delay to her normal schedule. The table was spread with ham, cheese and pickles, together with home-grown tomatoes, lettuce and crusty white bread, to be followed later by Edith's home-made cake – a special one, apparently, for my birthday. Oh, and my pet hate: canned apricots.

I watched as my father spread thick layers of butter onto his bread, and laid into copious amounts of ham. I decided now was the time to warn him of what was around the corner.

'Dad, I fear you're in danger. You've got to change your diet, and quickly.'

'What for?'

'I bet you've got high blood pressure. It could kill you within a couple of years.'

'Your nonsense gets worse by the hour. I've never heard such drivel!'

I needed to be firm with my warning, so decided to get it off my chest in one powerful rant.

'Dad, you're heading for a heart attack, and I'll tell you why. You're addicted to animal fat. I know what you had for dinner today, even though I wasn't there, because you have it every Sunday. Big slices of roast beef in thick fatty gravy. Then in the morning Mum will pack you off to work with bread and dripping left over from today's meat. And just look at you now, tucking into that ham like there's no tomorrow. You're a cholesterol nightmare!'

He flew into a rage.

'Get out! How dare you embarrass me like a spoilt brat in front of our hosts? Out! Go on, *now!*'

I slunk across to the door and down the stone steps before coming to rest leaning on the car. I could hear my father apologising to Edith – something about his son getting into bad company. I knew my mother would play her usual mediatory role, and within minutes she came out to persuade me to return to the table – where, thankfully, I'd just missed the apricot course.

My father said no more. Twenty to six soon came, and he, Mum and Edith went off to the little chapel, leaving me with old Tom. Rocking to and fro in his armchair and staring blankly into the distance, he couldn't make much in the way of conversation, leaving me to my own thoughts, which had begun to focus on the approaching night. For the first time since finishing that toasty breakfast I was starting to feel uneasy about the prospect of going to bed again, dreading the thought of falling asleep without knowing where I would wake up tomorrow. How many possible versions of the universe could there be? Might there be worse ones?

Dad's lips were buttoned as we drove home, but my mother tried to make small talk from time to time, complaining that I'd yet to open my birthday cards.

'They're still in their envelopes on the mantelpiece. It's not like you, Roger. You're usually keen to find out if there's any money inside.' When I didn't respond she turned to me in exasperation. 'You really need to get a grip on yourself, and fast. Is there anything else you need reminding of?'

'Well, Mum, actually there is. Could you tell me where I'm working tomorrow? Like, which department?'

'Good heavens, son! You're in a bad way if you can't remember that. You were there only the day before yesterday.'

'Strange to say, it seems to have slipped my memory.'

'I know you're only kidding,' she said, 'I guess it's your way of saying how much you hate the place. You've been complaining for the past month about the state of the saccharin factory.'

The saccharin factory! That explains the sweet taste in my bedroom. Saccharin is five hundred times sweeter than sugar, and it gets everywhere when you work in a factory full of the stuff. But my heart sank to the soles of my feet at the prospect of having to return to that dump-of-a-place in just a few hours' time. Perhaps I was already in the worst possible universe.

CHAPTER 5: The Big Idea

The saccharin factory looked old and run-down, which it was. The corroded window frames, the crumbling brickwork, the stench of acid fumes – it was as if I'd never left the place. A motley gang of men provided the labour, under the supervision of a works' manager and three foremen. Arriving with ten minutes to spare, I quickly reacquainted myself with the layout of the site, found the changing room without difficulty, and even identified my own locker within which, as expected, were my boots, goggles and boiler suit.

It wasn't necessary to say much to the other guys as I arrived. Just a quick, 'Morning!' The day workers were drifting in, while the night shift were having their showers before going home. I donned my overall and made my way to the tea room, where the men sat reading newspapers – the *Daily Mirror* and *Daily Sketch* being the most popular – their elbows resting on the long table in the middle. Their manner of speech was all too predictable, consisting mainly of expletives. The f-word was used liberally, apparently to mark the spaces between other words, while the air was thick with tobacco smoke.

At eight o'clock a siren sounded. I reported to the foreman, Stan, a small, affable bloke, five-foot-three in his brown smock, with deep-set, almost sad, eyes. Luckily for him he did have a life outside of this hell-hole. He was a trombone-player in his spare time, but the name of the band escaped me.

'There's some granulatin' to be done today,' he said.

Granulating, I recalled, involved feeding chunks of raw saccharin into a machine that broke it down into small grains. There was only one job worse than granulating, and that was 'kekking', in which the solid was fed into a high-speed mill – a Kek mill – that smashed it to a fine powder. Dust flew everywhere, and the operator was soon covered from head to foot in the white stuff, with its oppressively sweet taste. To make things worse, the mill shrieked intolerably loudly. A granulator was quiet by comparison.

'Look, do me a favour,' I said, 'and show me which batch needs granulating', hoping that Stan would take me to the machine, because, after forty-eight years, I'd forgotten exactly where it was.

He glanced at me wearily. 'Follow me, lad.' We headed up a flight of rusty iron steps. 'All that stuff needs to be done this mornin',' he said, pointing to a row of wooden casks before ambling away.

For several hours I fed the hungry machine with that ludicrously sweet solid. *What an existence*, I thought, secretly thankful to be working alone, where my posh accent wouldn't be exposed to ridicule. The monotony of granulating provided me with space to reflect on my lot. The bedside alarm had woken me at six forty-five, at which moment I wasn't sure whether to be dismayed or relieved to find that I was still in 1962. At least I wasn't somewhere even worse, and being eighteen rather than sixty-six did have its advantages, such as the prospect of meeting Nancy again. Absurd though it might have seemed, I couldn't take my mind off her, and spent hours planning what I'd say that evening. It would be tricky, and by mid-morning I'd formulated at least three different approaches, none of which sounded totally convincing. So busy was I in mind and body that by ten-twenty, the official break time, I'd finished granulating the entire batch.

I had a thorough wash, grabbed the sandwiches Mum had packed, and sat at the long table to eat them. The filling hardly mattered; in this place any type of sandwich tasted of saccharin. Out of the corner of my eye I snatched glimpses of the next man's newspaper, trying to get some idea of what was happening in the world. One event the papers certainly weren't reporting was the departure from Rotterdam, that very week, of a certain Lee Harvey Oswald, on a ship bound for America.

When the tea break was over I reported back to Stan. 'I've finished that batch.'

'What, already, duck?'

Duck is a common term of familiarity in Nottingham. Anyone, male or female, of whatever age, might be addressed as 'duck'.

'Right,' he said, 'for the rest of the day you're kekkin'.'

'Thanks, Stan. Thanks very much.'

One day in that God-forsaken factory was more than enough to convince me that if my arrival in 1962 was going to turn into a permanent affair, I must escape this wretched job as soon as I could. Surely I had a more important role to play in the world than shovelling artificial sweetener into the mouths of snarling machines.

Five o'clock eventually came, and I can only guess how many speed limits I broke on the journey home. By the time my father arrived from work I'd already finished my dinner, and the risk of another bust-up around the table was averted. Then it was a quick visit to the bathroom to smarten up before donning the least hideous clothes I could find for my date with Nancy. Shortly after seven I was ready to embark on what I imagined might be the most important mission of my life.

'Just popping out to see a friend,' were my words as I hurried toward the garage.

Apprehensive rather than excited, I rode once more in the direction of Nancy's home. Would she see me as promised? What if her parents were there, how would I face them? And what about her younger sister? I needed to speak with Nancy in private. The front door was already beginning to open as I walked up the short path.

'You can come in, but five minutes is the limit, ten at the outside,' she said, before leading me into the cramped but deserted living room. There was no friendly invitation to sit down.

'Debbie's up in her room. So, what do you want?'

'Just a brief chat.'

Even as I spoke, it occurred to me that there was something slightly indecent about a sixty-six year-old man trying to chat up a girl of seventeen.

'About what?'

I launched into my prepared speech. 'You may remember, when we were twelve or thirteen, I was very fond of you.'

'No, I don't recall that.'

'You know, I sent a message via Rose, saying that I loved you.'

'Nope.'

She couldn't recall what was to her a trivial incident, a total non-event. Back then, she'd seemed everything to me, whereas I'd meant absolutely nothing to her.

'So, what are you trying to say?'

My next words were formulated with great care.

'Since you were important to me then, I want to tell you about something amazing that's happened to me now.'

'Go on.'

'What would you think if I were to say that I can see into the future – in amazing detail?'

'Why? Is that the sort of thing you're intending to say?'

'Well, actually, yes.'

'I think you should leave now.'

'Wait, Nancy, please hear me out. When I woke up yesterday it was if I'd already lived to be an old man, and seen incredible things that had happened right up to the year 2000 and beyond.'

'You're bloody weird!'

'I know it sounds strange, but I'm serious.'

'Very well then, weirdo! David and I are getting engaged next month. How about predicting the date of our wedding?'

This wasn't turning out quite as I'd hoped. I was hearing things I'd have preferred not to, and what I said next didn't sound at all convincing.

'No, I can't, Nancy. I don't know the date of your wedding because I wasn't there to see it.'

'What the hell do you mean, Dumbo? Of course you weren't there. It hasn't happened yet!'

'But believe me, I *have* seen lots of future events,' I said, a note of desperation creeping into my voice.

'Go on then, tell me about something. Tell me about *anything* – anything important that's going to happen.'

This was the part I hadn't rehearsed at all well. I cast around for something that might grab Nancy's attention. I knew she liked rock music and had been a Presley fan. Right! I'd dazzle her with some predictions from the pop world.

'How about this? Next year a new rock sensation will explode onto the scene. They'll be big, perhaps even bigger than Elvis.'

'Really? No chance!'

'Just wait, Nancy. They'll bring a new kind of sound to the rock world. You'll love it!'

She wasn't impressed.

'And they'll be called, the Stones.'

'Stones? Are you serious?'

'Er – I mean *Rolling* Stones.'

'That's even worse!'

'Mark my words, Nancy. In the next few years you'll remember what I've said, and realise I was right, that I really can see the future.'

I decided to push my luck a little further by predicting the title of their first big hit. Was it *Satisfaction,* or did they have one before that? I was straining to remember, when an astounding thought hit me. It was an idea that I grasped whole, in an instant, like pure magic. I could remember loads of songs that had been hits in the sixties, seventies, eighties and nineties. I could recall the tunes, and at least a smattering of the lyrics. Just imagine, if I could write these songs, ahead of the times when they were originally composed, I could make a fortune! I didn't need to have been a pop enthusiast to be able to remember enough material to keep me going as a songwriter for years, and in most cases there was no rush; the songs hadn't existed until long after 1962. It was such a brilliant idea that I was ready to impress Nancy right away.

'And there's something else you ought to know. I'm going to be a songwriter. Many of my numbers will be international hits. Within a few years I'll be a millionaire. Wouldn't you like to share this future with me?'

'Get lost!'

By now I hardly cared what she said. I was gripped more by the implications of my amazing idea than by any designs on Nancy.

'And I wouldn't marry you if you were the last man in the loony-bin!'

'That's fine,' I said, my voice descending to a calmer tone. 'Look, it's been great to meet you again, and I hope you have a terrific future with the guy you marry. I trust I haven't wasted too much of your time this evening, and if you think I'm mad, just be patient for a year or two. I'm sure you'll look back on today with more than a little amusement, and be glad you met me again.'

Was she impressed? Heaven knows.

'You're certainly an oddball,' were her final words as I departed, and I guess she had a point.

Heading away, I was confident I'd never see her again. It had been an interesting experience, but I was almost glad she'd turned me down. It would take more than schoolboy infatuation to produce a worthwhile relationship, and I was now engrossed in other thoughts: the prospect of becoming a successful songwriter, almost effortlessly.

It wasn't quite half-past eight when I arrived home, so I went straight to the lounge and opened the lid of my mother's piano. Which tune to try first? The strains of *Love Is All Around* came to mind. It had been a big hit on its revival in the nineties, but was originally in the charts in 1967. Presumably it hadn't been composed as early as '62, so this could be my first song! Using one finger I started to find the notes, and switched key until the pitch sounded right, but soon realised it wasn't going to be as straightforward as I'd hoped. I could string the notes together for the first couple of lines of the melody, but how would I blend in an accompaniment? Then there was the tempo. How many beats to a bar? And the harmonies? I had to face the fact that I had next to no skill in writing music. Either I'd have to get some training before I could even begin to compose my first song or, better still, team up with someone who *did* have musical expertise. Yes! That was the answer. It would mean sharing the royalties, but the potential to compose more songs – quickly – would outweigh any disadvantage. Fame and fortune would await us! Hopefully.

I'd been tinkering on the piano keys for half an hour when my mother came into the room.

'What's that you're playing?'

'Oh, nothing, Mum.'

But it was what she said next that jolted me back to life's grim realities.

'It's your college day tomorrow. Would you like sandwiches for lunch?'

Alas, song-writing fame was, for the present, a mere pipe dream. I remained a cog in the industrial machine. What I needed was some sort of breakthrough, but wasn't sure how it would come about. Yet my encounter with Fangy had turned up a clue. I'd told him that I could predict the severity of the coming winter. Knowledge like that ought to be vital to the authorities. How about a role as a planning adviser? I reckoned I could forecast most of the major trends for the next forty years. But where to start? Perhaps I should approach a national newspaper. Surely I could astound any journalist with my insights. I might even be able to intervene in some of the wider issues that were looming in that one year of 1962 – a staggering thought. In some cases it wasn't merely important to tell the world, it was urgent! But would my meddling make things better, or worse? The implications were awesome.

CHAPTER 6: John and George

I parked my motorcycle by the college wall. The lads were gathering in the yard, some of them having a quick smoke before classes began. One by one I recognised them, and could even remember some of their names: Derek, Phil, Tony, Keith, Rob, Jagdish and Stuart.

Tony, who sported the most spectacular teenage acne north of the Trent, soon began haranguing me.

'It's time you got a bigger bike, Roger. Something with guts, like a 500cc job.'

'Why should I? This one serves me well.'

'But it's crap,' he insisted. 'What's your top speed?'

'About fifty-five.'

'Say no more. I rest my case. It's crap.'

'That's your opinion. As far as I'm concerned, a James Cadet is ideal.'

He stared at me curiously. 'You alright?'

'Fine.'

'That's not how you sound to me. Got a plum in your gob?'

Derek joined in. 'That's right, Roger, who are you trying to impress? You're talking like a bloody gaffer!'

Laughter broke out amongst the other lads who were overhearing our conversation.

Stuart glanced at his watch. 'Come on, you lot,' he said. 'It's almost nine o'clock. Old Rocky will be expecting us.'

Tuesday was our college day. The company provided day-release for its apprentices, in the hope that we'd pick up some useful qualifications, as we'd all left school without any. For me it was a welcome skive from the saccharin factory.

Mr Rockley was our physics lecturer, and today's lesson was about energy. After an hour's dictation – a classic case of information travelling from the teacher's notes to the students' notes without passing through the minds of either – Rockley seemed to get bored with his own existence and decided to lighten up the proceedings.

'Okay, lads, think about this. You all came here this morning on vehicles powered by petrol or diesel, some on motorbikes, others on the bus. I don't suppose any of you own a car, do you?'

On a wage of five pounds a week? You must be joking!

'Well, let's have some ideas about the transport of the future. How might we be using energy in twenty or thirty years' time?'

I could hardly believe my luck. Here was a chance to impress him with my incredible foresight.

'By 2010 people will be able to travel here by tram.'

'Did you say tram, Parnham? *Tram?* Good grief, lad, Nottingham got rid of those before the war. I'm talking about the future, not the past. Can you imagine anyone laying tram lines through the city streets again? Never! It's old technology. Haven't you got any better ideas than that?'

'Well, I could have a shot at predicting something that will happen in less than ten years, if you like.'

'Go ahead. Let's see if you can do better this time.'

'Do you mind if I write something on the blackboard?'

'Be my guest.' He grabbed the board rubber and cleared some space for my contribution. I wrote two words side-by-side:

CONCORD   CONCORDE

'What's this about?'

'Britain and France are going to build a supersonic airliner,' I said. 'They'll announce plans this autumn, and it'll be flying within ten years. It's just that our engineers will spell its name the English way, while *they* insist on spelling it the French way, with an 'e' on the end. And you know what? Before the thing flies, we'll have to agree to the French spelling, or they'll throw their toys out of the pram!'

Rockley wasn't sure where this was going. 'This lesson is about different types of energy, lad, not politics. Can't you think of something more original than trams and planes?'

'Windmills!'

39

'For crying out loud, Parnham! We're trying to imagine *future* power sources, not ancient ones. Why not tell us something about nuclear power?'

'No, windmills.'

'This is getting worse by the minute!' he boomed, his rich baritone voice now resonating like a well-tuned kettle drum. 'What about bloody windmills, then?'

'Fifty years from now they'll be sprouting up all over the place. Across the countryside, out at sea, even on city buildings.'

Sensing that Mr Rockley was trying to stifle a chuckle, the rest of the class joined him in a burst of laughter.

'This lesson isn't about the Middle Ages, Parnham. The human race has moved on a bit since it relied on windmills and water wheels.'

But now I was on a roll. I tossed half a dozen more predictions into the mix, developments I was sure would happen, yet these fared no better. The lesson came close to dissolving into chaos, something Rockley hadn't bargained for when he'd posed his original question, and he looked relieved when break time arrived and the rest of the lads shot off to the canteen. But I lingered.

'What is it, Parnham?'

'Sir, I think you were more impressed with what I had to say than you were prepared to let on.'

'Well, yes. I'd put you down as an original thinker, albeit a highly eccentric one.'

'And you've heard a mere smattering of my ideas. Don't you think I'm wasting my time, dragging sacks of chemicals around in the sludge?'

'Probably.'

'So, here's something I could do instead. Suppose I was to write a newspaper column about the technologies of the future?'

'Phew! A chemical worker is a far cry from a scientific journalist, and there's one big obstacle to changing your career. You're an *indentured* apprentice, tied to your employer for five years, with more than three still to go. There'd be legal complications if you tried to quit your apprenticeship early.'

He scratched his sideburn and gazed out of the window for a few seconds. 'But I tell you what, Parnham, a friend of mine is a reporter for the *Evening Post*. He specialises in scientific matters. I could mention this weird apprentice with way-out ideas. He's always on the lookout for original stuff. He may just be interested.'

'Oh, if you would!'

'Don't get too excited, lad. Does your home have a telephone?'

'Yes.'

'Then note down the number for me. I'll phone George this evening, and if he's interested he can contact you directly.'

A small flash of hope, but a significant one. The legal bit was daunting, but perhaps I could find a way around that.

By mid-afternoon I was bored out of my mind. Not that it was the fault of the teaching staff. I could answer their questions before they asked them, and in most cases fancied I knew more about their subjects than they did. After that, the ride home was a slow one. There'd been an accident on the ring road, and most of the town was snarled up with traffic. It was nearly half past six when I arrived. Mum was looking anxious, but it wasn't my lateness that was bothering her.

'Your dad hardly ate anything for his dinner, so there's plenty left for you.'

He was still sitting at the kitchen table. Taking the seat opposite I began to tuck into my meal, all the while sensing that something was wrong.

'What's up, Dad?'

'One of my mates dropped dead at work today. He was only forty-nine.'

'Any idea why?'

'People were saying it was a heart attack.'

I carried on eating, anticipating what might come next. It did.

'I've been thinking over what you said on Sunday, about me.'

'Well, Dad, I might have been exaggerating a bit when I said you've only two years to live' – I certainly wasn't – 'but the good news is that you can do something about it, right now. In fact, two things.'

'Go on.'

'First, your diet. Have much less meat – especially the fatty kind you're so fond of – eat more fresh vegetables, especially raw salad and fruit, and have as much fish as you like, but poached or grilled, not fried.'

'And second?'

'See the doctor right away. Get him to check your blood pressure, and if he prescribes pills to bring it down, take them.'

He didn't argue. Today he was willing to listen to my advice without a murmur of protest. A big improvement on Sunday's fracas.

Later that evening the telephone rang. Mum answered it. 'Roger, it's for you.'

I almost snatched the receiver from her hand. If the call was what I thought it was, it was mighty quick.

'Hello. It's George Lang from the *Evening Post*. John Rockley gave me your number. Is it convenient to chat?'

Yes, it was very convenient.

'John tells me you have some interesting thoughts about future technology.'

'What? He absolutely ridiculed them in class.'

George chuckled. 'You don't need to take everything he says seriously.' Then, 'How about coming to meet me at the newspaper offices tomorrow evening? Will five thirty be okay?'

'Sure, that's ideal.'

'Good. You'll have half an hour to enlighten me.'

Hmm…thirty minutes to impress this guy with a selection of ideas from the following forty-eight years. Quite a challenge.

Wednesday at the saccharin factory was as dire as any other day. The works' manager, known affectionately – or not – as The Chief Idiot, sat in his office, chain-smoking his way through the day's invoices – or, more likely, racing tips. The foreman, with or without trombone, was his usual melancholic self. The Kek mill screamed, the dust flew, acid fumes continued to corrode the steelwork – not to mention the operatives' lungs – and the men gathered around the long wooden table at break time to munch their sandwiches, tell dirty jokes, and curse the government.

When five o'clock eventually came I took off at speed for the headquarters of the *Evening Post* in Foreman Street, there to be met by George, a forty-something provincial journalist in a tired-looking grey suit and cheap plastic-rimmed spectacles. As he was ushering me into a cramped office, the all-pervasive sound was one that I'd almost forgotten: the 'tap-tap' of typewriters.

'John Rockley has told me a bit about you,' he said, stroking the dark stubble on his cheek. 'As it happens, I'm preparing a column on *New Technology in Everyday Life*. I could do with some fresh ideas.'

'Then how about this? Today your offices are dominated by typewriters, but well before the close of the century they'll all be gone. They'll be museum pieces.'

'What? We'll be back to handwriting everything?'

'No, it will all be done with computers.'

'Computers to do typing?'

'Effectively, yes. And much more than that.'

'Well, pardon me if I sound sceptical, but a few weeks ago I went to an exhibition that featured the latest computer from a company called IBM. Great lumbering thing, it would more than fill my kitchen. How many of those could you fit inside a newspaper office?'

'I'm telling you, by the mid-nineties there'll be one on every desk, each more powerful than today's largest. In fact, within fifty years a man will be able to walk around with a computer in his pocket, more powerful than all of today's machines put together.'

I must have sounded as if I knew what I was talking about, because George had gone quiet, allowing me to push my luck a little further.

'And your office will change in other ways. For instance, your photographers won't need film in their cameras, the pictures will be captured electronically. And they won't need a dark room, the images will be processed in computers. And then there's music. It'll be created and stored in computers, and—'

'Okay, Roger, slow down. For my column I need something more, shall we say, *homely*. Something your average Nottingham reader will latch on to. You might do better taking your ideas to an electronics magazine.'

'But there's something else. I'd like to dabble in political stuff as well.'

'That's definitely not my field, I'm afraid, but it's doubtless an interesting combination, technology and politics. You'll need a national paper for that.'

He then came out with something totally unexpected. Perhaps he

43

just wanted to be rid of me quickly, but he said, 'I tell you what, I have a contact on the staff of the *Daily Express*. He just might, and I stress *might,* be interested in talking to you.'

I was on the edge of my seat. 'That would be great!'

'Okay, keep calm. I'm going to speak to a chap called Andrew Barnet.'

He reached for the telephone and dialled. After half a minute of silence he put the receiver down. 'No reply at the moment, but I'll keep trying. Then I'll call you at home.'

'I know what he needs,' I said, 'an answer machine. Something else a computer could do.'

CHAPTER 7: Fleet Street Calling

Those saccharin days dragged on. Wednesday, Thursday, Friday passed, and still there was no call from George. With Saturday came the relief of not having to wallow in chemicals for a whole weekend. I rather enjoyed the lie-in, and it could have lasted until midday for all I cared, but was brought to an abrupt end by my mother.

'Your friend Paul is here. He wants to know if you're available.'

Twenty minutes later I was 'available'. After a wash, a mug of tea and three Weetabix, I joined Fangy outside, where he'd been banished along with all other purveyors of Sunday newspapers. At least he hadn't taken the hump and wandered off.

'Thought you might like a stroll, Roger.'

'No football?'

'Not today.'

'Okay. Let's head up the fields again.'

Soon we were perched for one final time on the fence overlooking the railway tracks.

'Just like the old days,' I said, 'when we were kids.'

'That's that sort of thing I wanted to talk to you about. I've been thinking over what you told me last Sunday. You tried to make out that you'd already lived to be an old man in another universe, and had just landed back here as a teenager. I know you're quite intelligent – even won the school prize for history – so it's got to be an act. It doesn't fool me, and it's unlikely to fool anyone else, but if you persist with it you could get yourself locked up.'

Now it was my eyes that were rolling.

'I mean it, Roger. The men in white coats and all that. So, when are you going to snap out of it?'

I was saved from having to give an immediate reply by the emergence of a particularly long goods train from the tunnel, during

45

which I decided to make one final attempt to convince him.

'Believe me, Paul, I know what's up ahead, and I can't let that knowledge go to waste – for the sake of humanity.'

He laughed. 'Oh dear, mate, you really are deluded.'

'No!' I protested. 'Just give me a chance and I'll prove that you're wrong. I'll show you I really can predict the future.'

'Go on, then, tell me something important that will happen soon.'

'Important? How about this? Next year the president of the United States will be assassinated.'

'You mean Mr Kennedy?'

'Yes. Shot dead.'

'Then why not warn him, so he can avoid the bullet?'

'That's a reasonable idea.'

'But if you did warn him, and he wasn't killed, your prediction that he would be assassinated would turn out to be wrong.'

'Er, yes.'

'So, if what you say is true – and I don't believe for one moment it is – then just by being here you're changing the past, so the future is bound to turn out differently from what you imagined.'

'Ah, very clever, Paul,' I said, at the risk of sounding more sarcastic than was necessary. 'I was wondering when you'd get round to that one. You've hit on the big conundrum of time-travel, and I don't think I have an answer to it yet.'

'So, how sure can you be that England will win the World Cup in 1966? The slightest difference can completely change the outcome of a match. A bad decision by the referee, an off-day for a player, a slight change in wind direction—'

'All true, but I'm still confident of the big things, like the polar freeze that's coming next winter. There's nothing humans can do to prevent that. It's down to massive forces in the atmosphere and oceans that no one can stop. In fact, I reckon I should be on television right now, warning the nation of the perils that lie ahead.'

'Huh. Don't you just fancy yourself?' he said. 'Touring TV studios and talking utter shite.'

'No! More like changing the future for the better. Perhaps even... saving the world.'

His cheeks expanded like a pair of balloons as he battled to contain an explosive laugh.

'So, what about that girl you were going to see? Have you changed *her* future?'

'Nancy? Yes, I reckon I have. She'll never think of me in quite the same way again when the Stones burst onto the scene.'

'Sorry, I don't know what you're talking about. Did you get off with her or not?'

'That'll be a *not.*'

This time he didn't attempt to stifle his mirth. 'Poor Roger!' he laughed. 'I knew from the start you were on a hiding to nowhere, pushing your luck with a girl who never fancied you in the first place. Completely out of your depth. One disaster on top of another!'

'You're wrong, Paul. Totally wrong. I admit it was an awkward encounter, but I've come out of it wiser and more determined, with a new plan to make my mark on history. Just wait. You'll be amazed!'

'There you go again, spouting total crap!'

'I don't have to listen to this,' I said, turning my back, dropping from the fence, and making off toward home.

'Hey, don't take it too seriously, mate.' He scrambled after me. 'We're still buddies, aren't we? How about meeting up again tomorrow, after my paper round?'

'I'm not sure about that,' I said, as we made our way down the path. It wasn't so much that I felt insulted, but more out of fear that he was getting too clingy, as had been the case when we were eleven. I didn't want the responsibility of becoming his special friend all over again.

'Perhaps I'll see you sometime next week,' I muttered, as we parted for the last time.

'A man phoned for you while you were out. Said he'd try again later.'

'Thanks, Mum. I'm not going anywhere for the rest of the day.'

I settled in the lounge with my dad's copy of Friday's *Evening Post* and a bag of peanuts, and waited. It was just after four when George called again.

'I've spoken to Andrew Barnet, and persuaded him to meet you. Do you think you could get yourself to London on Tuesday?'

'Sure.'

'You'll need to make your way to the *Daily Express* offices in Fleet

Street. Ask for Andrew. He's expecting you at eleven.'

But now I was left with a problem: how to take Tuesday off work. Apprentices didn't get much annual leave – mine was six days. Could I get a day off at short notice? I'd need to request it on Monday, but what if it was refused? A glance at the calendar made my heart sink, for I realised there was an even bigger problem. *That* Monday was a public holiday, Whit Monday, so I wouldn't even be at work to make the request. What should I do?

A cunning thought came to mind. Tuesday being college day, would I be reported to the firm if I bunked off lessons? If not, I might just get away with it. Hardly the honourable thing to do, but in some respects I didn't care if I got the sack. So I decided to live dangerously and take an unauthorised day off. Surely Mr Rockley would understand and be supportive. In fact, if I asked him nicely, he might even be willing to forge the register to make it appear as though I'd attended. Wicked thoughts! Where were they coming from?

Next was a quick ride to Nottingham's Victoria Station to enquire about trains to London. The woman on the ticket desk was even able to provide me with a Tube map, so that I could work out how to get to Fleet Street. All feasible by 11 a.m. It was just a matter of scraping together enough cash to get me there and back. A short-term loan from Mum would cover that.

When I returned home she was busy laying the table for a salad tea.

'Your dad's already taking the pills,' she said.

'Pills?'

'The ones the doctor prescribed for blood pressure.'

'Wow! He's taken my advice seriously. Good for him!'

CHAPTER 8: Pincher

That Tuesday morning I sensed the beginning of something big. Travelling to London to meet a journalist at a respected national paper, the prospect of making an impact on the world. If my arrival in 1962 was intended to serve a purpose, this surely was it.

The train drew into Marylebone station just before ten o'clock. With the help of the Tube map I found my way to Fleet Street. Not knowing one end of the street from the other, I'd allowed sufficient time to wander the length of it if necessary, in search of the *Daily Express* premises. But I needn't have worried. The building stood out from its neighbours as something special, even ultra-modern, I thought, unaware that it dated from the 1930s. The interior was almost as striking, its lavish décor adorned with gleaming metal, polished wood and expensive-looking marble. I felt distinctly out of place as cautiously I announced who I was and stated the purpose of my visit. Obediently I sat down and waited for this Barnet fellow to appear.

Eleven o'clock came and went. Then eleven fifteen and eleven twenty. I got the impression that my visit didn't feature very prominently in this guy's list of priorities. Would he forget me altogether? It was almost eleven twenty-five when a man in his mid-thirties, with close-cropped fair hair, a bright red forehead and shirtsleeves rolled up to reveal suntanned arms, came over to where I was sitting.

'Roger Parnham? Hello, I'm Andrew. Sorry to keep you waiting. Let's go somewhere to talk.'

We went up several floors and into a small meeting room. No one else was there, but a pot of fresh coffee stood invitingly on the table.

'Sorry for the delay', he said again, picking at the loose skin peeling from his left ear. 'We're preparing a feature on *Charles de Gaulle,*

Saviour of France.'

'De Gaulle, a saviour?'

'That's right. Five years ago the country was close to civil war. Army rebels from Algeria had taken control of Corsica and were planning to attack Paris from the air and with tanks. Imagine that! De Gaulle was elected president with the promise of saving the nation, and he did.'

'Fair enough. And since we offered him refuge here during the war, I guess he's a friend of Britain.'

'That's debatable. It's true he fled to London in 1940 when the Germans invaded France, and ran a government-in-exile here, but to say he *likes* us is a slight exaggeration. For instance, he'll do anything to keep us out of their club-of-six.'

'Uh?'

'Six countries. They're called the *European Economic Community.* Pincher reckons de Gaulle regards the British as quintessentially non-European.'

'Pincher?'

'Chapman Pincher.'

'*The* Chapman Pincher?'

'Of course.'

The mere mention of that name was electrifying. Pincher, the unrivalled expert on Europe, the Cold War, espionage, the arms race and more. I would have given my back teeth to meet him, not simply to pick his amazing brain, but also to point out a few places where he was wrong. The space race, for example. He was convinced that the Russians would be the winners, and put the odds against an American boot being the first to walk on the moon at something like 5:1. I craved the opportunity to point out that he was mistaken on that score – and more than that, to tell him how and when the Cold War would end. He'd hardly believe it, back in 1962.

'I'd really like to meet him,' I said.

'I'm afraid there's not much chance of that. He's seldom in this building. You don't get to unearth the machinations of world powers by sitting in an office. But that's beside the point, Roger. Why exactly did you want to see me? You've got forty minutes at most. I'm due at a recording studio in Luton later this afternoon.'

'A recording studio? Why? Are you a singer or something?'

'Heavens, no! But I was a sound engineer before I moved into journalism. I thought that was why George Lang referred you to me, because you have specialised knowledge of the latest electronic techniques. Tell me that's true.'

'I'm afraid it isn't.'

'Then I guess you've made a wasted journey. As I say, this evening I'm helping to record a session with a local singer-songwriter, a talent too important to miss. It could result in a best-selling album. Still, it's been nice to meet you,' he added, politely.

My heart sank. Everything I'd invested in that trip was in danger of coming to naught, and to salvage anything from it I'd have to resort to extreme measures. I decided that I was going to have to deploy my secret weapon much earlier than planned. I'd hoped to keep this bombshell in reserve for some later date, avoiding the need to unleash it prematurely, but, with so little time available, it would have to be detonated on the spot. I wondered whether I should let it go as cheaply as this, rather than biding my time in the hope of 'selling' it to a higher bidder. Yet this was, by my good fortune, the *Daily Express,* and if my device could provide an opening to meet Chapman Pincher, it would be worth it. Andrew was just reaching for the door handle to show me out when I pressed the 'fire' button.

'Guess what! A government minister has been having an affair with a teenage show-girl.'

'What?' His jaw fell open, but he hadn't heard everything yet. My missile had a second warhead.

'And a Soviet naval attaché has been having it off with the same girl.'

'You've got to be joking! That's bloody dynamite!' He was loosening his tie and fumbling for a pencil and notebook. 'Is this some sort of ploy to make me look stupid?'

'No, it's absolutely true.'

I knew the affair had broken as public news in 1963, but was pretty sure that most of the action had already taken place by the spring of '62. I reckoned the scandal was out there, waiting to be uncovered by some canny journalist, and I was gifting the story to Andrew. Suddenly the recording session was forgotten.

'Do you know which minister?' he said in an excited whisper, as though someone might be listening outside the door.

How much was I prepared to tell him? I ought to let him find some things out for himself, but maybe I should reveal just a little more, in case he be dismissive of the whole thing.

'It's Jack Profumo,' I said, mocking his whisper.

'Profumo? The War Minister? Sharing a girl with a guy from the Soviet military? Unbelievable! Bloody unbelievable!' Whispering had gone by the board.

'I thought you might be interested.'

'Interested?' he gasped. 'It could bring down the Government.'

'It probably will.'

He stared at me. 'Okay, Roger. Let's have the truth. I don't know where you've picked up this rumour, but it's got to be a hoax.'

'No, as I said, it's one hundred percent genuine.'

He continued to press me. Who was my source? Could they be relied upon? I told him I was deadly serious, and he could take it or leave it, it was up to him. I didn't care. I could easily offer it to another paper. That had him focussed. He wanted to know more. But no, I wasn't going to tell him the girl's name or any further details. He could earn his pay by doing his own nosing around. I wouldn't be presenting him with everything on a plate.

'You haven't told anyone else?'

'No one.'

'Then please don't.'

'I won't tell anyone in the immediate future, but I can't promise to keep it under my hat for ever.'

'Give me at least a couple of weeks.'

'Okay, three at the most,' I said, applying a little more pressure than was necessary, 'but there's something you could do for me in return.'

'Anything.'

'I really would like to meet Chapman Pincher. Could you arrange that?'

'Pincher? As I said, we don't see him very often, but I'll do what I can. Pour yourself another drink.'

He disappeared for a while. The coffee was lukewarm by now. Lulled by the distant sound of typewriters I sank back into the chair, wondering if I should warn Andrew of the dangers of sunburn. The risks of skin cancer were hardly mentioned in the early sixties, a time when many folk still reckoned the link between smoking and cancer was unproven.

When eventually he returned it was with a smile. 'You're in luck. Mr Pincher will be calling in this afternoon. I've asked that an urgent request be passed to him to see you before he leaves. He won't be arriving before two o'clock at the earliest, so you'll have at least an hour to get some lunch.'

'I don't have any money for food,' I said, bending the truth a little. 'I used it all on my fare to get here.'

Andrew reached into his wallet and brought out a five pound note. Then, looking at me wistfully, he slowly produced three more of them. Wow! What sort of people carry cash like that? It was something like a month's pay for an apprentice, and more than enough to cover my expenses for the whole day, even if I included a slap-up meal. Yet I reckoned he was getting the Profumo lead at a knock-down price. What a fortnight or so he was going to have! I didn't suppose his family would be seeing much of him for a while, and as for the recording studio, it would have to play second fiddle to his new obsession. What would it mean for British political life? The scandal would probably explode into the news months ahead of the 'original' timing, with the potential to change the course of history.

'Look, Roger, I'm sorry I can't come to lunch with you. I was due in a meeting half an hour ago. Can't miss it altogether. There are plenty of decent places to eat, but make sure you're back in reception by two, preferably with something to read. You may have a long wait. Oh, and here's my home phone number. Give me a call if you think of anything else. Now, I'll show you down to the lobby.'

I made my way along the busy street in search of a restaurant. True to character, I chose a place that didn't look too expensive. As a chemical worker I'd never had much money, and wasn't going to blow all of Andrew's twenty pounds just for the hell of it.

Eating slowly, I thought through what I would say to Pincher, knowing that this might be my only chance to make an impression on a journalist of his stature. On my way back to the *Express* building I bought a copy of an aeronautics magazine, and by two o'clock was seated once more in the reception area, thumbing through its pages. Among the contents I spotted a brief report of a new altitude record set by an American rocket plane, which had reached a height of over 200,000 feet. The pilot's name: Neil Armstrong.

It was shortly after three when I was approached by a smartly-dressed chap in his late forties, five-foot-ten and almost as handsome as my dad. I'd been expecting someone a little older, but no matter, it was the man himself, and he was willing to give up a little of his valuable time to hear what I had to say. Soon we were alone, facing each other across a desk in a small, cluttered office.

'Well, young man, what is it you wish to see me about?'

Pincher's voice was noticeably different from that of the Londoners I'd encountered since I arrived in the capital. While it had a 'posh' quality, underneath was a faint but distinct northern twang.

'I want to share some insights into the space race and the Cold War.'

'Very well, but be concise. I intend to be on the train in just over an hour.'

Here goes, I thought, and took a deep breath.

'I know you'll disagree with my first point, but I want you to know that the Russians won't win the space race. The first feet to walk on the moon will be American.'

He didn't interrupt me, so I pressed on. 'The Soviets took an early lead because they were already building massive rockets capable of carrying nuclear warheads halfway across the world, but they soon saw the chance to adapt them for launching satellites, and showed that they could put a whole ton into orbit, while the Americans could manage a few pounds at most.'

'Yes, and it scared the shit out of the Yanks,' he said, 'and they're still light-years behind.'

'But I guarantee they'll overtake the Russians, and before this decade is out the race to the moon will have been won. The US economy is more dynamic than its rival, and American capitalism will triumph.'

Pincher smiled faintly, passing a hand across his straight, swept-back hair. 'I don't need a lecture on the power of the free market,' he muttered, rising from his chair in readiness for showing me the door. Pretending to be oblivious to the body language, I persisted with my theme, steering the argument in a direction calculated to straighten that smug face.

'The Americans are going to the moon to prove the superiority of the capitalist system over the communist one, but in all other respects the programme is far ahead of its time. Once the initial flurry is over, no one will even attempt to visit the moon again until well into the next century.'

'What?' he exclaimed. 'Surely you don't need reminding how rapidly air travel progressed once the Wright brothers had shown it was possible. I'm in no doubt that within a few years of the first lunar landing we'll see the start of a permanent base on the moon. Such is the very nature of progress.'

I shook my head. 'You're mistaken. Once the Americans have shown it can be done, that will be the end of manned lunar trips for over fifty years.'

'Nonsense!'

'Alright,' I said, 'let's move on to something else. You know the Americans are getting sucked deeper into Vietnam.'

'Sucked in? Is that what you call it?' Pincher was now back in his seat.

'Yes, and sooner or later they'll face a humiliating defeat, and be forced to withdraw, allowing the communists to take over the whole country.'

He sensed something interesting. 'So, if South Vietnam falls, how much further will communism spread in the Far East?'

'Ah, the domino theory,' I said. 'Is that what you believe? One Asian state after another falling to the Reds? My answer is – not much further. In fact, communism will be in retreat well before the end of the century, and in Europe the Cold War will be over inside thirty years.'

'That's wild speculation, with absolutely no basis in fact!'

'But it will happen.'

'Very well, give me a plausible scenario for the collapse of communism in Europe. You can't, can you? Certainly not in thirty years – well, not without a world war, and that would mean the end of more than just communism.'

I knew it would be unwise to predict a precise re-run of history. The Gdansk shipyards, the Solidarity union – these might be involved, but differences were bound to arise. The election of a Polish pope had been a key step along the way, but the cardinals might make a different choice this time. Even so, I felt that the broad picture would be the same. Communism would crumble away in Russia and its satellite states before the close of the century.

'The collapse in Europe will happen quickly once it starts,' I said. 'You fear Asian dominoes, but I'm talking about a domino effect in the reverse direction, as one East European country after another shakes off the Russian yoke.'

'But all the trends are in the opposite direction, lad. Think of the monstrous wall they've just built around West Berlin...'

By now we'd both lost track of time. I don't know if our discussion lasted twenty minutes, forty, or even sixty, but Pincher's train journey didn't seem to matter any more. I remember at one point telling him that Vietnam would become a trendy holiday destination for western tourists, which brought the retort, 'Your version of the future is absurdly utopian: the Cold War ended, the superpowers at peace. Do you expect me to take you seriously?'

'It's not quite as simple as that,' I said. 'By the start of the next century the West will be preoccupied with a new enemy.'

'Let me guess. China.'

'Well, possibly, but I have a different threat in mind.'

'Namely?'

'That can wait. After all, you've ridiculed most of my ideas.'

'On the contrary,' he said. 'I'm riveted. There's something uncanny about your view of the world, and I say that, even though I think most of your theories are wrong. The point is, they provide imaginative new ways of looking at international affairs, and that's no bad thing. Tell me, have you shared these thoughts with anyone else?'

'No.'

'Then don't. I think a sort of partnership between the two of us would be well worthwhile. I'd like to run a feature about you in the *Express*. Not exactly an interview, more a profile, interwoven with your unique insights. What do you think?'

Inside I was glowing, on the surface I remained matter-of-fact. 'Alright, if you think people would be interested.'

'Interested?' Pincher rose to his feet. 'I'm going to find my editor. I want to run the idea past him. It may take a little while, so I'll have some coffee sent up.'

With that he disappeared. Minutes later a young woman delivered a pot of coffee together with a plate of biscuits. Pincher must have been gone for at least half an hour, for by the time he returned I'd drunk most of the coffee and devoured all but one of the biscuits. There was now an air of excitement about him.

'The editor has given the go-ahead. What I'd like to do is to meet you on your home territory, so to speak, to get a feel for your background. They tell me you're from Nottingham. Suppose I meet you there?'

'Sure. When?'

'How about Saturday? I'll be on my way north to meet up with friends in Sheffield, but I could break my journey at Nottingham for lunch.'

'That's fine by me.'

'Good. And by the way, you'll receive a fee from the paper, on the understanding that you don't share your story with anyone else.'

'That's fine, too. It's the sort of thing I agreed with Andrew.'

'Barnet? What have you told him?'

'Er – nothing. Nothing relevant to our conversation. We talked about something else altogether.'

'Alright, let me have your phone number. I'll contact you on Friday with details of when I'll be arriving. Oh, and it would be good to have a picture of you. Do you mind?'

It was as well that I didn't, for he'd no sooner finished speaking than a photographer arrived. Three flashes from various angles and he was gone.

'Heavens! Look at the time,' Pincher said. 'I really must fly. Are you going home by train?'

'Yes.'

'Which station?'

'Marylebone.'

'You can share my taxi if you like. I'm heading for Paddington, but I can get the driver to drop you off at Marylebone on the way.'

I wasn't saying no to that offer, and as a consequence was boarding my train back to Nottingham before the clock struck six. On the journey home I reviewed my finances. After paying the train fare and having a decent lunch, I still had most of Andrew Barnet's twenty pounds left in my pocket, and in London I'd left behind a couple of chaps who would be eternally grateful to have met me. Not bad for a day's work – much more lucrative than a normal Tuesday. It left me in two minds whether to bother turning up at the saccharin factory the next morning.

CHAPTER 9: *The Trip*

'Do you think there's going to be a war?'

My mother had been shopping in the town, but had made the fateful mistake of lingering in the sunshine of the Old Market Square rather than contenting herself with the delights of Marks and Sparks.

'People are scared, you know. Really scared. Most prefer not to think about it, but that doesn't make the danger go away.'

'You've been listening to the soap-box pundits, haven't you?' I said. 'Nutters to a man.'

The Square was Nottingham's answer to Speakers' Corner, where aspiring orators would hope to attract a willing audience, especially on a summer's day.   Socialists, communists, pacifists, anarchists, freethinkers, Mormons, hot-gospellers – and even normal people – might fancy their chances of drawing a crowd.

'One speaker made the point that a world war is due within the next two years. "Work it out for yourselves," he said. "The Great War started in 1914 and the Second World War in 1939. That's an interval of twenty-five years. Add another twenty-five to 1939 and what do you get?"'

'Hmm,' I said, '1964.'

'Precisely, and you can see it right now, on schedule. The build-up to World War Three.'

'Oh dear, Mum! Take no notice of these ruddy communists.'

'What? This speaker was a member of the Conservative Party!'

'Good grief, what is political discourse coming to these days?'

But she was right. That was the atmosphere of the early 1960s. And the '70s and much of the '80s, come to think of it. No wonder most people didn't invest in pensions. There was a general feeling that the chances of civilisation surviving to see the year 2000 were at best 50:50.

'Don't laugh, Roger. This chap reminded us that last October the Russians detonated a fifty megaton bomb in the Arctic. He said it was over two thousand times more powerful than the one that devastated Hiroshima. Just one bomb, and they've probably got thousands of them. If that's not scary, I don't know what is.'

'You're right, Mum, we do have to face facts. It's no use pretending otherwise.'

'And one trivial mistake somewhere in the world could cause the whole thing to spiral out of control,' she continued. 'No one knows where the next flash-point might be.'

Those words jolted my memory. Ah, yes! I did indeed know exactly where the next flare-up – a really *big* one – would occur, and it would be happening very soon! But I'd be keeping that close to my chest. When the prospects of war or peace rest on a knife edge, it's wise to avoid upsetting the balance. Only a fool would play with matches in a petrol station.

'Now we're on this subject, Mum, there's something you ought to know. I didn't go to college yesterday. I went to London instead.'

'You're kidding, aren't you? What on earth were you doing there?'

'I met a man – two men, actually – and one of them is coming to meet me in town on Saturday.'

'I don't get it. Why?'

'Well, we discussed the sort of stuff you've just been talking about: missiles, bombs, spies, the Russians and so on, and he thinks I've got some interesting ideas.'

'But Roger, bunking off college! Have you gone mad? You could get the sack.'

I could have said, 'That's precisely what I'm hoping for', but there was no point in piling on the angst. Meanwhile there were two more days of saccharin hell to be endured before the weekend.

Pincher phoned, as promised, early on Friday evening.

'I'll be arriving at the Midland Station at eleven twenty-five tomorrow morning. Would you like to meet me there?'

'No problem.'

'Then I suggest we head to a pub for lunch. Any ideas?'

'Well, Mr Pincher, there's *Ye Olde Trip to Jerusalem*, reputed to be

England's oldest inn.'

'That sounds an excellent choice. And, by the way, you can call me Harry.'

The next morning, rather than jumping on my motorbike, I caught the Number Ten bus into the Old Market Square, and from there walked down to the station. Pincher's train was on time, and we were soon enjoying lunch, at his expense, half-in a cave cut into the sandstone rock below Nottingham Castle.

'I know you're only young,' he said, 'but there's something I need to know. Have you had any contact with agents of the state?'

I must have looked bemused.

'I'm talking about the Security Services, MI5 and MI6.'

'No, never.'

'It's just that I'm mystified as to how you could be aware of some of the things you told me on Tuesday, unless you'd had contact with someone in the know. And by that, I mean a person working for our side, or for the other, or both.'

Now I looked baffled.

'Roger, be careful what you might be getting yourself into. Things aren't always what they seem. I'm pretty sure some characters are batting for both sides in this match.'

'Traitors?'

'Double agents. The Cold War isn't just about bombs and missiles. It's about propaganda, subversion and espionage. Take care not to become someone's useful idiot.'

'Is that what I am to you, a useful idiot?'

'No, of course not. Your insights go far beyond the immediate confrontation between East and West. It's as if you've already seen the future, or at least parts of it. In a sense it doesn't matter how wrong you are – and I suspect you *are* wrong on almost everything – it's your originality of thought that's so brilliant.'

'That's very flattering.'

'I mean it,' he said, 'and when we've finished eating I want to go over a few things with you again. In fact, let's sit outside, away from this ghastly smoke.'

I smiled. 'Well, Harry, if you survive into the early part of the next century, you'll be relieved to find that smoking is banned in public buildings.'

'What, even in pubs?'

'Yes.'

'If only I could believe you! Take my advice, Roger. Never touch a cigarette.'

We sat for a further hour in the sunshine, Pincher constantly scribbling in his notepad. Near the end of our conversation he reached into his case and drew out an Agfa Silette camera.

'Just a few snaps of you and the pub,' he said. 'My article should appear in the *Express* as early as next Wednesday, so look out for it. Oh, and let me have your full address. You'll be receiving a cheque for four hundred pounds.'

'*Four hundred?* That's almost twice what I earn in a year! I could buy a decent car with that.'

'It's mere chicken-feed to the paper. But beware, some of the things I'll be including in the article might attract unwelcome attention. Be on your guard. Oh, and I almost forgot,' he said, reaching deeper into his briefcase, 'your contract. Have a quick read. By signing it you're agreeing that the *Express* has exclusive rights to your story. Right?…Good! Now, would you like to stroll back to the station with me? My train leaves just after four.'

That decided it. I was determined to quit my job at the chemical works. Hopefully I wouldn't need a lawyer's services to escape my apprenticeship. Surely the firm would cooperate, but it would also require the consent of my father. In 1962 the age of majority was still twenty-one, so legally I remained under his wing, and it was he who had signed my indentures. However, I reckoned I'd only have to wave that £400 cheque under his nose to secure his acquiescence. Our home would be free from the taste of saccharin once more.

CHAPTER 10: The Call

Somehow I endured another Monday at the chemical works and another Tuesday at college, but when Wednesday came my plans were entirely dependent on whether Pincher's article appeared in that day's *Express*. If it wasn't there, I'd go to work as usual, but if it was, the wretched factory together with its foul emanations could go to blazes. Hence my seven o'clock dash to the newsagent to buy the paper.

And there it was! A double page spread, complete with pictures taken in London and at the *Trip*. I didn't hang around for the shopkeeper to identify me, but tucked the paper into my jacket, sped home and dived into my room to pour over every sentence. Overall, Pincher had done justice to what I'd said, with liberal helpings of his own views thrown in for good measure. He'd even implied that some of my ideas were his own – rather sly, I thought – and everywhere there were undertones of Soviet espionage and insinuations about double agents in British intelligence, even though I hadn't mentioned them once. I wasn't in a hurry to show my face to any of my acquaintances. Although Pincher hadn't revealed my full name, referring only to 'Roger, the remarkable teenager from Nottingham', he'd hinted at my day job, talking about 'the apprentice whose imagination pierces the walls of a chemical works with stunning originality'. The *Express* being a top-selling paper in the sixties, the chances were that my workmates would see it, as would my employer, the kids at the youth club, the neighbours – even the old crone from the post office who walked her poodle down the street every teatime. I hadn't anticipated how I would feel when exposed like this.

By the time I'd absorbed every last word an hour had gone by, and I was engrossed in other stories when my mother casually entered the room, only to gasp at the sight of her son sprawled on the bed, reading.

'Roger! It's gone eight o'clock. You should be at work. I thought I heard your motorbike leave over an hour ago. Why are you back? Are you ill, or something?'

'Mum, calm yourself, sit down and look at this.'

I watched her face as her eyes darted to and fro across Pincher's article. She couldn't have taken in more than a smattering of the words before she spoke.

'What have you got yourself into, Roger? How did this man find out about you? Do you trust him?'

'It's alright, Mum, you don't need to worry. I've decided I'm not going to work today. In fact, I don't think I'll ever darken the doors of a chemical factory again, but I'll need to contact the firm and explain. I'm sure the management will have seen this article before the end of the day, and they'll know what to expect.'

I decided to sort things out once and for all the following day, so on Thursday morning I made my way to the personnel department and met the 'gaffers' who'd arranged my apprenticeship back in 1960. I knew they'd never smelt a tank of industrial meths in their lives, nor battled to hold their breath when swilling ammonia around by the bucketful, but they were *awfully nice* to me, and even wished me well in my *new profession* – if that's what it was – and yes, they would release me from my apprenticeship *post-haste*, and would even cancel my indentures without my father having to be involved. Done and dusted!

While in town I visited the Midland Bank to set up a current account. None of my mates had one in 1962. Our wages were paid as cash in little brown envelopes every Friday afternoon – and some of the lads parted with at least half of it in the pub the same evening – but I would need the account when the cheque arrived from the *Express*. Reaching home mid-afternoon, I immediately checked the post. There was still no sign of the £400, but later that evening something truly remarkable happened. The telephone rang, and as had now become my habit, I leapt to my feet to answer it. The caller said he was a producer at Independent Television. I wondered how he'd got our number. Had he been phoning every Parnham in the Nottingham directory until he found me? But it was what came next that seemed unbelievable.

'Would you be willing to appear in a current affairs programme on

Monday evening? It's a live half-hour pilot with Edgar Lustgarten as the presenter.'

Lustgarten? I vaguely remembered the name. He'd been a barrister, and went on to present TV programmes on criminology. Why would they turn him loose on me?

'Mr Lustgarten will be interviewing you for about five minutes. A lot of interest has been generated by Wednesday's *Daily Express* article, and we want to get in first.'

'Get in first? But I've never been on television before. What sort of thing will I be asked?'

'Don't worry, we'll put you at your ease. Mr Lustgarten will be particularly interested in your views on the future of the arms race.'

I felt stressed, big-time. I had a matter of moments to respond. I could say yes or no, and that would be it. It seemed a daring thing to undertake. How would I cope with a live TV appearance? On the other hand, wasn't this just the kind of publicity I'd been seeking when I first contacted the press? I'd even implied as much to Fangy.

'There's no fee for your appearance,' he continued, 'but your expenses will be covered, including first-class travel, taxi fares and overnight accommodation in a hotel.'

'Okay,' I said. 'I'll do it.'

The producer sounded delighted. 'The programme will be going out at 7:30 p.m., but we'd like you to arrive by three thirty at the latest. Ask your driver to bring you to Television House, at the corner of Aldwych and Kingsway.'

I had barely four days to psych myself up for this ordeal. Lustgarten was known as a formidable interrogator, and I suspected he'd want to turn my arguments inside out. I feared making a fool of myself in front of thousands, perhaps millions, of viewers. My whole weekend was, to a large extent, ruined by my dread of what might happen in that television studio on Monday evening. There was one bright moment when my cheque arrived in Saturday morning's post, but as the banks closed at 3:30 p.m. on Fridays and didn't open again until 9:30 a.m. on Mondays, it would have to wait in my drawer for a few days. On Saturday afternoon I ventured into town to buy myself an off-the-peg suit – with borrowed cash, of course. It didn't fit perfectly, but was a big improvement on everything else in my wardrobe. On the Sunday I sneaked out early and bought three newspapers – definitely a sinful thing to do, but my father didn't need to know – narrowly avoiding another encounter with Fangy as he was finishing his paper round. Up on the fields I spent a couple of hours devouring everything related to world affairs in readiness for facing the awesome Lustgarten, before making my way back down the path and ditching the papers in a litter bin.

Back home my parents were getting into the car.

'There's something you need to know,' I told them. 'I'm off to London again tomorrow, and I'll be staying overnight.'

'What's it about this time? Have you got a real job now?'

'I don't know if you'd call it a *real* job, Dad. I'd call it a profession. It's all to do with high-powered journalism, and doesn't involve wearing a gas mask and rolling drums of chemicals through pools of noxious effluent, which I've been doing for the past two years.'

'There's nothing wrong with an honest day's graft,' he said, starting the engine. 'But these early morning strolls on Sundays are becoming a regular habit. Are they to avoid having to come to church?'

'I wouldn't say so. In fact, I reckon you could be closer to God up on the fields, with nature all around you, than in a stuffy building.'

He drove off in disgust, while I went inside to fiddle with my new suit.

CHAPTER 11: Miriam

Monday, the 25th of June, dawned brightly. Under any other circumstances I might have been happy, relaxed and carefree – perhaps even euphoric when I arrived on the platform at the Midland Station and realised that the eleven forty-five to London would be pulled by steam rather than diesel. The hiss from the boiler, the whiff of smoke from the funnel, the sunlight reflecting off the well-oiled con-rods – all were evocative of an age that was destined to pass before the sixties had run their course. And travelling first class, ordering anything I fancied from the buffet, being transported door-to-door by taxi – these were luxuries I'd scarcely known before, even in my previous existence as an underpaid industrial chemist. But what detracted from all this potential pleasure was the prospect of being eaten alive by the fearsome Lustgarten in full view of the world. I'd given up trying to anticipate his questions and rehearse my responses. It was too stressful. Better to put it out of my mind, if only I could. Yet had I known in advance just how fateful that day would turn out to be, I might well have jumped off the train and returned to Nottingham at the first opportunity.

On arriving at the television studios I was introduced to someone important – so important that I can't remember what his role was. There was a small army of producers, directors, floor managers, technicians and the like. He explained the basics. The show would last thirty minutes – twenty-three if you allowed for the commercials – and my involvement would be confined to the first five minutes. The studio set was designed to convey a relaxed informal atmosphere, with the participants seated in comfortable leather chairs. Edgar Lustgarten would be sitting to my right and I was to look toward him, not at the cameras. Thankfully there would be no studio audience.

I was then passed to another guy who took me through the types of questions Lustgarten would be asking: a bit about my background and what I did for a job, before grilling me on my 'outlandish' claims. Finally he would move on to the terrifying arms race. With America and Russia testing increasingly deadly weapons, how might it end? Would the world ever become a safer place, or was nuclear annihilation just around the corner? Quite a lot to pack into five minutes.

I then met a kindly middle-aged woman who unfolded a map showing the location of my hotel, just a few blocks away, and presented me with a form for claiming expenses.

'Make sure your claim is *ample*,' she said. Did that mean *inflated*?

After this I was taken to a room off the main studio, where a couple of women fussed over my appearance and seemed reasonably satisfied, although they insisted I wear a different tie. Why? This was mere 405-line black-and-white television. Would such a detail matter?

As things turned out, an even greater surprise was waiting in the wings. I hadn't quite finished straightening the new tie when someone came into the room to offer me a cup of tea, and at that moment my world changed, this time decidedly for the better, for I was looking straight into the face of a stunningly pretty girl. She was about my age – perhaps nineteen – with large, dark eyes and an exquisite smile. If I'd once thought that Nancy was beautiful, and surely I had, this girl was in a different league altogether.

'Er…tea…yes, please,' I said, looking her up and down as she turned to the trolley. Her hair was dark, almost black, matching the colour of her shoes, and between those extremities was a trim figure in a white blouse and knee-length grey skirt. It's strange that I can recall those details. I rarely have much of a memory for what people are wearing.

'Milk? Sugar?'

'Oh, no sugar, thanks.'

As I took the saucer from her, I felt her fingers briefly touch mine.

Pull yourself together, Parnham, I said to myself, *or you'll drop the bloody drink.*

The girl drew up a chair and sat down beside me. She smiled. 'Don't be nervous. Appearing on TV for the first time can be daunting, but you'll be fine.'

'Gee, thanks,' I replied, 'it's good to be reassured.'

Where had a dumb expression like 'gee' come from? It wasn't a word I normally used.

'Have you come far?'

'Just from Nottingham.'

'That's somewhere I've never been,' she said. 'What's it like?'

I was in a state of bliss, conversing with, arguably, the loveliest girl I'd ever seen, and she was taking an interest in *me* of all people. When I was eighteen I didn't have much confidence with girls. After all, the only one with whom I'd fallen in love had rejected me in no uncertain terms.

'Nottingham? It's great,' I said, exaggerating a little – in fact, a lot. 'What about you?'

'Daddy's a television producer. He has a flat in central London, but our home is in Dorset.'

'Did your father get you a job here?'

'Heavens, no! But he lets me come to the studio to help out. A bit of work experience, if you like. I'm at drama school, but we have Mondays off.'

She spoke impeccable English, but with a slight hint of a foreign – perhaps east European – accent somewhere in the background.

'Then you might be a television actress some day?'

'Maybe, but I mustn't get ahead of myself.'

All too soon she was called away to some duty more important than wheeling the tea trolley. My heart went after her, yet I hadn't even got round to asking her name. Would I see her again? My thoughts were barely on my TV appearance, but elsewhere, so to speak, which was probably a good thing.

Someone took me to the refectory. It was five thirty, and they wanted me to return to the studio by six forty-five. Although I could eat as much as I liked, I decided that over-indulgence would be unwise before the programme. It ended up being little more than a light snack.

Back at the studio I met Lustgarten for the first time. I got the impression I'd been foisted on him at short notice following publication of the *Express* article, and he didn't much care for my inclusion in his line-up. He had a government minister to interrogate, and I was merely the warm-up act as far as he was concerned, a tiresome detail intruding into his schedule.

Seven o'clock came and the studio was buzzing with activity. Managers and technicians were busy with final preparations. Seven thirty-one, and someone signalled that we were on-air. Lustgarten, immaculate in pin-striped suit and silk tie, began his introduction.

'I have with me a young man who has caused a minor stir in recent days. The weekend papers have been awash with reactions from commentators to the claims made by my first guest. One might even call them *prophecies.*' I thought I detected the hint of a sneer. 'His name is Roger Parnham, he's eighteen and is, or was, an apprentice with a chemical company. Recently he's attempted some predictions about what will happen, not just tomorrow or next year, but right up to the end of the century. He even forecasts the collapse of the Iron Curtain within thirty years.' Lustgarten turned to me.

'Now, Mr Parnham, how can you possibly know what's going to happen three decades hence?'

I tried to give him an explanation, but he ridiculed the whole idea.

'Surely, if you've had a private viewing of the future, you'll be able to pick the winners of races, the results of football matches and such like, and make yourself a tidy fortune?'

'No, actually I can't. It doesn't work like that.'

'Then your claim to be able to predict the future is nonsense, isn't it?'

'No!' I said. 'What I foresee is the broad picture, the way things are shaping up on a global scale.'

'But what you're doing is claiming privileged knowledge of events that are still a long way off,' he insisted, 'so there's no immediate prospect of being proved right or wrong. There's nothing clever about that, is there?'

I could sense that the interview wasn't going well. I couldn't get into the smooth flow I'd achieved in my encounters with newspaper columnists. My interviewer had only five minutes to make something interesting out of my appearance, and he seemed intent on doing a demolition job. My worst fears appeared to be materialising. I risked being made to look a fool.

'Well, I can predict next winter's weather if you like.' I knew it sounded feeble.

'Come, come, Mr Parnham. Weather prophets are two-a-penny. I don't think our viewers are impressed in the slightest. They are more concerned about the future of the arms race and the prospect of nuclear war. They want to know if the world will still be here in ten years' time.'

'Very well, Mr Lustgarten,' I said, 'listen to this.' I tried to get something going, stubbornly commencing with the weather. 'The coming winter will be the coldest for centuries, but the world will still be here in forty years' time, and the post-war division of Europe will be over by 1990.'

'That's pathetic,' he sneered. 'I put it to you that you've developed a knack of imagining future possibilities and passing it off as prophetic genius, when in reality it's a cheap charade. It's captured people's attention because they like what they hear, but you can no more foresee the real future than my Aunt Ethel. It's just an act.'

My excuse for what happened next is that he was goading me beyond endurance. I know that's a weak defence, and my reaction is something I later regretted profoundly.

'Alright, Mr Lustgarten, I'll tell you about the future of the world. In fact, I'll tell you about something that's happening right now, that has the potential to bring the planet to the brink of disaster before the year is out.'

I expected some response, but none came. He was staring at me, willing me to continue.

'At this very moment the Russians are building nuclear missile bases on the island of Cuba, just a few miles from the USA, from which they'll be able to devastate American cities without warning.'

Lustgarten looked stunned. His jaw muscles twitched as if he was about to speak, but it must have been five full seconds before anything came out. 'Am I hearing you correctly? Surely you can't be serious—'

'I'm deadly serious.'

'But that's a momentous allegation! The Americans couldn't possibly tolerate such a threat.'

He was right. The Cuban missile crisis was *the* big international event of 1962. In the autumn of that year there was a nerve-wracking confrontation between the superpowers, with many people fearing imminent nuclear Armageddon. I was fairly sure the Americans hadn't become aware of the construction of the missile bases until later in the year, so I would in effect be tipping them off several months in advance, if they were listening. I should have realised that my outburst would reverberate far and wide beyond that studio.

'Are you sure of your facts? Who else knows about this?' Lustgarten was trying to press on with the interview with some semblance of normality, but by now his script, if he had one, had fallen by the wayside.

'The Russians and the Cubans know. That's all.'

From that point on, things became increasingly chaotic, with Lustgarten demanding to be told how I could possibly know what was happening in Cuba, and I insisting that my story was correct. Eventually someone behind the cameras gave a signal, and he brought the interview to an abrupt close, thanking me for 'providing some useful insights'. On the far side of the set, the politician who was Lustgarten's second guest was awaiting his cue, but he too was visibly shocked. Someone beckoned to me to leave my chair and exit left. As I moved out of the bright lights and toward the studio door, I came face to face once more with that dark-haired beauty.

'You were great,' she whispered. 'I was watching it all from the control room.'

Such was my delight at meeting the girl again, I promptly forgot the stresses of the show and the gravity of what I'd just revealed to the world. Once outside the studio we were able to speak normally.

'Would you like to come out for a drink?' she asked.

'What, just the two of us?'

'Of course.'

Was this actually happening? Over the past three weeks I'd questioned the reality of my whole situation many times, but by that evening I'd begun to settle into my new life, even to accept it as normal. But now, could *this* be real?

'Er, that would be great,' I said. 'I'll just collect my overnight bag and we can be off.'

This was magical. Not only would I have the girl to myself for a while, I would also be well clear of the studio before the end of the programme. I didn't relish another encounter with Lustgarten, fearing he might corner me after the show and challenge me to reveal more. I'd already said too much. Better to make myself scarce.

I grabbed my bag, the girl put on her coat, and we made our way out. It was not yet eight o'clock on that June evening, and shafts of bright sunlight were falling between the tallest buildings.

'I'm sorry, I don't even know your name.'

'It's Miriam,' she said. 'Come on, there's a friendly pub about five minutes away.'

She led me along Aldwych in the direction of Covent Garden. A bolt of fear that I might be recognised was quickly quelled as I remembered that very few bars had television sets back in 1962.

'What would you like to drink?' I said, as we settled into a quiet alcove.

'I'll have a shandy.'

Queuing at the bar, I kept glancing over my shoulder, hoping she wouldn't suddenly wander off, or worse still, succumb to a chat-up line from some opportunist bloke twice my size. I still needed assurance that this was real. Safely back at the table, sipping a cool cider, I felt my confidence beginning to return.

'This is nice, Miriam,' I said, wetly, then tentatively added, 'I hope your boyfriend won't mind.'

'I don't have one.'

Could things get any better?

'Your performance in front of the cameras was stunning,' she said. 'At one point, Lustgarten nearly fell off his chair. The papers will be full of it in the morning.'

'That's what I'm afraid of. Gee, Miriam, what have I done?'

There I go again, another bloody 'gee'.

'You're not scared, are you?'

'Of course not,' I lied, desperately needing to appear cool.

'Tell me, where do you get your information? How do you know what's happening in Cuba?'

'Well, I know this sounds odd, but I really can see into the future.'

'But you were talking about what's happening in Cuba right *now*, not in the future. How do you know? Are you part of a spy ring?'

'Heavens, no!'

Miriam wouldn't let go of the idea that I was linked to some kind of espionage network. It was that aspect which intrigued her the most. Eventually I got her off the subject, and we started discussing our childhoods – or rather, *my* childhood, the details of hers were hazy. At first I was reluctant to disclose my working-class background, and tried to disguise any awkward facts with half-truths – or, in some cases, downright lies – but she listened sympathetically, all the while drawing me closer into her confidence. An hour went by, then another. It was surreal. Barely three weeks earlier I'd said goodbye to Nancy, deciding I could manage without romance for the foreseeable future, and here I was, mesmerised by a girl I'd met only a few hours earlier. It wasn't just that she was unbelievably pretty. She was blessed with that special combination: good looks *and* kindness – to me, at least.

By ten o'clock I'd downed no fewer than three ciders – only half-pints, but well in excess of my usual consumption – and was wondering how the evening might end, when she said, 'Are you free tomorrow?'

'Tomorrow? That's Tuesday, isn't it? Well, come to think of it, I'm free all week.'

'Then how about another day in London?'

'Why, are you offering to—'

'Show you around? Why not?'

Was I hearing this correctly? Did she actually fancy me? Was I in with a chance? Surely things like this didn't happen to nondescript guys like me.

'Yes, of course, I'd love to spend the day with you. No need to hurry back home.'

'Then you're on. What would you like to see?'

'Er, what about you?'

'I spend most of my life in London, I can see it any time. You choose.'

'Well,' I said hesitantly, 'how about the Science Museum?' It was hardly romantic, but I'd been captivated by the place ever since my parents took me there as a small child. To me it had been a wonderland, but I feared it wouldn't seem cool enough to a sophisticated young woman like Miriam.

'Okay,' she said. 'That's one place I've never been. I'll meet you at

South Kensington Underground Station at eleven o'clock.'

My pleasure was multiplying by the minute. I was sure that if Miriam had seen me covered in dust, kekking in the saccharin factory only a few days earlier, she wouldn't have given me a second look – but now I'd entered another world, where life was full of incredible promise.

'How will you get home tonight? May I take you?'

'No problem,' she said, 'I'll phone for a taxi. Just wait here.'

She went off 'to find a telephone box' while I remained at the table in a blissful stupor. She seemed to be gone for ages. I was pretty sure we'd passed a row of phone boxes shortly before entering the pub. Surely it didn't take over ten minutes to phone for a cab? I should have been more suspicious, but in that besotted state my cognitive processes weren't at their most acute.

'That's fine,' she said when at last she returned. 'The car will be here in five minutes.'

We went outside and waited on the pavement. It was now practically dark, and the passing vehicle lights were flickering on her face. I could hardly take my eyes off her, and wondered how she might react if I were to give her a kiss – just a little one, perhaps a peck on the cheek – but, sadly, I couldn't summon up the courage. Still, I had the whole of tomorrow to remedy that.

With one last smile and a wave she was gone; gone in a type of car I didn't recognise. It certainly wasn't one of those traditional black cabs.

I consulted the map and set off in the direction of my hotel. Minutes later I was checking in. Amazingly, there was a television set in my room, with *both* channels, BBC and ITV. I say *amazingly*, for something strange had begun to happen. Why would someone who'd lived into the 21st Century be surprised to find multi-channel television in a hotel room? It was a minimum expectation in 2010, whereas fifty years earlier most people had never so much as seen a TV set in a bedroom, even at home. I imagined it was rare for hotel rooms to have television in the 1960s. Perhaps this one was part of an experiment by the management, but the eerie truth was that I'd begun to react as if life in the sixties was completely normal to me. It wasn't that I'd forgotten my previous life, it was just that I didn't feel part of it any more. Instead, I felt I belonged right here, in 1962. Already I'd ceased to miss the technological conveniences of later years, the microwave ovens, mobile phones, laptops and the like, which was astonishing. Although, to be honest, I did miss having a mobile phone, just a basic one, but that was all. How could a change like that occur in just over three weeks? What was happening to my mind?

I turned the TV on and, not having the benefit of a remote control, crouched in front of it in readiness for switching between channels. After twenty seconds or so the grainy black-and-white picture appeared. I was hoping to find a news bulletin, but no such luck. One channel was screening a film, the other an arty-farty discussion. I'd have to wait until morning to find out what sort of impact my interview was having on the world outside. Meanwhile, I would spend a few minutes with my map of the Tube, working out how to get to South Kensington.

My emotions were hovering midway between terrified and ecstatic. I may have blundered badly on television, but as a result, sweet romance was surely coming my way. The good life was almost within reach. It had to be a massive improvement on my previous lot as a worn-out, sixty-six year-old divorcee.

Settling down in the large double bed, I listened to the unfamiliar din of London traffic for a while before dozing off. My final thoughts were of Miriam, although I don't recall actually dreaming about her. But she, of all the people I'd met, had made my day.

2010 could take a running jump.

CHAPTER 12: Running Scared

It was a new experience for me. The anxiety, even desperation, not to be recognised. This was, I imagined, the sort of predicament faced by many a wanted criminal. You try not to look people in the eye, try to deflect attention away from your face, spend a lot of the time looking down at the ground. In pubs and cafés you sit to one side, your back to everyone else. If possible you wear a hat, or have your collar turned up, and hold your hand up to your face, especially when talking to strangers.

Such was my state on that Tuesday morning, in the cool light of day. Not that I was a wanted man. There weren't posters across the land displaying my picture. The police weren't looking for me, but I'd appeared on television for just over five minutes the previous evening, and what I'd said had almost halted the show. For some viewers the memory would still be fresh, and there was a danger that someone would recognise me.

Over breakfast I scanned every morning paper I could lay my hands on. None of them had splashed my outburst across the front page, although two carried 'stop press' items making brief reference to it. I guessed that few journalists would have been glued to their TV sets at seven thirty on a Monday evening. The programme hadn't been billed as anything special, and they would have received no prior notice of a sensational announcement, so a hurried piece with few details was the most they could conjure up, and certainly no pictures of me.

Leaving my overnight bag at the hotel reception, I headed for the Underground. On the train to South Kensington I stared resolutely at the floor, looking up only briefly to keep track of the stations. Miriam was constantly on my thoughts – hoping she would turn up, hoping she hadn't been a mirage designed to torment a poor gullible youth.

Reaching our appointed meeting place with fifteen minutes to spare, I bought a copy of the *Daily Express* and stood near the station entrance with it close to my face, half-expecting to find an article on East Germany or Vietnam or China written by the tenacious Pincher. I'd perused half a dozen pages when the paper was suddenly flicked by a female hand, and a familiar voice had my attention.

'Hi, Roger!'

It was Miriam. And no, I hadn't imagined it. She was a stunner, even more delectable in broad daylight, now wearing a light blue sweater and dark jeans – the ladies' type, with a zip down one side.

'See, I'm hiding behind a newspaper so as not to be recognised.'

She laughed. 'I'm sure you overestimate the danger of that. No one knows you, and you were on screen for only a few minutes. Try to relax.'

I should have been the happiest guy around. I had a whole day to enjoy in the company of this amazing girl, whom I even dared to believe had fallen for me; yet I was wondering whether her presence would be an advantage or not. On the one hand she was the sort of creature to turn heads, and so would draw attention away from me. On the other, some blokes would be curious to know who the lucky dude was who'd pulled this gorgeous chick, and I might come under the spotlight too. I knew that dark glasses were a standard piece of kit for disguising one's appearance.

'Could we find a shop that sells sunglasses?'

'But it's dull, even gloomy, this morning.'

'Yes, but it might brighten up later… Oh, alright, I admit it. I want to make my face less recognisable.'

I didn't want to lose favour with Miriam by fussing too much, but she seemed to be amused and tolerant of my idiosyncrasies. We found a pharmacy, and with her help I chose a large pair of glasses that didn't look too hideous on me, anxious as I was that nothing should ruin my chances on this once-in-a-lifetime date.

We reached the Science Museum shortly before noon. I had the sense not to do what I would have done as a child: to spend hour after hour examining each mechanical exhibit in minute detail. This trip was simply a means to an end. It was Miriam's enjoyment that was paramount. Hence it turned out to be my shortest ever visit. We were in the place for less than two hours.

Leaving the museum we found a café, and sat down to scones and a pot of tea. I didn't have room for anything more substantial after helping myself to a huge hotel breakfast. By now I was feeling more relaxed, and able to dispense with the dark glasses for most of the time, since no one had shown the slightest sign of recognising me.

'What would you like to do for the rest of the afternoon?' she asked.

'The museum was my choice. Why don't we go for one of your favourites?'

'How about a cruise on the river?'

'Sounds great.'

It was time to pay the bill. Opening my wallet, I felt a stab of panic as I realised how little money I had left. There was enough to pay for the snack, but what would a river cruise cost? And what would Miriam think of a guy who'd offered to take her out for the day and then couldn't pay for it? There was no point in pretending. My cash would soon run out, and there weren't any hole-in-the-wall machines in 1962. I didn't even have my cheque book; it was back in Nottingham. I would have to come clean.

'Miriam,' I said awkwardly, as we made our way back to the Tube station, 'I know this sounds stupid, but I'm running out of cash. I brought just enough to last overnight. The television company was paying for everything else.' I didn't want her to think I was *poor* and therefore unsuitable as a potential boyfriend, so I added, 'Of course, I've got plenty of money back home. The *Express* paid me hundreds for the Pincher interview.'

'Don't worry,' she said, 'I always carry a bit.'

She opened her shoulder bag and drew out a purse. It was stuffed with pound notes and fivers. Where did a drama student get cash like that? Having a TV producer daddy must have had something to do with it.

Half an hour later we were nearing the Thames embankment and heading for the pier where the river cruiser was moored. I grabbed Miriam's hand as we crossed a busy road, and held on to it when we reached the other side. She didn't pull away. I was walking on air.

The sun came out as we sat on the open deck. I feared running out of things to talk about, feared she might find me a bore, but it was

Miriam who drove the conversation. She kept returning to the 'Cuba' thing. How did I know the Russians were building missile bases there? Was I in contact with spies? I was tempted to say yes, if that was the kind of thing she found attractive in a man.

The cruise over, we were both hungry. She knew this part of London well, and headed for a decidedly up-market restaurant. I felt uncomfortable that she was doing all the paying, but there was no alternative. It was about half past six when we finished our meal, and I was wondering what might happen next; how the day would end.

'Why don't we go back to my parents' flat? I'd love to introduce you.'

My heart leapt through my chest.

'Of course, that would be great,' I said, before we headed for yet another Underground station.

'I'd better phone Daddy to let him know we're coming. I'd hate him to be out.'

It occurred to me that my own parents would be wondering where I was. They would have expected me to be back in Nottingham by now.

'I ought to call home too,' I said, 'to let them know I'll be late.'

'As late as you like,' she whispered.

Boom!

She dived into a phone box while I waited outside, trying to hear what she was saying above the traffic noise. She was extremely brief. I heard something like, 'We'll be there in half an hour,' but no mention of whom she would be bringing. Then it was my turn, after which a short Tube journey followed by a brief walk got us to the flat. This area of the city was smart but unimposing, and the apartment block was in a nondescript side street. Miriam unlocked the outer door and led me up two flights of stairs. As we entered the flat she called, 'Hi, Daddy, we're here!'

She took me into a small sitting room and disappeared, presumably in the direction of the kitchen. Moments later a man in smart casual gear, taller than Pincher and even better looking than my dad, came in and smiled warmly in my direction.

'Hello, Mr Parnham,' he said, shaking my hand. 'I've been looking forward to meeting you.'

How did he know my name? Perhaps he was at the TV studio last night. He might even have been the producer of the very programme in which I'd appeared, although I couldn't recall seeing him there. He was certainly handsome, as befits the father of such a beautiful girl. Somewhat overawed, I was about to make an ingratiating remark about his daughter, when I heard more footsteps entering the room. Thinking it was Miriam returning, I glanced over my shoulder. Another man, this one shorter and stockier, was closing the door behind him.

What's this? I thought. Who are these guys? The first man must have noticed my look of unease.

'Please, Mr Parnham, sit down.'

'What's going on?' I said. 'Where's Miriam?'

'You won't be seeing her again.'

What *was* this? And what is a chap supposed to feel in such circumstances? Fear, panic, terror? I looked toward the door again. The stocky geezer was barring the only way out.

'What the heck—?'

The tall man smiled again. 'It's alright, Mr Parnham. You're in no danger, I can assure you of that. Please, do sit down.'

'But who are you? What do you want?'

'We'd just like a brief chat, then you'll be free to go.'

'If you don't mind, I'd rather leave right now.'

'I repeat, you're quite safe, and we would be grateful for the chance to talk with you for a few minutes – if that's alright with you.'

Soothed by that velvet voice, the feeling of dread began to subside. Perhaps the situation wasn't as menacing as I'd first thought. Maybe I was overreacting, but I knew I'd been duped. What a mug, taken in by a pretty woman! Twenty-four hours of heaven had been brought to a cruel end. Her interest in me had been so much trickery.

I sat down on the sofa and stared up at the tall man. He was the embodiment of politeness and civility, calm, relaxed, self-assured – everything that I wasn't. Then it came to me in a flash. These chaps must be members of what Pincher called the Security Services, wanting to know where I'd got my Cuba tip-off. If so, their approach was a little over the top. Surely they didn't need to go through such an elaborate rigmarole to contact me. They could simply have come round to my place for a cup of tea and a chat. Mum wouldn't mind. I felt confident enough to register a protest.

'Did you really need to use a teenager to lure me here?'

'Milena? She's twenty-two.'

'Still a rotten trick.'

'Please, Mr Parnham, don't take it too hard.' Smiling again, the tall man took a seat in the armchair facing me. 'But now to business. We've studied the article in the *Daily Express*, and watched you on television last night.'

Ah, I was right, they were indeed secret agents.

'We think you may have an important contribution to make to the cause of world peace.'

Really? That sounded rather grand.

'How would you feel about spending a few days in pursuit of that goal? We would make it worth your while.'

A few days? I could tell them all I knew about Cuba in a couple of minutes. Still, if they wanted me to take longer over it, fair enough. All part of one's patriotic duty.

'You have profound insights into the course of world history, and events that will affect the peoples of our countries in the coming years.'

Our countries. That was a strange expression to use.

'What exactly do you have in mind?'

The man's smile broadened even further. 'I'm authorised to offer you five hundred pounds if you'd be willing to stay as a guest for two or three days at the Soviet Embassy in London.'

Ugh! The Russians, I thought. The sense of terror returned.

'I repeat that you're not, and won't be, in any kind of danger. We're not asking you to become an agent for a foreign power, but simply appealing to you to do something to further the cause of understanding between our two nations.'

He certainly was a charmer, and five hundred was a hell of a lot of money in 1962, but it wasn't enough to tempt me. In fact, a million wouldn't have persuaded me. There was a hint of treachery in what they were suggesting, and if I were to agree to their proposal to go to the embassy, I had no confidence that I'd ever be free again.

'I'm sorry, but no. It isn't something I feel I can do. In any case, I think you're overestimating what I know.' And then, in order to shield myself further, I added, 'It's all guesswork really,' trying my best to sound casual, even flippant. I feared that things might become very unpleasant. If I failed to respond to their bribe, they might move on to some kind of coercion. But I remained firm, and although the man tried several more times to persuade me, I declined.

Finally he said, 'Very well, Mr Parnham. You're free to leave now, but please bear our offer in mind, and call this number if you have second thoughts.' He handed me a card bearing a single handwritten telephone number.

I was already on my feet. The thickset guy stepped aside, and even opened the door for me. I just wanted to get the hell out of there. I didn't trust either of them. Feared a bullet in my back. As I descended the stairs I was scrutinising every corner in case someone was lying in wait. In the street I listened for the slam of car doors, the threat of abduction. I walked as fast as I could in the direction of the Tube, keeping well away from dark recesses and alleyways. At the station I glanced up at the Underground map to work out how to get back to Marylebone. Fortunately I could make it in one hop.

Down on the platform I was willing a train to come. After ten long minutes one arrived, and I sprang aboard. At Marylebone a Nottingham train was waiting at the platform. Flashing my return ticket, I jumped on and scurried to the first-class carriage.

Should I go to the police and tell them about the agents at the flat? I didn't know the address, but I reckoned I could lead them to it. On the other hand, it was doubtful whether the men had been doing anything illegal. They were probably employees of the Soviet Embassy, going about what they would consider to be legitimate business.

I began to feel easier as the train drew out of the station. I had a coffee – if that was the appropriate term for what British Railways served up – and a quick snack on the journey. Right, I thought, as I finished my supper, I can at least fill in the expenses form for the television company. Now, where did I put it?

Oh, shit! I've left my bag at the hotel, with the wretched claim form inside. I'd have to get it back somehow, but there was no way I'd be going anywhere near London in the foreseeable future. I would have to call the hotel and ask them to send it on.

Back in Nottingham I hurried to catch the Number Ten bus, but they didn't run very frequently in the late evening, and I'd just missed one. Indeed, it might have been the last bus of the day.

Who cares? I thought. I've just enough cash to pay for a cab, and I can claim it back anyway. I've seen how people like 'Milena' spend their money. I'm in their league now.

'Taxi!'

CHAPTER 13: Malcolm and Gail

It was nearly midnight when the cab deposited me outside my parents' bungalow. They were waiting up for me, their normal bedtime long passed.

'The neighbours say they saw you on television last night,' my father said. 'Of course, we don't watch *that* channel.'

'And they say you caused quite a stir,' Mum added. 'Well, what have you got to say for yourself?'

'Look, forget it. It was a mistake. A bad mistake. I'd rather not think about it.'

'Then it's back to the factory tomorrow?'

'No, Dad, I'm not that desperate. Tomorrow I'll have four hundred pounds in the bank, with more to follow once my expenses have been paid. Oh, I've just remembered. I'm going to have to make a call to a hotel in the morning. After that, I'll think of something. You won't believe this, but I was offered a further five hundred earlier this evening.'

'Five hundred pounds? Where can you come across money like that, lawfully? Careful, son, you don't want to get involved with the wrong crowd, what with all this television and newspaper nonsense. They're an ungodly lot.'

'Don't worry. I've drawn a line under it.'

Perhaps that was wishful thinking, but it was exactly how I felt: regretful, chastened, foolish. I knew I'd bitten off more than I could chew. It was time to assume a low profile, a very low one.

The following morning, after speaking to someone at the hotel and getting an assurance that they would forward my overnight bag without even charging for the service, I couldn't resist a quick dash to the newsagent to grab Wednesday's *Daily Express*. The shopkeeper gave me a strange look, and opened his mouth as if to ask a question as I handed over the cash, but I was gone before he could utter a single word. One glance at the paper revealed that the repercussions of my TV debacle were making front page news in the *Express*, as well they might have done. It was their scoop that had kicked the whole thing off.

Mum was waiting at the back door as I scuttled up the driveway.

'There was a call for you a couple of minutes ago. I said you weren't home, but the man asked me to give you a message.'

'What was that?'

'He was increasing the offer to a thousand — whatever that meant.'

Cunning swine, I thought. *They even know our phone number!* They must know where I live. How did they find that out? Had I been followed last night? Probably not. All they needed to do was to consult the local telephone directory. There weren't all that many Parnhams. Someone must be anxious to secure my cooperation. I didn't think I'd been recognised as I strolled around London, but this was Nottingham. Lots of people would know me here.

I could sense Russian vultures circling. Perhaps they merely wanted a chat, but what I had to say would hardly satisfy them. How had an eighteen year-old discovered one of the Soviet Union's best-kept secrets? When the men in the flat reported back to their superiors, more drastic action might be ordered. The heavy brigade could turn up at any moment. At the same time I was furious with myself. If Lustgarten hadn't been so aggressive I wouldn't have mentioned that wretched island. But it was my own silly fault. No one forced me to react in that way. What had I let myself in for? I had to make myself scarce.

'Listen, Mum, forget the thousand pounds. I need a break. The press aren't going to give up on me just yet. There will be more "reporters" ferreting around. They might phone you, or even come to the house. I ought to move out, at least until things have quietened down. I don't want to be pestered by journalists, however much they offer. But where can I go?'

'What about Gail's place?'

'Do you think she would have me? It could be for quite a while.'

My sister was almost nine years my senior. She'd moved to the West Country when she married, and now lived in a quiet Somerset village with her husband and twin daughters aged four. Her home, far from Nottingham, would be a near-perfect place to hide.

'I'm sure she wouldn't mind,' Mum said, without a second thought. Whether or not Malcolm would mind wasn't discussed. 'Why don't you phone her?'

A call to Gail yielded positive results almost immediately. *Of course* I could stay there. This was before I hinted at how long it might last, but there wouldn't be a problem for a couple of weeks at least. I could help to keep the kids entertained. But Malcolm wasn't so much as mentioned.

'And I can pay my way, Gail. You'd be amazed at how much cash I've suddenly got.'

'So, when will you get here?'

'Not before tomorrow, because to be honest, I've next to nothing in the bank at the moment; not till I've paid a whacking cheque into my account. I'll do that today and call you again later.'

I turned to my mother. 'Right, I'm going to dash into town on my bike, visit the bank and the station, and be back for lunch. At least my helmet will serve as some kind of disguise.'

By late afternoon all the necessary arrangements had been put in place. I could get from Nottingham to Bath, changing trains at Birmingham and Bristol. From Bath there was an infrequent but reliable bus service to Gail's village. It could all be done in a day. I called my sister to confirm the plan.

'And there's something else, Gail. Don't tell anyone about my visit, not even your neighbours.'

'Why? Surely you're not going to hide indoors all the time.'

'Hopefully not, but the neighbours don't need to know who I am. I could be a student or a lodger. Or better still, just keep quiet about it and hope people don't notice.'

'Well, I should warn you, Uncle Roger, you won't get away with refusing to take the girls to the swings. They'll see to that!'

My father's old suitcase was large enough to hold the stuff I needed for my trip. It was duly packed before I went to bed. Early the next day I was ready to leave. My parting words were, 'Don't tell anyone where I'm going, not a soul, and if you get calls from reporters just say I've legged it, but you don't know where.'

I didn't think I was being followed as I headed to the Midland Station for the nine twenty-five to Birmingham. I was inclined to view every other passenger with suspicion, even though I had little idea how to recognise an Eastern Bloc agent if one were to sit down opposite me. After all, Milena's 'father' looked as Anglo-Saxon as our next-door neighbour.

It was a hideously slow journey. Three trains followed by a bus from Bath to my sister's home. Sound asleep on the second train I almost missed my connection. The trip seemed to take all day – which it did – but at long last I was plodding up the final gradient to a honey-coloured stone cottage on the edge of the village. Gail was peering out of one of the leaded windows as I approached the front door. Aged twenty-seven, she didn't bear much resemblance to either of our parents, in appearance or temperament. With a broad face and straight dark hair she was a free spirit, always aspiring to be independent, and determined to live far away from the 'dismal' Midlands town where she'd spent her entire childhood. Marriage, doubtless undertaken hurriedly, had provided an escape route from the domination of our overbearing parents. As for me, while I felt completely at ease in Gail's presence, I knew that confronting her husband would be problematic, to put it mildly, and there was no mistaking Malcolm's surprise when I appeared in the hallway, mouthing a falsely cheerful, 'Hi!'

Tall, bearded, thin as a concrete lamp post and fourteen years older than my sister, he glared down at me icily and muttered something distinctly unpleasant under his breath. I knew he'd never liked me, but it wasn't until that moment that I realised the depth of his hostility. I must have offended him in some way as a young child. Perhaps it was the time when, clumsily, I'd smashed his Japanese bone china vase; or that summer's day when I'd trampled his runner bean plants during a game of hide-and-seek in the garden. But now, as an adult, I had to wonder how my sister, warm and caring, had ended up with an individual so unlike herself, a man apparently fashioned from cold stone. It was instantly apparent that he hadn't been informed of my visit until I turned up on the doorstep – a serious misjudgement on Gail's part – and he didn't waste any time in letting me know what he thought of my 'ridiculous antics', brought to his attention when a work colleague had showed him the previous Wednesday's *Daily Express*. The couple didn't have television; it was 'too trivial and distracting' for Malcolm.

The twins shared a bedroom and were already asleep. Gail showed me to their tiny spare room, then prepared a light supper. The atmosphere was strained as we nibbled and sipped in the dimly-lit dining room, with Malcolm dropping hints about bedtime, even before ten o'clock. As for me, I was happy to retire at ten-fifteen, far out of harm's way at last.

Malcolm had departed for work, Gail was laying the kitchen table for breakfast, and the twins were squabbling over which one should sit next to me, when the telephone rang.

'We're in trouble, Roger!'

I could hear the tension in my mother's voice, and knew that Gail, who had originally picked up the receiver, could sense it too. This wasn't the best of starts to a Thursday morning, and had Malcolm still been at home, what I was about to reveal would doubtless have caused ructions.

'It's the police,' Mum said. 'Two plain clothes officers came to the door this morning, asking for you.'

'What did you tell them?'

'I did as you said. I told them you'd gone away and I didn't know where.'

'Good.'

'It's all very well saying "good"! I could be charged with misleading the police, with obstructing their enquiries. I could get myself arrested.'

'Hang on, Mum. How do you know they were police officers?'

'They said they were.'

'But did they show you any identification?'

'No.'

'Then there's a good chance they weren't real police. Don't worry. I'm sure you've done nothing wrong.'

'But what if they come again?'

'Ask to see their identification. I bet they won't have any. It's ten-to-one they're newspaper reporters.'

Reporters? Agents of a foreign embassy, more like. But this was getting serious, deadly serious. A phone call from them was one thing. Coming to my home suggested a deeper threat. After the call I decided I had to come clean with Gail.

'There's something I haven't told you, because I didn't want to cause alarm, but it has to do with my real reason for being here.'

'Go on.'

'The day after my TV appearance I was approached by men I suspect were Russian agents, and was offered a massive bribe to go with them to the Soviet Embassy. They think I'm some kind of spy.'

'Heck, Roger! What are you playing at? You should go to the police.'

'What, the village bobby?'

'Be serious! Phone the county constabulary, or even Scotland Yard. You know, Whitehall one-two-one-two.'

'I hear what you say, but I'd prefer to contact a friend who happens to be an authority on espionage. I'm sure he'll help. Might even put me in touch with British Intelligence. They'd be preferable to the police.'

'I hope you know what you're doing. Think of the rest of us, Roger.'

'I'm confident you're in no danger. No one knows I'm here – well, only Mum, and I've told her to keep quiet about it.'

My sister was far from convinced, but my immediate problem was that I didn't have a phone number for Pincher. However, tucked away in my back pocket was Andrew Barnet's number, and it provided my best chance of contacting Harry.

I could feel Gail's eyes in the back of my head as I dialled. Someone answered right away: a woman, presumably Andrew's wife. He was at work, but she would try to get hold of him as a matter of urgency. There followed four anxious hours as we waited. It was nearly one o'clock when Andrew rang.

'Roger! Great to hear from you. Is this by way of a reminder that my three weeks is nearly up?'

'What? Oh, don't worry about that. Take as long as you like over the Profumo investigation. I've got a problem, a big one, and I need help.'

'I'll do what I can.'

'I need to contact Chapman Pincher – fast.'

'Strange that you should mention that name. Only yesterday I bumped into him, and *he* seemed desperate to talk to *you*. You caused quite a stir on Lustgarten's show, and Harry wants a piece of the action.'

'I bet he does! But can you get hold of him now, quickly?'

'I'll do my best.'

Again, all we could do was wait. As the afternoon wore on, Gail became more restless.

'How long before you go to the police?'

'I'll give it until tomorrow morning. If my friend hasn't contacted me by then, I'll have no alternative.'

The call came just after three.

'I see you're keeping up the good work,' Pincher said.

'How do you mean?'

'Soviet nukes in Cuba. You kept that one up your sleeve, didn't you? Look, can we meet? I'm keen to know more.'

'Later, perhaps. Right now I need help – urgently.'

'Really?'

'Yes. I'm in trouble over what I said on TV. I've been approached by what I think were Soviet agents. In fact, they virtually held me prisoner in a London flat on Tuesday evening.'

Even over the phone line, Pincher's excitement was tangible. 'Good God! What happened?'

'I was offered five hundred pounds, and that was increased to a thousand yesterday.'

'To do what?'

'Go to the Soviet Embassy.'

'My boy! That proves you're on to something.'

'Yes, but what should I do? I've had to flee from home and go into hiding. Meanwhile, back in Nottingham, my parents might be at risk. Should I go to the police?'

He thought for a moment. 'No, but we must act quickly. I have a contact in the Security Service. I'll put him in the picture. Don't go away from the phone. I'll call you again as soon as I have news.'

'I hear what you say, but I *will* be contacting the police if I've heard nothing by morning.'

'So, where precisely are you?'

'Sorry. It's not that I don't trust you, Harry, but I'm not divulging that to anyone. Not even to you.'

'Okay, I understand. What's your nearest town, then?'

'Bath.'

'Right, leave it with me.' With that he hung up. Now we had yet another wait, another two hours of suspense before the next call.

'All is arranged,' Pincher said. 'Can you be in Bath for eight thirty this evening?'

I looked at Gail. 'When's the next bus?'

'Twenty past six, and it's the last one.'

'I can be in Bath by seven twenty-five.'

'Then wait discreetly. Go for a drink or something. The car that's coming to pick you up won't be there until after eight. Wait in front of the abbey, across from the Roman Baths, holding your case in your left hand. At exactly eight thirty you'll be approached by a man who'll say, "It's a cool night for walking by the river." He'll take you to the car, and you'll be looked after from there on.'

'Understood.'

'This sounds like the real deal,' I said to Gail after he'd hung up. 'Coded messages and all that.' But it was obvious she didn't share my enthusiasm. Only profound unease.

Malcolm arrived from work just minutes before I was due to leave. We didn't venture to enlighten him, but simply let him think my departure would be permanent.

'Just when I was getting to like you,' he said, with a sarcastic sneer.

'I don't know when I'll see you again,' I told Gail as I set off for the bus stop. My brother-in-law muttered something that sounded suspiciously like, 'Good riddance.'

CHAPTER 14: Gallimore

I was in Bath well before the appointed time, and did a circular walk over two river bridges to pass half an hour before strolling to the front of the abbey to wait. It was a dull, chilly evening and I'd begun to shiver when, just before eight twenty, a man wearing a brown suit approached me.

'It's a cool night for walking by the river.'

I almost replied, 'Hi, I'm Roger Parnham,' but feeling it would sound silly, promptly followed him around the corner to where a car was waiting. Car? Its size and style placed it firmly in the limousine class as far as I was concerned. He opened the nearside rear door and I sank into the plush leather seat. A glass screen separated me from the driver. When the first man was seated beside me, but at a comfortable distance, the car moved off.

My escort seemed distant, aloof. A little conversation would have been reassuring, but he showed no inclination to talk. I felt like giving him an 'I'm not a robot' box to tick. One feature of his appearance did, however, stick in my memory. There was a curious notch cut into the upper portion of his left ear, aligned with a two-inch scar that ran toward the rear of his head. Visions of a sword fight came to mind, with an opponent's blade flashing across the side of his skull, or perhaps a bullet had passed that way. Truly a close shave.

We hadn't gone far before blinds were lowered around the whole of the rear compartment, so that I couldn't see out of the vehicle in any direction.

'Standard procedure,' said my host. 'Security is paramount at all times.'

He spoke in the flawless English of a BBC announcer, the accent I'd only recently claimed to be imitating. In fact, I was able to make a direct comparison, for moments later the radio came on. It was

93

tuned to the Light Programme, with *Friday Night is Music Night* playing at full blast, making conversation impossible. Presumably the blinds and music were intended to confuse my senses, so that I would lose track of our direction of travel, but I did make a point of timing the journey. It lasted just over an hour. Eventually, I could feel the vehicle moving slowly over relatively uneven ground, and shortly thereafter it came to a halt. The engine was cut, and the blare of the radio faded.

'We've arrived, Mr Parnham. It's a reasonably comfortable place, well out of reach of foreign powers.'

I could hear metal shutters closing behind the car as the door was opened for me. We were parked in what appeared to be a cavernous but bare metal garage – or perhaps it was an agricultural barn, but if so, cattle, sheep and pigs were nowhere in evidence. The stale odour was oily rather than mammalian. A single fluorescent tube flickered into life overhead, providing sufficient illumination for me to discern a half-open door in the brick wall that formed one side of the enclosure. My escort beckoned me to follow him through the doorway and along a short corridor that opened into the spacious hallway of a large house. There were no carpets on the tiled floor, and our footsteps echoed across to a broad staircase. Apart from my guide and the driver of the car, there was apparently one other person in the house, and he was short, middle-aged, bespectacled and wearing an apron.

'This is Gallimore. He'll ensure that you're well fed during your stay.'

'Good evening, sir. If you'd like to bring your case, I'll show you to your room.'

Gallimore led me up two flights of stairs, across a wide landing and into a room with a single bed. In keeping with the rest of the house it was clean but sparsely furnished.

'The bathroom is the first door on the left, sir. When you've settled in, come downstairs for supper.'

I reached across to the small window and drew back the curtain, a pointless exercise, for it simply revealed a closed wooden shutter beyond the glass. 'Settling in' entailed very little effort. Other than socks and underwear, I had one spare pair of trousers and two shirts in my case, together with a few toiletry items. Before returning down-stairs I visited the bathroom, another room-without-a-view. It seemed that every window in the house was boarded up, covered with blinds, or fitted with obscure glass. I imagined that the average resident in one of Her Majesty's prisons enjoyed better views than this, but how would I know? I'd never set foot inside a jail. Still, as the man said, 'security is paramount'.

Off the hallway was a brightly-lit dining room, with a kitchen beyond.

'What can I offer you, sir?' Gallimore asked. 'Tea, coffee, a beer?'

'Tea, please. No sugar.'

On the large table was an ample selection of food: wholemeal bread, cheese, a can of sardines, some freshly-cooked meat, biscuits, cakes, and bowls of salad and fruit.

'I also have some soup. Could you be tempted?'

Tempted I was. In contrast to the other men, who had disappeared without trace, Gallimore was positively loquacious.

'This is all new to me,' I said. 'I mean, the security precautions, and not knowing where I am.'

'You can't be too careful, sir. In fact, there will be someone on watch all night.'

'Just how many personnel are there here?'

'Only four, but one of us will be based in the hallway at all times, so you'll be safe.'

'You won't be having much sleep, then?'

'Each watch lasts two hours. My turn is first, and once I've done my stint I can get to bed for the rest of the night, so as to be up to prepare breakfast. I've heard that one of the top brass from London will be travelling down to meet you personally.'

'Top brass? Who?'

'We just know him as "Boyle".'

I wanted to ask more. For example, who was the invisible fourth person in the house? And why hadn't he or she been introduced? But Gallimore had retreated into the kitchen once again, and was busy preparing more food, presumably for tomorrow's breakfast. Hopefully my questions, of which there were many, would be answered in the morning.

Back in my room the lack of a view was frustrating. It would be dark now, and I might have been able to see the lights of other buildings – although, judging by the lack of traffic noise, we weren't in a built-up area or near any main roads. As I drifted off to sleep I fancied I could hear the soothing strains of cattle lowing on some distant field, but little else. However, part-way through the night I was woken by very different sounds: a car drawing up on the gravel outside, and doors being opened and closed. Perhaps it was the 'top brass' arriving. From the sound of footsteps in the hallway I reckoned several people had entered the house. There was some shuffling to and fro, and after a while I could hear the low murmur of voices: two men in prolonged conversation. I lay quietly, trying to make out what they were saying, but the sounds were faint and muffled. Curiosity getting the better of me, I slipped out of bed and moved over to the door. I didn't want to risk opening it, but by lowering my head to floor level I was able to listen through the wide gap at the bottom. I couldn't make any sense of what was being said. They were speaking a foreign language, but which? Straining to pick up every sound, I gathered that it was an eastern European tongue, and before long was convinced it was Russian!

This was slightly unnerving. Why was I hearing Russian spoken in a British Intelligence establishment? There could, of course, be a perfectly rational explanation. Our agents would need to understand the enemy's lingo, and surely they would have aimed to recruit ethnic Russians to our side. Fair enough, I could sleep peacefully again. Except that I didn't. For the remainder of the night there was the nagging suspicion that the people who'd picked me up weren't British agents at all, but Soviet ones. It was a nerve-jarring thought. Yet how could it have happened? Harry had told me where to wait, and he'd given me the exact phrase that the man would use. Only he and the MI5 operatives involved in the pick-up would have known about the arrangement. Was it conceivable that Pincher himself was 'batting for the other side'? Or was it the work of a mole in the Security Service?

Eventually the conversation ceased, and there was further movement in the hallway, followed by the sound of a car being driven away. Lying there in the silence, I tried to frame a strategy for the morning. Perhaps, as a precaution, I should behave as if it was true that these were Soviet agents. If this were the case, there would be one item above all on their agenda. What was the source of my information on Russian military plans? So what could I say under questioning that wouldn't land me in further trouble?

A possible approach came to mind, one I might call the 'Lustgarten defence'. I would tell them that all my predictions were simply inspired – or not-so-inspired – guesswork. That I'd hit on a way of inventing scenarios for the future, and to my surprise my little game had turned out to be highly lucrative. And what about the specific issue of Cuba? Could I explain that away? Well, Fidel Castro had come to power in the revolution a few years earlier, making Cuba the one and only communist state in the western hemisphere. It would make sense for the Russians to capitalise on this and turn it to their military advantage. I could say I was just making an educated guess when I claimed they were building missile bases on the island. It was simply a natural part of my act. Would that convince them? Perhaps. But what if they were genuine British agents after all? Well, it wouldn't matter if I gave them the same explanation. After all, they wouldn't believe the real one, and I could provide an alternative version at some later date, when I knew it was safe to do so.

With my strategy settled, and early dawn beginning to break on that June morning, I fell asleep once again.

CHAPTER 15: Bluffing

The clumsy sound of a hand bell being swung woke me at 7:30 a.m. I took the hint, and was down in the dining room before eight. My only breakfast companion was Gallimore, but I gathered from the pile of unwashed plates and dishes that he'd been serving other diners shortly before my arrival.

'Did that Boyle fellow arrive in the night?' I asked.

'No, sir. No one came.'

Really? Who did he think he was kidding?

A surge of panic began to grip me. How had I managed to land myself in this mess? Had I been a fool to trust Pincher? He'd seemed so plausible, even warning me of double agents, when he might have been one himself! I had to flee this place: make a run for it, across open countryside if need be. But how would I get out?

By eight forty-five, with breakfast finished, I was looking for my opportunity. As soon as Gallimore disappeared into the kitchen I slipped into the hallway. Ahead of me were the elaborately-glazed front doors of the house. I tried the polished brass handle. The doors were locked, with no sign of a key. Glancing to my right I had a view along the corridor that led to the garage. It offered my only possible escape route. The rattle of dishes indicated that Gallimore was occupied at the sink, so I tiptoed forward, praying that I would find the door into the garage unlocked. I was just about to reach for the handle when I heard a voice behind me. I froze.

'Good morning, Mr Parnham. I trust that you slept well.'

I turned to see the man with the notched ear approaching. There seemed to be an air of menace about him. I thought quickly. 'It's my habit to take a walk in the fresh air every morning.'

'I'm afraid there's no time for that today,' he said. 'A senior officer from London has arrived and will be joining us in the lounge shortly.'

He beckoned me back along the corridor and across the hallway into a dingy sitting room, with thick curtains drawn across the one window on the far side. He reached for a switch. The lights came on to reveal a sparsely furnished parlour, with a sofa and three chairs arranged around a coffee table, but a total lack of ornaments or pictures on the walls.

He rubbed his hands together. 'It's chilly in here' – hardly surprising with the windows boarded up. 'I'll switch the electric fire on. There, that's better.'

'What's going to happen today?' I asked, doing my best to hide my nervousness.

'We'll be debriefing you, for as long as it takes.'

'Debriefing?'

'We'd like to know how you came to be involved with Soviet agents, and if you have sources of information likely to be of value to Her Majesty's Government.'

While he was still speaking, the 'senior officer' entered the room. The newcomer looked to be in his mid-sixties, about my height, nearly bald and somewhat overweight. I couldn't help seeing a distant resemblance to Nikita Khrushchev...surely a coincidence. Once the three of us were seated, Boyle, if that was his name, peering over half-moon glasses, began the interrogation.

'Mr Parnham, I've been following recent events with interest, namely, the *Daily Express* article, your television appearance, and the rumours that are circulating about your involvement with the Russians.' His English was perfect, with no hint of a foreign accent.

'But I'm not involved with the Russians,' I protested. 'My encounter with them was entirely against my will.'

'Let's not pursue that for the moment. The first thing I need to do is to clarify some aspects of your background. Now, I understand you're from Nottingham...'

For twenty minutes he questioned me in detail regarding my family, schooling, employment, personal interests and political affiliation – of which there was none – before moving on to my involvement with Chapman Pincher, and the inevitable question of how it was that I apparently had 'special sources of information'. At this point I activated my carefully-rehearsed plan. How convincing would it sound? And who were my hearers, were they working for 'us' or 'them'?

'Look, this is slightly embarrassing, and I'm sorry if I've caused the Security Service unnecessary concern.'

'Go on,' said Boyle.

'Well, as you've probably guessed, I can't *actually* see the future. Rather, I've latched on to a clever wheeze that promises to be lucrative, provided people like yourselves don't take me too seriously.'

'Meaning?'

'The truth is, I *pretend* to be able to foresee the future. The trick is to hit on the right sort of prediction. Something that's unexpected, yet just within the bounds of plausibility, preferably a scenario that people would *like* to believe, but not so utopian as to seem impossible. For instance, take the big issue of our time, the fear of nuclear war. The confrontation between East and West has a feeling of permanence, as though it will go on for ever. People of my generation have known nothing else. The widespread anxiety is that sooner or later it will lead to World War Three and the end of civilisation. So, my claim that it will fade away peacefully within thirty years, though barely plausible, offers a glimmer of hope that the world just might have a future.'

Boyle was frowning. 'And what about your claims of Soviet involvement in Cuba?'

'That's the amusing part,' I said, putting on a fake grin. 'It happened almost by accident. I'd no idea what a fuss it would cause. Of course, being scary, it's an exception to my normal rule, but I was feeling a bit mischievous at the time and thought I'd drop in a spine-chiller. It was fun to turn the tables on Lustgarten, and watch him squirm. I could easily imagine military cooperation between Castro and the Russians. After all, the Yanks have plenty of missiles threatening the Soviet Union, so it's only natural that the Russians would jump at the opportunity to correct the balance.'

'So, let's get this clear. You're saying that you have no real source of intelligence about Cuba?'

'Heavens, no! Where would a chemical apprentice get that?'

'So, do you know if the Russians actually have missile bases on the island?'

'I've no idea.'

'Well, Mr Parnham, you may have hit on a clever way to line your pockets, but can't you see it's highly dangerous?'

'I suppose so, but you must realise that I was reacting to provocation from an insufferably pompous barrister.'

He pressed me further, but I stuck to my explanation to the point where both of my inquisitors appeared to believe it. They warned me against pursuing my new career, and in order to satisfy them, I agreed to confine my interest to things that were of no immediate military consequence.

'You've got to admit,' I said, 'that the collapse of the Soviet empire within thirty years is an intriguing prospect. But guess what? I have another trick up my sleeve. You see, as a result of my predictions, the pundits have started to speculate about life after the Cold War: a golden age of peace and prosperity. But I'm going to tell them it won't be so great after all, because by the end of the century America will have a new enemy, one with the potential to absorb its energies almost as much as the communist threat does today.'

'And what is this supposed new menace?' Boyle demanded, his tone implying that my game was becoming more than a little tedious.

'You're not going to believe this.'

'Try us.'

'Islamic extremists.'

The two men glanced at each other, and I detected faint smiles on their faces. I think this was the turning point in my interrogation, the moment when they began to accept that I was just a gifted crank. Perhaps not entirely harmless, but a crank, nonetheless. Even so, they didn't let matters drop immediately. They continued their probing for another hour, then disappeared, leaving me to lunch with Gallimore. Presumably they were reporting the results of their morning's work to their superiors, and seeking further instructions. It was a strange feeling, not knowing if they were genuine British agents, but whoever they were, I was beginning to feel smugly satisfied with my performance.

They returned early in the afternoon and grilled me on some aspects of my claims yet again. I stuck to my guns, and even invented a few further predictions that they found almost as amusing as the 'jihadists' line. When finally they departed I was left feeling, if not exhausted, at least a little jaded.

At four-thirty the man with the injured ear returned. 'We're making arrangements to take you home. Could you be ready in fifteen minutes?'

'No problem.'

I hurried upstairs to gather my things. 'Home', where would that be? Should I get them to return me to Gail's place? No, that would risk revealing my only hideaway. Better, I thought, to ask to be taken to Nottingham. If these people were Soviet agents, and I still wasn't sure, they would probably know my parents' address anyway.

Once again the blinds of the limousine were lowered, but we were spared the distraction of the radio. It was the same driver, and the same brown-suited man as my escort. They didn't argue with my request to be delivered to Nottingham, although that might have entailed a journey of some considerable distance. The previous evening we'd travelled an hour from Bath, but in an unknown direction. Had it been to the south, I estimated that would put us about five hours from Nottingham, as there were no motorways to the West Country in 1962. As it turned out, the trip took just over three hours, so I judged the country house to have been roughly north of Bath, perhaps in the Cotswolds or the Severn valley.

As we approached the city, the blinds were raised so that I could indicate where I wished to be dropped. I directed them to the suburb where my parents lived, but not all the way to the bungalow, asking instead to be put down at the Number Ten bus terminus, several hundred yards short of my destination. As the car stopped, something strange happened. The man with the scarred ear got out and came round to my side of the vehicle, as expected, to open the door. But then, as I stepped on to the pavement and he closed the door, the car started to move away without him. Why was he being left behind? The guy stood between me and the car until it was out of sight, then turned and hurried after it. What the hell was going on? It was only later that a possible explanation came to mind. By blocking my view of the car, he'd prevented me seeing the number plate. Reflecting on this, I could have kicked myself for not having noted the number earlier, in Bath or at the country house.

'What in heaven's name are you doing back here?'

My mother was confused rather than fretful. 'Only three days ago you were desperate to make yourself scarce!'

'The danger's passed, Mum. Things have settled down. I'll be alright now, but I ought to give Gail a quick call.'

I closed the kitchen door so that my parents wouldn't overhear the conversation from the phone in the hallway.

'Hi, Gail. I'm back in Nottingham,' I whispered.

'What happened?'

'I was picked up outside the abbey as planned, and taken to a country house for the night. I spent most of the day answering questions, after which they brought me here.'

'Listen, Roger. Someone called Harry has been trying to contact you. He's phoned umpteen times already today.'

'Did he leave a number?'

'Yes.'

'Then let me have it.'

I dialled and he answered immediately.

'Where are you now, Roger? And where have you been?'

'I'm back home in Nottingham.'

'Why weren't you at the pick-up point last night?'

'I was.'

'So what happened?'

'I was picked up.'

'By whom?'

'By British Intelligence, I assume.'

'Good God, Roger! When our men arrived there was no sign of you.'

'But they were ten minutes early.'

'No, you blasted fool! You were told "at *exactly* eight thirty". *They* must have been someone else. And what they were able to do is truly frightening. How on earth did they pull it off? I'm sure my contact in MI5 can be trusted. I alerted him, and him alone, to your predicament, and he made just one call back to give me the details of the pick-up. Yet someone intercepted those messages and contacted the other side, and in a matter of hours they were able to organise the car to take you away. They even knew the precise phrase you'd been told to listen for.'

'Well, to tell you the truth, Harry, there were times when I wondered if *you* were working for the other side!'

He chuckled. 'Look, I'm sorry I was a bit sharp with you a moment ago. That contact line could have fooled anyone. So, where did they take you?'

'To this country house, miles from anywhere, maybe in the Cotswolds, but I'm not at all sure.'

I began to relate most of what I could remember about my encounter with the 'opposition', including brief descriptions of the men involved. 'I think I know who the bald chap is,' Pincher said. 'The one who looks like Khrushchev. They may have called him "Boyle", but his real name is Volkov. MI6 denote him by the codename Laika.'

'So, are our boys looking for a country house with a Russian owner?'

'I doubt it. Wherever it is, it's almost certainly owned by a Brit, one secretly loyal to the Bolshevik cause. There are plenty of them, you know. Treacherous scumbags, with more money than decency. But listen, Roger, I smell the makings of a great news story, a follow-up article to our previous one, with a detailed account of your latest experiences. It would be sensational!'

'Don't even think of it! For my own safety it wouldn't make sense to have my story splashed across the pages of the *Express*. Life's been scary enough already. I need some peace and quiet.'

'It would be worth at least a thousand, probably more.'

'No! Perhaps in the future, but now is definitely not the time to tempt me, with however much cash. Speaking of which, do you realise how long we've been on the phone? I dialled *you*, so this call will be on my parents' bill. Long distance, it'll cost them a fortune!'

'Sorry, Roger. I'm sure you can make it up to them. Anyway, my guess is that the Security Service will still want to interview you.'

'They can if they wish, but they'll have to come to Nottingham. I don't mind meeting them here, but is it really necessary? After all, I reckon I did a good job of persuading those nerds that I'm not a threat to Russian security.'

Reluctantly he accepted my need for a break. 'We must keep in touch,' he insisted, as I brought the conversation to a close. After that, only one thing mattered. A solid night's sleep in my own bed.

CHAPTER 16: Ted and Nicola

Sunday began with bright sunshine, waking me as it had done on that fateful dawn just four weeks earlier. As I pushed back the bedclothes in readiness for facing another day, fully intending it to be a relaxing one, something came to mind that I'd forgotten in the recent frenzy of activity. What was it that I'd told Nancy before wishing her a final goodbye? 'I'm going to be a songwriter', and even more fancifully, 'a millionaire'. And something else had passed me by. I remembered a comment that Andrew Barnet had made when I first met him. That he needed to be in Luton for a recording session with a someone whose talent was 'too important to miss', a detail that hadn't registered with me at the time, preoccupied as I'd been with other plans. But now…

As soon as my parents left for church I reached for the phone. Yet another long-distance call to add to their bill.

'Oh, it's you again,' said a female voice when I dialled Andrew's home number. 'I'm afraid he's not here. He's been working long hours recently. I can try the *Express* office and leave a message if you like, but I don't know when he'll be able to get back to you.'

Surprisingly, he got back to me before lunchtime.

'I've been stuck in traffic half the morning, and on a Sunday, too! You won't believe this, Roger, but London's blanketed in thick fog. On the first day of July, for Pete's sake! Who'd have believed it? In winter the smog's an absolute killer, but it's still a wretched nuisance in summer. Oh, sorry, what was it you wanted?'

'I'll be brief, because I know you're busy. Remember when we first met, you had a date at a recording studio in Luton?'

'Hmm…yes. A lot seems to have happened since then.'

'You mentioned a singer-songwriter?'

'Yes. Ted Cunningham.'

'An amenable sort of chap?'

'Sure. A nicer fellow you couldn't hope to meet.'

'And do you have a way of contacting him?'

'Why?'

'I'd like you to put us in touch.' I knew I could twist Andrew around my little finger. 'Don't ask why, it's nothing important.'

'Okay, I'll do my best. It ought to work one way or the other. Either, I ask him if I can give you *his* number so you can phone him or, I give him *your* number so he can phone you. Alright?'

'Right!'

Andrew was true to his word. A call came at lunchtime the following day. Sure enough, it was this guy Ted. He sounded very pleasant over the phone, but took ages to explain anything, digressing profusely over each point. Eventually I brought him round to the issue in hand. Could he use some fresh ideas for songs, both lyrics and tunes? Probably. Always on the lookout for new material. I had some promising ones. Very well, he'd give them a hearing. I asked him where we might meet.

'You can come over to my place, Roger. Tomorrow, if you like, but bring your pyjamas and toothbrush. If your ideas are as good as you make out, we might need a couple of days. I'll pick you up from Luton station. Okay?'

'Yes.'

'You'll easily recognise me.' he said. 'Just look for the short, tubby character with the red beard and scruffy jacket. I'll certainly recognise you, having seen your mug in the papers.'

He was waiting on the platform as the train arrived on that Tuesday morning. He matched his self-description reasonably well, although the redness of his beard was beginning to weaken in favour of grey, as one might expect for a man in his mid-fifties. I felt at ease with him almost immediately, and we were soon bouncing and swerving along the country lanes of Hertfordshire in his untidy old estate car.

He lived in the kind of cottage that looked as though it ought to have been thatched, but wasn't. Pushing his way past piles of magazines in the porch, he steered me into the living room which, with its low-beamed ceiling, small windows and open fireplace, was even more disorganised than his Vauxhall. I sat down on the sofa beside a ragged-looking cat that paid absolutely no attention to my arrival.

'I'll put the kettle on,' he said. 'Help yourself to a sandwich.'

The kettle whistled and the cat stretched. Ted reached behind a chair for one of his many guitars, then perched on a high stool beside the fireplace. 'I'm all ears, Roger.'

'Here goes,' I said, and began my tentative rendition of *Love is All Around*. I don't have much of a singing voice, but the melody spoke for itself.

'Hey, fella, that's really cool. Sing it again.'

Ted was already picking at the strings of his guitar. 'Raise the pitch a little...there, that's better.' Then, 'Let me grab some manuscript paper. I'll start to jot it down.'

I had to improvise some of the lyrics, but Ted contributed his own improvements, and after a solid three hours' effort he'd produced an almost finished score on paper. If only I had that kind of skill!

'Well, Roger, I'm hungry for more. Let's have another cuppa to keep us going, then you can introduce your next big idea.'

I'd just begun to hum the tune of *Annie's Song* when there came a clatter from the direction of the porch, after which the living room door swung open with such force that the handle knocked a piece of plaster from the wall.

'Hi, Dad! I'm starving.'

The girl flung her school bag into one corner and kicked off her shoes. 'Only two more weeks until the end of term. I can't wait—', but then she dried up as she noticed a stranger in the room.

'Hi Nicola!' her father said. 'Meet Roger.'

She stared at me, dumbstruck for a few seconds before saying, 'Are you famous? Haven't I seen you on TV?'

Rather on the short side for a fifteen-year-old, slightly overweight and wearing a tight-fitting school blouse, she swept aside her chaotic strawberry-blonde hair and collapsed on to something I took to be a bean bag, though it might have been a sack of laundry. Weighing her up within seconds, as would any eighteen-year-old, I'd have ranked her as reasonably pretty had her nose been a bit smaller, and her knees not quite so far down her legs.

'A fortnight more of school and then I'll be leaving for good,' she said. 'And not a day too soon.'

'What are you going to do – for a job, I mean?'

'I'm going to train as a hairdresser. What do you do, Roger?'

'Well, I guess I'm in training too, to be a songwriter, believe it or not, but my tutor's going to need a heck of a lot of patience.'

Ted intervened with a suggestion. 'Nicola, be a sweetie and start to prepare dinner for us, would you? There are three large potatoes for the oven; they'll need just over an hour. Then boil some eggs and get the pack of ham out of the fridge. You'll find plenty of salad in there as well, but be sure to wash it thoroughly. Oh, and there's a chocolate cake if you want a bite straight away—'

'But I've only just sat down, Dad,' she protested. Then, with a glance in my direction, added, 'Oh, alright. Since you've got someone important here, I'll make a start on the spuds.'

Once they were in the oven she disappeared upstairs.

'Her mother passed away when she was nine,' Ted explained. 'We get along well together, but it goes without saying she'll want to make her own way in the world before long, and that's fine by me. My only regret is that she's not in the slightest bit musical.'

He reached for his guitar again. 'Now, what did you say? A number called *Annie,* or something?'

I nodded. In this case I could remember the lyrics perfectly, and the melody was a doddle.

'Simple,' he said. 'We'll easily have it scored before bedtime.'

Composition was interrupted briefly by the evening meal. Our young caterer took her food upstairs on a tray, possibly to avoid having to clear the remaining junk off the small dining table. The moggie was now wide awake, and spent the whole time rubbing itself against my leg. After dinner we remained at the table to finish our efforts on the second song, and by nine o'clock Ted expressed satisfaction with the result.

'These numbers are great,' he said. 'I'll get them to my publisher as soon as possible, and as for the second one, I'm going to record it myself. It's perfect for my voice. Might even add it to the album I was recording a couple of weeks ago… No! Come to think of it, it would make a fantastic single—'

'And where does my cut come in?'

'Fear not, young Roger. You'll go down as joint composer.'

He rose from the table and shuffled across the room toward a wine rack. 'I reckon we should do a third number in the morning. Any further ideas?'

'Plenty.'

'Excellent! But for now, I think we ought to round off the evening with a bottle of something. What do you say?'

'I say, red.'

'Then red it shall be, and I think you'll agree that a slice of chocolate cake would be the perfect accompaniment.'

He stood the wine bottle on the table and disappeared into the kitchen to fetch a couple of glasses, after which I heard him call, 'Nicola! Where's the chocolate cake?'

Half a minute later her feet clattered down the staircase. 'Sorry, Dad. I've polished it off… Hey, don't look at me like that. I told you I was starving.'

I felt the sofa groan as she landed beside me.

'Do you know what?' she said. 'We don't live far from London, but I hardly ever get to go there.' She was addressing her words in my direction. 'I'd love a day in the city. How about you?'

'What, you want *me* to take you there?'

'How about it?'

I knew I had to get out of this without sounding too unkind.

'To be honest, Nicola, when I last left London I was glad to get out alive. It can be a dangerous place.'

'What *are* you talking about?'

Ted decided to chip in with his two-pennyworth. 'No harm in a trip to London. Why don't the two of you go to a show?'

Blast! I thought, or something earthier. It seemed as though the two of them were ganging up on me, so instead of a resolute, 'No,' all I was able to muster was, 'Maybe we could see about it', hoping to put off the evil day indefinitely. I'd come here to establish my songwriting career, not to be trapped by yet another girl. This was starting to spoil what had otherwise been an immensely satisfying day.

Nicola disappeared up to her room again, while Ted opened the bottle. 'Shame about the cake,' he sighed.

I sipped my drink slowly, so as to avoid any pressure to be topped up. One glass of wine is my limit. Ted went on to finish the lot.

'Any more, Roger?'

'No thanks. In fact, I'm ready to turn in for the night.'

'Okay,' he said. 'The bathroom is facing you at the top of the stairs, and the spare room is the door on the left.'

The room was in keeping with the rest of the house in terms of disorder, but at least it had a large and comfortable bed. My plan was to return home the following afternoon, by which time we should have completed a third song. After lying awake for a while trying to decide which it should be, I was on the verge of drifting off to sleep when I heard a movement from a few feet away. I've long had a dread of rats, and this seemed to confirm my stereotype of an old cottage: rife with vermin. Lying motionless, I realised that the sound was coming from the direction of the bedroom door. Not a rat, for I could hear the door handle slowly turning. I sprang out of bed and intercepted it just as a girl's face peered around the gap.

'Nicola!' I whispered. 'What do you think you're doing?'

'I just wanted to see you on your own' she said, too loudly for my liking.

'Shh! Your dad will hear.'

'Don't worry. He sleeps like a log when he's had his fill of wine.'

She was still making too much noise, so I opened the door wide enough for her to slip in.

'There's no way you're getting into my bed, Nicola.'

'I just want a kiss.'

'But think. I'm a guest in your father's house. How would he react if he knew I was messing about with his daughter? And you're only fifteen, for God's sake! Go back to your room.'

'I'm not going until you've kissed me.'

'Keep your voice down,' I insisted.

'Well, are you going to kiss me or not?'

'Alright. Just a quick one, then you must go.'

Nicola wasn't going to be content with a mere peck. She pressed her lips against mine, and clung on until I summoned up the strength to pull away. Once she'd gone, I felt along the edge of the door until I found what I needed: a small bolt that could be slid into position to prevent any further access. Now I could sleep.

When I woke it was broad daylight and someone was knocking on my door. It was Nicola again, but at least she was fully dressed this time, and bearing a cup of morning tea. She was also carrying a newspaper.

'It's eight o'clock,' she said. 'I've already been out and bought *The Times*. I thought we could see if there's a show we could go to.'

Persistent little cow, I thought. Why couldn't she just lay off?

She left the paper with me. What was I to do? Flicking through the pages, not sure what I was looking for, I spotted an ad for an event taking place in London in just over two weeks' time. It was a concert featuring Jacqueline du Pré, a chance to hear the renowned cellist at the very beginning of her public career! Dare I travel to the city for such an opportunity? It was tempting, and it occurred to me that if I were to offer to take Nicola to that sort of event, she'd probably decline. After all, her dad had described her as 'not in the slightest bit musical'. She'd hardly be turned on by the prospect of two symphonies and a concerto. It seemed a good idea. Offer her something she'd reject, and I'd be off the hook.

I joined Nicola and Ted for breakfast. She was downing a final glass of orange juice before dashing off to school, but there was just enough time for me to do a bit of thinking out loud.

'The only thing that could possibly tempt me to venture into London again would be a classical concert a fortnight on Saturday.'

Nicola was quick on the uptake. 'That sounds nice. I'd love to go.'

Surely she didn't mean that? Probably wouldn't know one end of a bloody cello from the other.

'It's really highbrow stuff,' I said. 'You'd be bored out of your mind.' But it was clear she was willing to endure almost anything for the chance of a day in London – *with me*.

Moments later she was hurrying off to catch the school bus, with a final wave in my direction. I told myself there was a good chance she'd forget the idea in a day or two, and in any case, I'd be far away in Nottingham by the date of the concert. There was no way – *absolutely* no way – that I could be trapped into taking Nicola, even if I dared to go myself, which admittedly was tempting in spite of any perceived danger.

My plan for Wednesday was twofold. To complete at least one further song with Ted, and to be well on my way home before Nicola returned. I still hadn't decided what our third number should be, but when Ted pressed me I plumped for *Fields of Gold*. By early afternoon we'd all but completed it, and Ted expressed his satisfaction with our work.

'You and I are going to be a great team.'

'Cunningham and Parnham,' I said. 'A duo to rank with Jagger and Richards.'

'Who?'

For lunch we went to the village pub. I'd already made it clear that I wanted to be on the four o'clock train from Luton, and saw to it that we didn't linger over our meal.

'Come over again as soon as you have more ideas,' Ted said as he saw me off. 'Just give me a call when you're ready.'

But I was thinking, Couldn't we find somewhere else to meet, well away from your daughter?

'Or you could come to Nottingham…'

CHAPTER 17: *Royal Children*

'That pesky newspaper man has been calling for you again,' were the words that greeted me as I arrived home. 'I told him I didn't know where you were, which was true, but he insisted on leaving his number for you to call.'

'Well, I'm not going to, Mum. I don't want him leaning on me again. Besides, if we wait for *him* to contact *us*, the call will be on *his* bill, not *ours*. How about that?'

Early the following morning, when the tenacious spy-hunter called again, my father almost swore at him – and would have done so, had he not been a good Christian – but Pincher somehow persuaded him to hand the receiver to me, and the pleading began in earnest. What a story I had to tell, he said, of virtual kidnap by foreign agents, of secret locations in London and beyond, of pressure to reveal military secrets and—

'But you're the one pressurising me, Harry. Be reasonable. Why would I risk putting myself in harm's way again?'

It was as if he wasn't listening. He rambled on about Soviet plots, the infiltration of British Intelligence by foreign powers, the danger of nuclear confrontation—

'I'm sorry, pal, but I'm keeping a low profile. You can see my point, can't you? I felt in real danger last week. It just isn't worth the risk.'

'Yet no actual harm came to you, did it?'

'No, but who knows what might happen if I cross them again?'

'Ah, but wait, you haven't heard everything yet. What you don't know is that the *Express* is willing to pay fifteen hundred pounds for your story.'

'Fifteen hundred? You've got to be joking!'

'Think about it, Roger. Together with the previous four hundred you could buy yourself a nice little house in some out-of-the-way place. You'd have financial security and a means of keeping out of the public eye. An offer like this may never come your way again.'

It was the sort of silly money designed to gnaw at anyone's resolve – unless they were a millionaire already – and from my hesitation he could sense that I was weakening.

'What precisely would it entail?'

'Can you imagine what a stir you've caused behind the scenes?' he said. 'You're a major contributor to the current paranoia about nuclear war. Your testimony would provide vital evidence: how you were lured to the flat, the inducements offered in exchange for collaboration, your treatment after being intercepted in Bath. I would blend your experiences with my own knowledge of Eastern Bloc methods. It would be a cracking article.'

'But I'd be asking for trouble. I got out of a tight corner by hoodwinking them, even pretending my talk of Cuban missiles was mere guesswork. They apparently fell for it, and it got me off the hook, but now you're asking me to risk getting into deeper trouble. It would be as though I was gloating over my success in fooling them.'

'I'm sure you exaggerate the supposed danger. Basically they wanted to know if you were part of an espionage network. Clearly you aren't – although I'm totally baffled by your "guesswork" – and now they've satisfied themselves of that, I reckon they'll leave you alone.'

'It's easy for you to say that, Harry. It's not your neck that's on the line. Yet I have to admit to being sorely tempted. If I was to agree, and I'm only saying *if*, I'd need to have a plan in place to go into hiding in advance of the article being published, and remain there for weeks, if not months, until the furore blows over. And just in case you're about to offer, it couldn't be at your place. That would be too obvious.'

'Don't worry, Roger, that's not an option. But what do you say?'

'I don't even know if I can trust you, Harry. I'm not so naive as to think you're proposing this out of fatherly concern for my financial welfare, rather than to advance your own journalistic career. But you do have a knack of putting temptation my way, damn you.'

I could hear a faint chuckle over the line. 'The choice is yours, Roger.'

'Then I'll state my terms. Are you listening?'

'Yes.'

'Number one. My supposed knowledge of Soviet missiles in Cuba *must* remain guesswork. Two, I've never had the slightest connection with espionage. And three – *note this particularly* – I didn't make fools of my abductors. These are my red lines.'

'Fair enough.'

'Also, how and where would you want to meet me? I certainly wouldn't want to go anywhere near London.'

'I can meet you in Nottingham again if you like, but we mustn't be seen in the same pub. It was identified too clearly in my first article. You'd need to find somewhere else. So, are you saying yes to the interview?'

'No, not until I've had time to organise my disappearance. I'll need to arrange a hideaway first – a secure one. Can you wait twenty-four hours for my decision?'

'Okay, I'll call again tomorrow. After that I'm tied up with other commitments over the weekend, so the earliest I could meet with you would be Monday.'

So, I'd set myself a problem. If I were to go ahead with this crazy plan I'd need to make myself scarce – very scarce indeed – potentially for months. Four options came to mind. Number one, stay in a cheap hotel or guest house in some remote part of the country…but even a cheap place would eat away at my savings if my stay ran into months. Two, return to Gail's place. A quick call to my sister yielded a not-altogether-unexpected result. She would welcome seeing me – my last visit was all too short – but Malcolm's reaction didn't bear thinking about. There was no way he'd tolerate a stay of weeks, let alone months. So Somerset was ruled out. Three, a more distant relation had a caravan on the windswept Norfolk coast…but I'd have to vacate it in time for their family holidays in August, and in any case it didn't have mains electricity, just bottled gas, and no bathroom. So that, too, was out. Four, there was my musical buddy in Hertfordshire. I guessed he wouldn't be averse to an offer of more songwriting collaboration, at least for a week or two – not sure how long after that – but there was the downside of his unbearably irritating daughter. In the end, with so little time to arrange anything else, I decided that Ted's place would be my best bet. If after a while it didn't work out, I might have to switch to the hotel option as a last resort.

When I called him, Ted jumped at the idea.

'It might be in about a week's time,' I said, without revealing why I needed a hideaway. 'I'll phone you again in a few days.'

Pincher's call came early on the Friday morning.

'Okay, Harry, I'll do the interview.'

'Good man! So, is it Nottingham?'

'Yes.'

'And do you have a pub in mind?'

'We could try the *Royal Children*. It's easy to find. Just think "castle". You know where the *Trip to Jerusalem* is, that's Castle Road. Walk further up the street, with the castle rock on your left, until you come to Castle Gate. Turn down there and you'll find the *Children* on the left.'

'Understood. Now listen, Roger. We'll need most of the day to cover your story, so I'll be arriving on an early train. There's one that gets into Nottingham at five to eleven on Monday. How's that for you?'

'Fine, but I wouldn't call 10:55 early.'

'It'll be early enough when I catch the train at my end.'

'Alright, Harry, I'll meet you outside the pub at eleven fifteen. And one final thing. Make sure you bring proof that the offer is fifteen hundred. Anything less and the deal is off!'

I was outside the *Royal Children* at eleven o'clock on Monday morning. I had a long wait. It was eleven thirty-three when Pincher turned up.

'They're making an almighty mess of your home town, aren't they?' he said, nodding in the direction of Maid Marian Way.

'That's Siberia City for you.'

'And what's that monstrosity across the road from the *Trip*? You know, the big white block. It looks totally out of place next to the medieval pub and castle.'

'That's the People's College.'

'Good God!' he said, with a twinkle in his eye. 'The reds are everywhere.'

'How do you mean?'

'You must know what I'm getting at. In communist states everything is "*the people's* this" or "*the people's* that". The people's republic, the people's party, the people's congress, the people's democratic—'

'Your problem, Harry, is that you see reds under every bed. That building has nothing to do with communism. There's been a People's College in Nottingham since 1846, so I bet the name predates *Das Kapital*. And in any case, around here The Reds are a football club, not a political movement.'

He laughed. 'Let's go inside. I need a drink.'

We found a quiet corner and Pincher began his probing.

'I happened to be watching the Lustgarten programme when your face suddenly appeared. There was no mention of it in the *TV Times*, but what you had to say was truly show-stopping.'

'That's what bothers me, Harry. I'm digging myself deeper into a hole, and I don't seem to be able to give up. Just agreeing to this interview is near madness, but I need the fifteen hundred quid!'

'So, fill me in. How did you get invited on to the show? And did you notice anyone behaving suspiciously at the studio?'

'Suspiciously? I've no idea, but there was this pretty girl who took a close interest in my—'

'Girl?' His eyes lit up. 'How did that turn out?'

'I spent the whole of the next day with her in London.'

'*What!*' His eyes were like headlamps. 'And don't tell me, let me guess. She lured you to the flat!'

'It's not funny, mate. I was scared.'

'But this is classic stuff, Roger. It's a standard ploy the Soviets use, trapping naive Westerners with offers of sex.'

'Wait a minute,' I protested, 'there was no sex involved.'

'Come off it, son. What do you expect when an attractive girl invites you to her apartment in the evening?'

'Honestly, it wasn't how you imagine.'

'Maybe not, but they were exploiting the same old weakness, the weakness that men have where a pretty woman is concerned. In some cases it involves blackmail through photographs taken in compromising situations. You know, "cooperate with us or your wife will see these". In your case you were enticed into a trap because you'd fallen for an attractive girl. No blackmail needed, you were easy prey.'

'No need to rub it in.'

'Sorry, Roger, but this story is getting better by the minute, and as regards money, there's a good chance I'll be able to persuade the paper to bump up your fee when they realise there's a sex angle.'

'What did I just tell you? *There was no sex.*'

A woman at a nearby table looked round when she heard my raised voice. I cringed. Pincher was grinning.

'Alright, I believe you, but a little ambiguity in the wording will go a long way. Stimulating the reader's imagination, that's the art of journalism, the sort of thing that sells newspapers.'

'Well, Harry, I must say I'm shocked. I'd always taken you for a serious investigator.'

'Ah, but there are exceptions to every rule, and this is one of them.' He reached for a second pencil, having snapped the first one in his excitement. 'So, describe this gorgeous filly.'

Thus he built up the story. Aside from the sensationalism, he was keen for me to describe in detail the men I'd seen, both at the flat and the country house, as well as the premises themselves. Names didn't matter, they were probably false ones anyway. I told him all that I could remember.

By a quarter to one we were both hungry, and ordered food. By one-thirty the pub was too crowded – and too smoky – for the interview to continue.

'We'll have to get out of here,' Pincher said. 'Is there somewhere else we could go?'

'Remember what I told you yesterday? "Think castle". As it's a fine day, I'll take my own advice. Let's wander into the castle grounds. There's plenty of space up there – and fresh air.'

And that's where the remainder of our conversation took place, in the elevated grounds of Nottingham Castle. It looked initially as though we were going to have to sit on the grass, which was decidedly damp, but a seat soon became available, and we spread out along it so

NO DEALS, Mr PRESIDENT

that no one else could join us. Later in the afternoon Pincher returned to the subject of the pick-up in Bath, eager to highlight his own role as the point of contact with MI5.

'You didn't make a very good job of it, did you, Harry? I was picked up by the wrong people. Do you realise that at one stage I even suspected *you* of working for the other side?'

'That's a mystery still to be solved,' he said. 'I've long suspected that the whole of our Security Services are riddled with communist sympathisers, but I've no reason to suspect my particular contact in MI5. Yet once the pick-up at Bath Abbey had been arranged, a number of other people would have been in the know, and it would require only one traitor to jeopardise the whole plan. It's the timing that's staggering. They had only a few hours to organise that car to intercept you, and only a matter of minutes to pick you up ahead of the British. Some aspects of the operation must have been planned in advance. They wanted to get you, and were ready when the opportunity presented itself. "They", whoever they are, clearly have personnel available, and the use of premises in the country. Have you no idea where they took you?'

'I can only say it was an hour's drive from Bath, and three hours from Nottingham.'

'That narrows it down.'

By five o'clock Pincher seemed to be satisfied that he had all the information he needed. 'And finally, your contract,' he said. 'The wording's almost identical to the previous one. Just sign and date it, here...Good! Now, I'm hoping the article will be in Friday's paper. Bear in mind that its publication will make it all the more likely that the Security Service will want to interview you. Be prepared for that.'

'So, if they do approach me, how do I make sure I'm not talking to a double agent?'

'Good point, Roger. Be vigilant, keep a low profile and watch your back.'

That, I decided, was no answer.

'Don't worry. Before this appears in print I'll have disappeared without trace.'

'Then you'll need advance warning,' he said. 'I'll call you two days before publication, so you can make your getaway.'

Back home I encountered my father sweating over a spade on his vegetable patch, and took the opportunity to drop a hint about the sort of fee that would be coming my way, knowing that I was about to trouser more cash from that one newspaper story than he would have earned in three years of hard graft.

'Have you thought about the tax you'll have to pay on these huge sums?'

'Tax?' I grimaced.

'Yes. You'd better set aside enough to pay the Inland Revenue when they demand their cut next April.'

I'd only ever paid income tax in the form of PAYE. 'Couldn't I just keep quiet about it?'

'And risk going to jail?'

That took some of the shine off my deal with the *Express*. All the more reason to hope that Harry could coax them into being a little more generous.

CHAPTER 18: The Hideaway

Pincher called two days later, on the Wednesday morning. The article would appear in Friday's *Daily Express*.

'And you'll be pleased to learn that I've persuaded the editor to increase your fee to two thousand.'

'An extra five hundred quid for the non-existent sex? That's a bargain, Harry!'

'Well, the boss thinks this is a story that will run and run, and he doesn't want to risk losing you to a rival paper when you have further beans to spill.'

'Maybe I won't have any "further beans". It depends on what sort of write-up I get this time. Just be careful what you say about me, alright?'

'It's too late now, Roger. The editor has approved the final draft. But rest assured, there's no mention of any impropriety on your part.'

'*Impropriety?* That word rings a bell. It's the precise term John Profumo used in the House of Commons to deny—'

'Profumo? The War Minister? What are you saying?'

'Forget it,' I said. 'I was rambling. It didn't mean anything.'

'Do you know something that I don't?'

'I told you, forget it. And speaking for myself, there was certainly no impropriety in my encounter with that girl.'

'And, as I told you, none is alleged in the article.'

'And none implied?'

'That's down to how the reader interprets the situation.'

'You're a sly old devil, Harry,' I said. 'Anyway, we'll talk again some time. Now I must arrange my getaway.'

I gave my parents a minimal briefing. I'd be going away 'for a short while', and no, I couldn't tell them exactly where, nor could I give them a contact number. However, I'd call them regularly to check if any mail had arrived. And I explained to Mum how to pay cheques into my account at the bank. As regards life's necessities, I managed to squeeze everything I needed into Dad's old suitcase, plus a rucksack. I didn't need to inquire about train times, I'd take the same one as before, arriving in Luton late morning. Ted – unsuspecting Ted – would be waiting for me. What could go wrong?

There were surprises on both sides. Unexpectedly, *very* unexpectedly, the following nine days turned out to be the happiest episode of my whole experience of being back in 1962. Songs flowed from my memory, while Ted's skills deftly converted them into musical scores, with the result that we completed at least one 'new' number every day. Then, when evening came, I even dared to leave the cottage for country walks with Nicola, wearing my dark glasses with the excuse that the sun was low at that time of day. And, of the few people we passed on local footpaths, none showed the slightest sign of recognising me.

However, the biggest change was in my attitude to Nicola herself. I soon realised I'd misjudged her on my previous visit, brief as it had been. This time, to my great surprise and pleasure, things felt very different between us, to the extent that I genuinely grew to *like* her. Not that I could actually fancy her – or at least, I didn't think I could – but she was great fun to have around: easygoing, one of nature's sanguine types, almost my polar opposite. Conversations with her were – mostly – relaxed and natural, without any need for pretence or pressure to win arguments. True, we did have arguments, with lashings of banter, but they were always good-natured and simply added to our mutual enjoyment. If ever I felt down, Nicola's presence was guaranteed to lift me up; and, as I soon realised, she was exceptionally happy because my arrival at the cottage coincided with her final day at school, and her sixteenth birthday.

'Are you having a party?' I asked, eyeing her cards on the kitchen shelf.

'I was going to, but then found out you were coming. So, I thought, *I could party with Roger.*'

What exactly did that mean? I hardly dared think.

'Didn't you tell me you were going to be a hairdresser?'

'Unfortunately, yes.'

'Why unfortunately?'

'Well, Roger, I have other hopes. What I really want to be is – *don't laugh* – an artist…'

She paused, as if expecting an instant reaction.

'I wouldn't dream of laughing.'

'…and I'm talking fine art,' she said.

'So?'

'Dad says I need to get a proper job, so hairdressing it has to be, but my training won't begin until August.' Her slightly sullen expression was quickly replaced with a mischievous look. 'Hey, I could give *you* a trim if you like. You look as though you need it.'

'What, me? Be your guinea pig?'

'No, that's my dad. I've been practising on him for years, beard and all.'

Later that evening, after she'd done her worst, or rather, *best* on me – and it was reasonably good for an amateur – Nicola showed me a couple of card tricks she'd learnt at school, then introduced me to a game she called Canadian Rummy. After several rounds, which she won hands down, I decided to express my feelings out loud.

'You know what? Life feels as though it's become worth living again. Perhaps it's something in the Hertfordshire water, but I could really fancy having my own cottage in the country, much like this one.'

'I'd prefer the exact opposite,' she said. 'If I had my way I'd live in London, at the centre of it all.'

That mention of the capital was a cue for me to change the subject – *fast*.

'Did I tell you I used to work in a dirty factory? No? Well, you may be surprised to learn that it's barely a month since I escaped the place.'

'How do you "escape" from a factory?'

'You walk out and don't go back.'

'Then why were you there in the first place?'

'I needed the money.'

'And now?'

'A newspaper keeps shovelling shed-loads of the stuff in my direction.'

'For what, exactly?'

'Hmm…let's say, for my *imagination*. One morning last month I woke up and imagined that I'd lived far into the future, and seen some incredible things.'

'Like what?'

'Well…let me think…cucumbers wrapped in cling film.'

'What's that?'

'Cling film? In the case of cucumbers, it's a sort of tight plastic coat.'

'But why would anyone do that to a cucumber? Is that the sort of thing you call *incredible?*'

'Why not? Have you ever seen a cucumber treated like that?'

'Of course not, and I agree it's incredible, but surely that's not what the newspaper is paying you for. Fantasising about cucumbers!'

'You're right, but if you want to know more, wait until the morning. Come to think of it, there's something you could do for me. I'd like you to go to the newsagent's before breakfast and buy a copy of the *Daily Express*. Then, as they say, all will be revealed.'

'Well, Mister Cryptic, in the meantime let me tell you something "incredible".'

'I'm all ears.'

'You didn't know it, but when you used the word *imagination* you lit my blue-touch paper. You got me all fired up.'

'Sounds dangerous.'

'It could well be. Let me tell you about *my* imagination. I bet it's even more deadly than yours.'

'Go ahead, Miss Arty.'

'Alright, but be warned, I could get angry, and I mean *really* angry. You see, my imagination has always been frustrated – thwarted, even – by people like Cowpat.'

'Who?'

'One of my teachers, Miss Gormley. Now my ex-teacher, thank God. Taught us art. She was an absolute *cow*, bad-tempered, moody, opinionated. I hated her, and the feeling was mutual. One day we discovered that her first name was Patricia, after hearing another teacher call her Pat. So, what do you call a cow whose name is Pat?'

'Let me guess…Cowpat?'

'Exactly! And once someone hit on that nickname, it stuck. Stuck like...well, have you ever trodden in one?'

'I try to avoid them. But why are you telling me this?'

'Because I need you to understand, Roger.' She moved closer and looked me straight in the eye. *'I need you to understand. Right?* Cowpat had a permanent downer on me. Always ridiculed my artwork – my imagination. After all, what is art really about?'

I stared at her animated young face, not sure what she was getting at.

'Come on, Roger, concentrate. What is art really about?'

'Sorry, I don't know the first thing about art, but I'm guessing you want me to say, imagination.'

'That's right! See, it wasn't difficult, was it? So, if you're getting paid handsomely for your imagination, what about me? Will I never be more than a hairdresser?'

'Don't even think like that, not when you're just sixteen. If you believe in yourself, there are endless possibilities, but you have to be realistic. Most artists don't make a fortune from their work. Unless you're very lucky, you'll still need your hairdressing skills to put food on the table and pay the bills.'

'You think so? Well, you haven't seen my paintings. They're imaginative alright. In fact, they're *fantastic* in every sense of the word. Yet Cowpat couldn't, or wouldn't, understand. And since they didn't fit neatly into her artistic straitjacket, she always marked me down.'

Nicola paused, as if having second thoughts about slandering the unfortunate art mistress. 'To be fair, I guess it's something to do with her age. The fact that she's old, and I mean *really* old. At least fifty. So it's hardly surprising she's on a different wavelength from me. She must have been born long before rock 'n' roll.'

She spun round in her chair. 'Here, let me show you one of my pictures. You'll be stunned.'

She began rummaging through a stack of papers wedged into the corner by the chimney breast. 'Bother! I can't find it now. I hope Dad hasn't binned it. He doesn't seem to bin anything else.'

She returned to the table. 'Anyway, you can't imagine how excited I was when he told me you were coming to stay with us again – and on my birthday, too. He reckons you've got a brilliant imagination, so I'm disappointed, Roger. All I hear from you are plans to suffocate cucumbers!'

'Look, forget the sodding cucumbers. I wish I hadn't mentioned them.'

'Then what, precisely, will be "revealed" in tomorrow's paper?'

'I can't be bothered to explain it all now. A friend of mine called Harry will put you in the picture. My picture. My *fantasy*, if you like.'

'Alright,' she said, feigning a sigh of resignation as she gathered up the playing cards and made as if to deal once more. 'Now, how about a final round of rummy before bed?'

'But it's nearly midnight. Your dad went upstairs over an hour ago. Another game could take at least twenty minutes.'

'Poor Roger! He doesn't want to miss his beauty sleep, does he?' She moved her face closer to mine. 'And don't think I don't know why you bolted your bedroom door the last time you stayed here. It was to keep me out, wasn't it?' Then, close enough for me to feel her warm breath on my cheek. 'Perhaps you could leave it unlocked tonight, just this once? After all, I am sixteen now.'

Pincher's masterpiece had to be seen to be believed. It occupied three inside pages in addition to a flash on Page One. He hadn't, technically speaking, crossed any of my red lines, but he'd come within a whisker in each case. He was uncharacteristically sensationalist throughout, quite out of keeping with his usually staid reputation. There was even an artist's mock-up of what Milena might have looked like, with amplified curves to make her look as sexy as possible – but the face was hopeless. What the article didn't have were any fresh pictures of *my* face, thankfully. When Ted saw my copy of the paper and glimpsed the article, he promptly went to the shop to purchase his own. As a result, we didn't get a single song completed that day.

'So you see why I wanted to come and stay with you,' I said, making out that it was to avoid further publicity rather than because of security concerns. Ted nodded. For his part, he found the whole thing hilarious rather than sinister, especially after I explained that I hadn't actually been kidnapped. Not ever.

Saturday saw us return to musical composition, which went smoothly for a further four days, but on the Wednesday, when I began to introduce Abba songs, Ted seemed to lose some of his spark.

Perhaps they weren't folksy enough for his taste. That said, he really liked *Our Last Summer*. The problem was that while I had the tune firmly in my head, I could remember only a smattering of the words, so we ended up with lyrics that were more about Blackpool than Paris, and even after two whole days' work Ted still hadn't finalised the score. His childhood holidays in Lancashire were a fading memory.

A call home on Thursday afternoon confirmed that my cheque had arrived from the *Express,* and Mum had paid it into my account. That evening, after a particularly long card game involving all three of us, Nicola brought up something I hoped she would have forgotten: the concert in London. She'd even saved the ad from *The Times* of two weeks previously.

'Look, here it is, Roger. *Arranged at short notice, a performance by the notable young cellist, Jacqueline du Pré, at the Royal Festival Hall at 7:30 pm on Saturday, July 21ˢᵗ.* '

'For God's sake, Nicola, you've heard me say several times that I don't feel safe in London. You've seen what it said in the *Express,* how I was held prisoner in a flat—'

'No you weren't,' she said. 'I've read the article. You went there to have sex with that Russian girl.'

'Huh, Miss Gormley was right to challenge your imagination, because that's what it is, pure fantasy.'

I folded my arms as if in a gesture of defiance. 'And, in any case, there's no proof she was Russian,' I teased. 'She could have been Ukrainian, or Latvian or—'

She reached across and rested her hand on my shoulder.

'But you *will* take me, won't you, Roger?'

'Well, it's difficult—'

'Of course you will, Roger,' Ted interjected. 'It will do you both good.'

'Yes, and I'll take care of you,' said Nicola.

'What *is* all this,' I said. 'I can look after myself!'

'Yes, and you'd better take good care of my daughter, too.'

'Of course I will!'

Shit! What had I just said?

But it was too late. That was the unfortunate moment when I capitulated; when the emotional pressure overcame my fears, not to mention my better judgment.

'Alright,' I said. 'We'll go to the concert. I'd better give them a call in the morning to check if there are any seats left.'

I could have lied. After I'd called the box office on the Friday morning, I could have said, 'I'm afraid they've sold out', but didn't have the heart.

'We're in luck. There are plenty of seats left. What about trains?'

'Don't worry,' Nicola said, 'there's a regular service from Luton to St Pancras.'

'I'll give you a lift to the station,' Ted offered, 'and pick you up in the evening, if you let me know what time you'll be back.'

'Right,' I said, 'so here's the plan. We'll catch a train that allows us just enough time to reach the hall by Tube, collect our tickets, and get to our seats for the start of the concert.'

'That won't be much fun,' Nicola protested. 'I'll hardly see anything of London. What's the point?'

'The point is to go to the concert of course!' I said, and nearly added, *and don't you just love the sound of the cello?*

'But I want to see more. I want to spend the whole day there.'

'No way! No bloody way.'

'Couldn't you arrive at a compromise,' her father said, in his interfering – or, as he would see it, helpful – way. 'You could have an early lunch here and get into St Pancras for, say, two o'clock, and have time to see a little of the city before the concert.'

'Alright,' I said, feeling backed into a corner. Then, turning to Nicola, 'You'd better think about what you'd like to see in the afternoon because, once the concert is over, we'll be getting a taxi straight back to St Pancras. I've no intention of wandering the streets after dark.'

CHAPTER 19: Wallace

Minutes after the train pulled out of Luton station, Nicola reached into her bag and drew out a small leather case, bringing with it an item that clattered to the floor.

'Oh, that's my front door key. Would you look after it, Roger?'

'And the case?'

'It's my dad's camera,' she said. 'He doesn't know I've got it, but I saw him putting a new film into it yesterday morning, so thought I'd bring it along.'

'To take photos of—?'

'To be precise, for *you* to take pictures of *me* at some famous landmarks. I've made a list. I want to be snapped on Westminster Bridge, by Big Ben, in front of Number Ten Downing Street, by Nelson's Column and at Covent Garden market. I'll probably think of more, but those will do for a start.'

'Then I suggest we catch the Tube to Westminster, and start our walking tour from there. Let's hope for dense crowds to lessen the chance that I'll be noticed.'

'You're not going to spend all day fretting about that, are you?'

'Well, no. After all, I've got you to take my mind off it.'

She smiled. 'That's right.'

As expected, the city was busy with summer visitors as we emerged from Westminster Underground Station and strolled on to the bridge.

'Two for the price of one,' I said. 'The bridge *and* Big Ben on the same photo, but you'll look tiny if you want me to get the full height of the tower in the picture.'

'That's alright,' she said. 'At least you'll get a close-up of me in front of Number Ten.'

When we reached Downing Street there was no chance of capturing Nicola alone. There were too many tourists jostling for a spot in front of the famous black door, and she had to make do with a shot that included a bunch of Italian visitors.

'Here's something for your imagination, Nicola. In thirty years' time you won't be able to get anywhere near this spot. There'll be massive security gates across the entrance to the street to keep the likes of us out.'

Leaving Downing Street we strolled along Whitehall, where Nicola found at least five more posing spots before reaching Trafalgar Square. There we looked for a vantage point that would allow the full height of Nelson's Column to be fitted into the frame along with Nicola in the foreground. I decided that a good place for her to stand would be at the top of the steps leading up to the National Gallery. From there I could capture Nicola, Nelson and even a smidgeon of Big Ben in the distance.

'I do hope it's a colour film,' she said, 'but it might be only black-and-white.' She paused for a moment to take in the scene. 'Anyway, let's sit down for a couple of minutes. There's no hurry.'

We squatted on the low wall surrounding one of the fountains, and spent a few minutes people-watching. I happened to be gazing across toward the nearest of the lions when for a brief moment I glimpsed what I thought was a familiar face staring back at me. The owner of the face quickly turned his head when he realised I'd spotted him, and slipped away out of sight, but in those moments, to my profound shock, I was almost certain that I was looking at the man with the injured ear, who'd met me outside Bath Abbey. At a distance of twenty-five yards I couldn't make a positive identification, but was sufficiently unnerved to consider heading back to St Pancras right away.

'I'm not sure that we should carry on with this outing.'

'What's wrong, Roger? You're looking pale. Is it something you ate on the train?'

'No, I don't think so.'

'Then cheer up. I thought you were enjoying the day.'

'I was, but—'

'Come on,' she said, 'let's press on to Covent Garden.'

Our pace was agonisingly slow as we made our way along the crowded pavement of the Strand. My plan was to cross Waterloo Bridge in order to buy our tickets from the box office in advance of the concert, leaving time for an early evening meal on the South Bank, but Nicola was adamant that she wanted to visit the Market.

'Let's turn off into one of the side streets,' I said, grabbing her hand. 'It might be less busy than the main road.'

I almost dragged her into Bedford Street and across toward Henrietta Street. 'We're nearly there,' I said.

Those were the last words Nicola heard. I'm not sure what happened next, but I was close to the kerb, with Nicola on my left, when I heard a loud, sharp noise to my right, followed by the screech of tyres as a car accelerated away. Her hand slipped from my grasp and the next thing I knew she was sprawled on the pavement, motionless. She'd gone down without uttering a sound.

'Nicola! Are you alright?' was my feeble, dazed reaction.

A man who'd been walking a short distance behind us hurried forward.

'Can I help?' he said, crouching down to see what was wrong. As he cradled Nicola's head in his hands, I saw, to my horror, a pool of blood forming on the slab below.

'Send for an ambulance!' I yelled as people started to gather round. Someone ran off in the direction of a phone box.

'What's happened?' I asked the stranger. He shook his head.

'She's bleeding from the neck. I don't know why. Some sort of injury.' He took out a handkerchief and pressed it against the wound. 'She's still alive, but needs urgent attention.'

A woman placed a coat over her. 'Best to keep her warm,' she said.

An ambulance turned up in less than ten minutes, by which time most of the colour had drained from Nicola's cheeks. The crew transferred her to a stretcher.

'Are you with her?' one of them asked.

'Yes.'

'Then get in.'

As the vehicle screamed through the London streets, the ambulance man who was looking after Nicola turned to me and said, 'This looks like a gunshot injury.'

'What?'

'Yes. The entry and exit wounds are plain to see.'

Minutes later we were entering the hospital casualty department, and Nicola was whisked away. Sinking into a chair, I must have looked as though I was at death's door, but the staff were too busy to notice. In a shocked stupor I sat and waited. After twenty minutes some thoughtful soul brought me a cup of tea.

'Are you with the girl?' the woman asked.

'Yes. How is she?'

'She's in the operating theatre right now.'

'Will she be alright?'

'It's too early to say. What happened?'

'We were walking along the street when I heard a bang, and she fell to the ground. The ambulance man thinks she was shot.'

'Then the police must be notified,' she said, and scurried away.

Half an hour later my very worst fears were realised. I was approached by a doctor, who asked me to follow him to a room away from the public waiting area.

'Please sit down,' he said. Then, 'I'm sorry to have to inform you that the young lady has passed away.'

If life had ever begun to be 'normal' for me, here in 1962, this was where normality ended. I could forget my clever schemes. Reality had caught up with me in a most brutal fashion. If only *this* were a dream! If only I could turn the clock back a day or two, or even forward several decades.

The doctor could see that I was trembling uncontrollably. 'I'll organise another drink for you,' he said.

When at length I could bring myself to utter a few feeble words, they were, 'What was it?'

'A bullet through the neck. We've informed the police.'

Two plain-clothes officers arrived. One of them, a gaunt, thin-faced man with straight black hair and matching pencil moustache, flashed his identification in front of my face: Detective Inspector Norman Wallace. There was something about him that reminded me of rodents.

'I'm sorry, but we need to ask you a few questions.'

He and his sergeant sat down opposite me. 'We've already spoken to the medical staff, and taken a preliminary look at the corpse.'

Corpse? The reality hit home. 'That's poor Nicola,' I almost sobbed.

'There are plenty of villains in London,' said Wallace, 'but it's still rare for someone to be shot dead in the street in broad daylight. And a teenage girl: that's particularly shocking. We'll get the scumbag.' Bold words from a rat-faced sleuth.

He reached for his notebook, 'So, who is she?'

'Nicola Cunningham.'

'Your girlfriend?'

'Er…no…more like brother and sister.'

Somewhere, deep down, I sensed that my answer wasn't quite one hundred percent true, but it was a good enough approximation under the circumstances.

'You know her address?'

'Not exactly. It's a cottage somewhere, but I have her father's phone number.'

'Then let me have it.'

'Surely you're not going to call him – with the ultimate bad news?'

'Of course not, but from the number we'll be able get an address, and a local officer will pay him a visit.'

Poor Ted! What horror awaited him. The loss of his only daughter, and as far as I knew, his only child.

'We believe the girl was shot in the neck at close range. Were you with her at the time?'

'Yes.'

'Then tell us how it happened.'

I related as much as I could. I couldn't even remember the name of the street. 'The ambulance men will know,' I said. 'In fact, they'll be able to take you to the exact spot.'

Wallace instructed his sergeant. 'I want the ambulance crew traced immediately. And call for back-up. We'll have the street closed and a forensic team examine the area without delay. Let's concentrate on finding the bullet.'

He turned to me. 'Did other people see what happened?'

'They must have. The street was crowded.'

'Then we'll put out an appeal for witnesses. If the shot was fired from a car, someone must have seen the vehicle.'

At that point I felt I ought to volunteer some information, and tell the inspector something that had been blindingly obvious to me from the moment I'd been able to think rationally about the incident.

'I think the bullet was meant for me.'

'Someone was out to kill *you?*'

'I'm afraid so.'

'But why?'

'Did you happen to read last Friday's *Daily Express?*'

'I don't think so,' he said, looking puzzled, but as soon as I began to relate the content of Pincher's article, Wallace knew precisely what I was talking about.

'It's been a hot topic among my fellow officers,' he said, 'particularly the extent to which the Ruskies have infiltrated our intelligence services. So, you're the kid who was abducted...'

I perceived that for him this particular evening was turning out to be considerably more exciting than was usual for a Saturday.

'This changes things. We'll adjourn the interview and get you to the station. No doubt Scotland Yard and the Security Service will want to be involved.'

My state of mind was only one degree above total confusion, but I have a vague recollection of leaving the hospital in a police car. On arrival at the station, Wallace, whom I hadn't yet forgiven for calling me a *kid,* was joined by one of his superiors in the interview room. Later, detectives from Scotland Yard arrived, and grilled me even more intensively. By midnight I was exhausted.

'You realise we can't let you leave here tonight,' said Wallace.

'Why? I'm not under arrest, am I?'

'No, but it's a matter of your own safety. If what you've told us is correct, and we have to assume that it is, you could be at risk as soon as you step outside. Whoever attempted to kill you might try again.'

That was certainly true. I'd no choice but to resign myself to whatever they, in their wisdom, decided. I would be accommodated at the station overnight, with an armed officer on duty for as long as I remained there.

The next morning, after a basic breakfast, I was faced by two officers from MI5 (or MI6, I'd no idea which. They were from 'Security'). Now reasonably alert, and slowly recovering from my state of shock, I asked a question of my own before they could start firing theirs.

'How do I know you're genuine British agents? Only a couple of weeks ago I was interrogated by men who claimed to be just that, but turned out to be working for the enemy. Can you show me your identification?'

'Members of the Security Service don't carry the kind of identification that police officers have,' replied the older man. I'd no idea if he was telling the truth. 'You'll have to be content to know me as Patrick and my colleague as Martin. But you feel safe here, don't you? You're in a London police station, for God's sake, not in some dive in the country.'

I took that to imply they'd already been briefed about my previous experiences. From that point on, the interview proceeded according to their agenda. Whereas the police had questioned me about the circumstances of Nicola's death and nothing else, these guys were interested in everything that had happened after my television appearance. I got the impression that they knew the flat to which I'd been taken, and perhaps even the identity of Milena, but when it came to the events following my abduction from Bath Abbey, they were totally in the dark. They insisted I describe the country house, and the people I'd met there, in as much detail as possible. This took most of the morning. After a brief pause for lunch, the interrogation continued until mid-afternoon. Eventually they left, saying they needed to talk over certain issues with the police. When someone returned to the room, it was DI Wallace.

'We're making arrangements to transfer you to a secure location,' he said. 'It's for your own safety, but also because we may wish to interview you again.'

'How long will I have to be at this "location"?'

'Who knows?'

'Look, sir,' I said, 'I feel I ought to return to Hertfordshire to be with Nicola's father. Heaven knows he needs it.'

'As far as we know, Mr Cunningham has already moved out. We

believe he's staying with his brother on the south coast.'

'But all my stuff is there, and look…' I fumbled in my pocket, '…I have a front door key.'

'So, you've actually been living with Nicola and her father?'

'Er, yes,' I said, thinking quickly, 'I'm the lodger.'

Forgive me, Ted! Saying *that* was a matter of expedience. Your cottage is my only hideaway until I can organise an alternative, and I'm desperate not to lose it.

'And you want to return there? What about your real home?'

'No, not there. The enemy already knows where my parents live, but they've no idea of the Cunningham's' address – so long as you keep Nicola's identity secret for the time being.'

'We'll certainly do that,' said Wallace, 'but I'll have to discuss any change of plan with the intelligence people.'

He was gone for over an hour. A uniformed officer brought me some refreshments at four o'clock, and Wallace returned at four-thirty.

'We've considered all the options, and we're prepared to let you stay at the Hertfordshire address on the strict understanding that you don't leave the house under any circumstances, and you must not try to contact anyone while you're there – not even the great Chapman Pincher,' he said, apparently relishing the opportunity for a dig. 'You'll be given a number to call if you experience any problems. It'll get you through to an officer in Luton CID. Is that understood?'

I wasn't sure of the legal position, and doubted they had any authority to impose these restrictions on me, a free citizen, but I went along with what Wallace was saying. I'd no reason to feel unsafe at Ted's cottage.

'I ought to contact my parents,' I said. 'They haven't seen me for ten days.'

'Fair enough. We can arrange that. You can have use of the phone for five minutes.'

Ratty's generosity was underwhelming. Of course, I didn't tell Mum and Dad where I was, or what had happened. I simply led them to believe I'd be staying with friends in the south of England for at least another week.

'We'll be moving you under cover of darkness,' Wallace told me after the call. 'You'll be travelling in an unmarked police car, with a second vehicle close behind. There'll be an armed officer in each vehicle, and the aim will be to get you to the cottage without anyone even suspecting it has happened. It isn't dark before ten, so you won't be there until nearly midnight.'

It was 10:30 p.m. when we got under way. Two cars slipped quietly out of central London, with no sirens or flashing lights, and headed north. When we reached the cottage, the officers watched as I unlocked the door and entered, then hung around for a further ten minutes before driving off.

It felt unbelievably strange, occupying the home of a dead girl, with her father hundreds of miles away. Even the cat had vanished. I flopped into a chair by the cold fireplace, and cried.

CHAPTER 20: America Beckons

The pips of the Greenwich Time Signal rang out like hammer-blows.

'It is nine o'clock on Monday, the twenty-third of July. Here are the news headlines. There are reports that an American spy plane has been shot down over the island of Cuba, amid escalating tension between the United States and the Soviet Union. Police in London are appealing for witnesses to the shooting of a schoolgirl in Covent Garden on Saturday afternoon...'

So far that morning I'd managed to make myself a cup of tea and switch on the transistor radio, or 'radio' as it would have been called in 2010. The announcer was giving more details of the main story.

'It is believed that the U2 was brought down by a Russian missile fired from the ground, and that the pilot has been captured.'

To me this was proof of the Americans' desperation to know if those missile bases were more than a mere figment of my imagination. There were echoes of the Gary Powers affair in what had just happened. He'd been shot down while flying a U2 over the Soviet Union in 1960, and had been released in a spy-swap in Berlin just five months ago. Now the CIA were up to the same tricks over Cuba, apparently with similar results.

Ted's fridge was well stocked, and by late morning I'd summoned up the presence of mind to throw together a simple meal. Still in my pyjamas, I was eating it at the small kitchen table when the telephone rang. I froze for a good ten seconds, but the ringing continued until, at length, I dared to lift the receiver. It was a voice I recognised.

'Hello, Roger. It's Patrick from the Security Service. How are you?'

'How do you think? Dreadful.'

'Sorry, but we need to come over and discuss an urgent matter with you.'

'About Nicola?'

'No. It's something else altogether.'

'Like what?'

'We can't discuss it over the phone.'

'So, when would you want to come?'

'Ideally this afternoon. We could be with you about three.'

'Okay. My diary's fairly empty this week – and the next, come to think of it. At least it'll be a chance to experience some human company, however anodyne.'

'Right. Watch out for us. It'll be Martin and me. Don't let anyone else in – but I guess you don't need to be told that.'

I got dressed, had a shave, sorted out the things I'd dumped on the floor the previous night, and even tidied up some of Ted's stuff to make the living room look more presentable. There was still no sign of the moggie.

My visitors arrived shortly after three.

'How come you're living here?' Martin asked, prompting me to wonder if my motivations were any of his business, such was my state of mind that day.

'It was arranged by the police. And I don't know if I'm glad to be "living" at all, but let me tell you something. Nicola has to be the unluckiest kid in the land. What happened to her was all down to my hair-brained scheme to write songs with her dad, *and* to my stupidity in allowing myself to be goaded into – how should I put it? – playing with matches in a petrol station. And it's Nicola who's paid the price. That's how badly I've messed up!'

'We absolutely get it, Roger. You're distraught over what happened on Saturday – but you didn't fire the shot. There's a murderer on the loose, probably still in London, and who knows? He might even be able to claim diplomatic immunity, in which case the most we can do is to kick him out.'

'But why were they trying to kill *me*? I wasn't any kind of threat.'

'Could they be sure of that?'

'I don't see why not.'

'Then let's just say, they regard your existence as *inconvenient*. That's all it takes to make you a target.'

'But if only I hadn't—'

Patrick interjected. 'We do have something important to tell you. How about making yourself a coffee?'

'Oh, sorry, gentlemen. Would you like a drink, too?'

I ended up making tea for all three of us, and emptying a packet of biscuits onto a plate.

'So, what's this urgent matter?'

'It's about our friends on the other side of the Pond. They've been taking a close interest in you. They've seen the *Express* articles and asked for a transcript of what you said on TV. They're curious to find out what more you know.'

I was slow on the uptake. 'Friends?'

'The CIA. Life's complicated for them at the moment, Cuba having turned commie, the Soviets getting a foothold there, and now your talk of nuclear weapons on the island. The downing of the spy plane shows the Cubans already have highly effective anti-aircraft missiles, probably SAMs operated by Russian technicians, so the Yanks are taking your claim about nukes very seriously. And we get the impression that there's something else they want to see you about.'

'See me about? They want to see *me?*'

'Yes.'

'So they're coming here?'

'No. They want you to go to America.'

I must have looked stunned. Was this a joke?

'Seriously, they want you to go to Washington DC. There's someone over there they'd like you to meet.'

'Someone for me to meet? But what would I be letting myself in for? The CIA don't exactly have a reputation for kidglove stuff. What sort of pressure might they put me under?'

'Absolutely none, as far as we can tell. You'd be free to return whenever you wish. The British Embassy will be informed, and you'll have a number to call should you feel the need.'

'But this is so unexpected. I don't know what to say. It seems a lot of trouble and expense for the Americans, for very little in return.'

'What's a few bob when US security is at stake?'

'So, how long would they want me to stay?'

'We can't say. It's unlikely to be less than a week, and could be longer, but there's no pressure. You don't have to go if you'd prefer not to. If you want more time to think it over that's fine by us, but the CIA would like a prompt response.'

'But my every move so far has made things worse, not better. I feel like saying no to everything.'

Patrick tried to encourage me. 'It would be a chance to get away from your present situation, confined to this house. You'd be safe in Washington, far away from whoever tried to kill you. No one over there knows you, and, as far as we know, you'd be free to come and go from your accommodation.'

Now, that *did* sound attractive. I was beginning to warm to the idea. 'I feel inclined to say yes.'

'Good,' he said. 'If all goes smoothly you could be on your way in less than a week. I don't suppose you have a passport?'

'Never had one.'

'No problem. We can organise that. In fact, we'll take your photo right now.'

Martin reached into his briefcase and pulled out a camera, while Patrick unfolded an application form.

'You'll need a visa as well. There are documents to be completed, but we can expedite things with the US Embassy.'

This form-filling occupied the best part of an hour, partly because of the many questions that kept occurring to me.

'What will I need to take?'

'Just clothes and personal items.'

'What about money?'

'Your basic needs will be covered as a guest of the CIA, but we'll provide you with some American currency before you go.'

'And can you provide me with a decent suitcase?'

I showed them Dad's old one, which raised a brief chuckle. 'No problem.'

'I ought to let my parents know I'm going to America. They'll be astounded.'

'Forget it,' Patrick said. 'The cops told you not to contact anyone, and they were deadly serious. Whoever tried to kill you won't be satisfied with one failed attempt. They'll be out looking for you, so don't leave this house for *any* reason, and if the telephone rings, lift the receiver but don't say anything until you're sure it's us or the police.'

'Well, I know your voice, but what if the police call?'

'Didn't they give you a password?'

'No.'

'Okay. Choose a name.'

'What do you mean?'

'I mean, *choose a bloody name!*'

'Any name?'

'Yes, unless it's your own.'

'Er – Nancy.'

'Very well. We'll make sure that if the Security Service or the police call you, they'll say, "This is Franklin. Is Nancy there?", and then you'll be free to speak. If you don't hear that specific phrase, say nothing and put the receiver down. Understood?'

Martin was gathering up the documents. 'Is there anything else you want to discuss?'

'I'm still puzzled about this person I'm supposed to be meeting in America.'

'Sorry, we can't help you there.'

They started to make their way toward the door. 'We know it's a lot to take in all at once, but we'll be in touch again, in due course, with news of your travel details.'

I could see them eyeing Ted's collection of junk as they negotiated the hallway. No corner of the cottage was unused, no shelf not crammed.

'Hey, there's a bottle of milk in the porch,' Martin remarked as he squeezed past a grandfather clock. 'I bet it's going off in this warm weather.'

'It must be Ted's daily delivery,' I said. 'I hadn't realised it was there.'

'Well, if you crouch down and reach around one side of the door, you'll be able to grab it without anyone seeing you from the road.'

He did a little demonstration.

'Take care now.'

Days of waiting passed. The nights were unbearable, with too many waking hours spent thinking of Nicola lying cold in the morgue and Ted grieving at his brother's place, while an imposter occupied their home. Every day I wondered if Ted might suddenly turn up, and if he was to do so, how he would react to finding a squatter in his house.

I tried to lose myself in reading. Around the cottage were masses of books of all vintages. I began with two of Jack London's tales: *White Fang* and *The Call of the Wild*. Then it was on to Dickens, with *A Tale of Two Cities* and *Bleak House*, which I abandoned after the first fifty pages in favour of more modern stuff. In this way a whole week went by, during which I heard nothing from anyone. A second week threatened to be similar. This was ridiculous. If the CIA wanted to see me urgently, why were they taking so long? Surely they had agents in Britain? Why not interview me over here? I wondered what their real agenda was.

It was early on the second Wednesday when the telephone rang. It was Patrick's voice. I didn't need the password, but he insisted on using it.

'We're coming to see you this afternoon, no later than two. Okay?'

That was okay by me. 'Tell me, have they identified Nicola's killer?'

'Not yet. It's a joint Scotland Yard-Security Service operation. It'll take time. Anyway, we'll see you in about five hours.'

Yet again I made an effort to tidy the sitting room before my guests arrived. When they did appear, Martin was lugging a bulky item that he placed at my feet.

'Your new suitcase. Like it?'

'It's much bigger than I need, but I guess I'll want to buy some extra clothes over there.'

I felt its weight. It wasn't as heavy as it looked. 'I assume the fact that you've brought it means that I'll be going.'

'Correct. You're flying to New York on Saturday.'

'*This* Saturday?'

'That's right, August the fourth. A police car will pick you up at 6 a.m. Your flight leaves London at ten, and you'll be met on the other side by a CIA officer who'll accompany you to Washington. There you'll be accommodated in a hotel. All the necessary documents are in order.'

He reached into his briefcase and brought out a number of folders. 'Passport, visa, plane ticket, advice booklet for UK citizens travelling abroad, emergency telephone numbers including the British Embassy, and two hundred US dollars in new notes.'

'This sounds serious. What am I letting myself in for?'

'You're not getting cold feet now, are you?'

'No. I'll definitely go, but I have to admit to being apprehensive about the mysterious someone I'm supposed to be meeting. Can't you give me a clue?'

'We would if we could,' Patrick said, 'but we're equally in the dark. Anyway, you'll get a call from the police on Friday confirming the pick-up. Once again, don't leave the house or contact anyone, under any circumstances.'

'But someone ought to cancel the milk.'

'Forget it. After a few days the milkman will cotton on to the idea that it's not needed.'

Once they'd gone I had some stocktaking to do. In a way, I was glad to be leaving my 'prison'. I was nearly out of fresh food, and some other vital supplies were running low. Also, I had a serious job to attend to: my laundry. I hadn't washed any clothes since I'd left home, and the situation was fast approaching critical. In one corner of the kitchen I'd spotted a twin-tub washing machine, the sort my mother used in the sixties. It was more laborious to operate than an automatic, but I'd do my best. Then there was the matter of drying. There was a clothes line in the back garden, tempting to use on a warm August day, but if I went outside someone might see me from a neighbouring property and I'd be breaking the cardinal rule, so drying would have to be done indoors. Last was the ironing. That was well beyond my expertise, but I'd seen Nicola using an ironing board, so I was determined to have a go. Then I'd devote Thursday and Friday to preparing to move out, confident that I'd be leaving the cottage for ever.

CHAPTER 21: Simon

Transatlantic airliner flights were relatively novel in 1962. It was less than four years since the British Overseas Airways Corporation had introduced its first jet service from London to New York, using an ill-fated plane called the Comet, but now my flight was on the very latest aircraft to be employed on the route, the Boeing 707. At New York International Airport, later to be renamed in honour of President Kennedy, I was met by a brown-haired muscular fellow in his late thirties, who politely, but without the faintest flicker of a smile, introduced himself as Russell Chalmers. A CIA operative? I guessed so, although he didn't say as much.

'We'll be taking an internal flight to Washington DC almost immediately,' he said, leading me to another section of the terminal. 'Here, let me carry your suitcase.'

There was the air of a poor man's Lone Ranger about him, the makings of a Western hero, but palpably devoid of charisma. Our conversation didn't extend beyond the mundane, presumably because he was unwilling to touch on sensitive issues within the earshot of other passengers. In any case, he didn't seem to be the kind of guy to engage easily in light-hearted chat. Issuing orders appeared to be more his forte.

After landing at Washington he took me to a waiting car. 'You'll be staying at the Langton Hotel with another youngster by the name of Simon Blake. He'll show you around and help you settle in.'

Late afternoon at the Langton felt more like bedtime to me. Meekly, I followed Chalmers into the foyer, where he asked the staff to let this Blake person know we'd arrived.

'He went out after lunch and hasn't returned yet,' said the receptionist.

'That's damned inconsiderate!' Chalmers said, thumping the desk and giving the poor woman a start. 'He knew we were coming!'

He turned to me. 'I'll show you to your accommodation. You're in Room 207, and Simon is in 211.'

My room was pokey, with no *en suite* facilities and, unlike the London hotel, no TV set either. It also had very little by way of a view, as the window faced a tall building immediately to the rear. Was this the best the US government could offer a VIP? I wasn't impressed.

'The evening meal is in half an hour,' he said. 'Let's go down and get some coffee to keep us going. Simon should be here soon.'

This Simon, whoever he was, failed to appear at all, even for the meal. By seven-thirty I'd eaten my fill and was struggling to stay awake.

'You'll need to adjust to the time difference,' Chalmers said. 'Best be getting to bed. I'll make sure Simon catches up with you in the morning.' He handed me an envelope. 'In there you'll find some useful information, including a local map. There's also my telephone number, and fifty dollars in cash.'

'Thanks,' I said, keeping quiet about the two hundred I'd already received.

'Before I go,' he said, 'a reminder that tomorrow is Sunday. You'll need a day to get over your journey, so I'll see you again on Monday morning. A car will pick you and Simon up at nine-thirty sharp.'

With a feeling of security I'd lacked for the last two weeks, sleep was effortless. I must have snoozed for my normal length of time, for when I woke my watch was indicating 8:30 a.m. Since I hadn't adjusted it since leaving England, I reckoned the time in Washington would be more like three-thirty. Wide awake, even though it was the middle of the night, I put the light on, poured myself a fruit juice, and lay there wondering who this Simon was, and why he was staying at the same hotel. I guessed he was some sort of minder assigned to look after me. There was also the prospect of our appointment on Monday. If the American government wanted to know about Cuba, I'd be able to tell them little more than they knew already. I could recall the missile crisis of the coming autumn, and how it had ended with a Soviet climb down, but I didn't have any technical details to pass on. They might think they'd gone to a lot of expense for very little in return.

Still, that was their problem, not mine.

I went down to the dining hall as soon as breakfast was served, and had just finished eating when a young man strode into the room. He glanced around, then made a beeline for where I was sitting.

'You must be Roger,' he said.

'And you're Simon, I presume.'

He was a little taller than me, slim rather than skinny, with short, sandy-coloured hair and a liberal complement of freckles over his forehead, cheeks and arms. 'I'll grab some food and join you.'

'What do you think of Washington DC?' he asked, between mouthfuls of cereal.

'I've hardly seen it yet. Done little more than sleep since I arrived.'

'Then I'll show you around later. We've got all day.'

'Is that your job, to take care of me while I'm here?'

'Not exactly, but if you want to know more, it'll have to be in private, not in a room full of guests.'

'Fair enough, but I was just thinking, if you're supposed to be looking after me, why weren't you here yesterday evening?'

'As I said, I'm not here strictly to "look after" you. Still, I guess I should have been around for supper, but I happened to go for a drive in the afternoon, and found myself at a bar in the country, where I met a couple of stunning girls…'

'Please, don't talk to me about girls.'

'Why? Have you had some bad experiences?'

'You could say that.'

'Anyway,' he admitted, 'it was after midnight when I got back to the hotel.'

'That guy Chalmers wasn't too pleased.'

'Shh! Don't mention his name in here. Wait until we can speak in private.'

Breakfast over, Simon took me to his room, which was larger than mine, with two chairs as well as a double bed.

'Mind if I smoke?' he said.

'Yes, I loathe it. It makes me feel ill.'

An exaggeration, perhaps. As an apprentice I'd shared locker rooms with men who smoked incessantly, but now—

'Fair enough,' he said, 'and in any case I'm trying to give it up. But listen, Roger, even in here we ought to speak in subdued tones. I have a vague idea why they've brought you to America. It's because they think you have some special intelligence about what's happening in Cuba. The stuff you said about missile bases was widely reported over here. You appear to know what the Russians are doing before the Russians themselves are aware of it.'

'How do you mean?'

'Well, you claim that they're installing nuclear weapons in Cuba, but you've jumped the gun. They've barely started the job yet, but they *are* planning to build the bases, and you appear to know about it in advance. No wonder they're out to get you! It's not so much that you might have a contact in Cuba, but rather in Moscow itself, in the Kremlin strategic planning department.'

'How do you know the Russians are out to get me?'

'Chalmers briefed me a couple of days ago.'

'What else do you know about me?'

'Very little.'

'Okay, so you think I've got it wrong about the construction of the missile bases, because they don't exist yet; but if that's so, how do *you* know the Russians are even planning them?'

'Well, it's complicated. How long have you got?'

'All day, until I fall asleep again.'

'Right,' he said. 'Now bear with me, because I'm going to be saying some weird things. You may well think I'm crazy, because it'll sound like I'm speaking in the wrong tense, but please suspend judgment for a few minutes.'

'Go ahead. I'll listen to anything.'

'So,' he said, 'the story goes like this. When I left college I went into the computer business, which was in its infancy in those days. My home was in Virginia but I relocated to California and joined an IT company. Within ten years we were developing microprocessor applications, and five years after that I moved to the market leader in the field. I was well on my way to becoming a millionaire before I was forty.'

'Hold on. You called this a story. In what sense were you using the term, *story*?'

'In the sense of *life story*.'

'But wait a moment. How old are you?'

'Nineteen.'

'Then you can't have done all those things yet – and in any case you don't look like a millionaire.'

'Why? How do millionaires look?'

'Never mind that. What I mean is, you were describing a *possible* career path. Your personal career plan, your ambition, which is reasonable enough.'

'That's right, but it's also my *actual* career, viewed from the future.'

That was the moment my tiredness evaporated – temporarily at least – in a burst of adrenaline. It was as if I was witnessing a collision of worlds.

'What do you mean by, "viewed from the future"?'

'I said it was going to be complicated.'

'Right,' I said, 'but now I'm going to complicate it a whole lot more.'

I decided to tell him *my* story. His reaction couldn't be worse than Fangy's, or Nancy's or – God help me – Lustgarten's.

'Listen, Simon. As you spoke, something incredible started to dawn on me, so I'm going to hazard a guess. Tell me if I'm wrong, but would I be right in thinking that something happened to you on June the third this year?'

He gasped. 'Why did you pick that date?'

'Well, I have a hunch about the thing that "happened", and I don't think you're in the least bit crazy. I believe everything you've said. So, would you like to hear my story?'

'Go ahead,' he said, sinking back into his chair, as if suddenly taken ill.

'Then here goes. I was an apprentice with a chemical firm until I was twenty-one. See, *I'm* speaking in the past tense now. I worked hard and went to night school to get extra qualifications, which was tough, with a wife and baby girl in tow. Unlike you, I had no chance of becoming a millionaire – which might explain why Jane divorced me after seventeen years – but eventually I became deputy under-manager of a weedkiller plant, and remained there until my retirement in June 2010, when—'

'You suddenly woke up in 1962!'

'Yes! Exactly! What have we stumbled on, Simon? What was it that happened in 2010?'

'All I know is that I went to bed in San Diego and woke up in Virginia, forty-eight years earlier, and forty-eight years younger.'

'So whatever *it* was, it happened to both of us. Do you suppose it might have happened to anyone else?'

'Who knows? Until a few minutes ago I thought it had only happened to me.'

'Same here.'

'But then, it's unbelievably odd, anyway,' he said. 'Consider this. If we've come back to the *real* 1962, why don't things happen exactly as they did before? And when you think about it, for me to have come back from 2010, I must be *guaranteed* to live until then, however reckless I am now. Suppose I were to get myself killed in an accident tomorrow. How could I then live until 2010? And if I didn't live till 2010, how could I have come back from there in the first place?'

'I know what you mean,' I said, 'it does my head in, too. But let's imagine a possible explanation that doesn't involve any contradictions. Suppose for a moment there's more than one universe, or if you like, more than one version of *this* universe. It's not such a crazy idea. If you remember, by 2010 many respectable scientists were talking about a *multiverse*.'

'True.'

'So, all that needed to happen was the transfer of our consciousness from one universe to another, but with the timings out of sync by forty-eight years.'

'Is that possible?'

'It could be. No one knows what consciousness really is, or even why it exists.'

'Of course we do. Consciousness is a function of the brain. It's the electrochemical activity of neurons and synapses. So when the brain dies, consciousness dies.'

'Are you sure of that? Can you prove it?'

'If you were to press me, no, and I guess my simple materialism has been challenged by recent events.' He stood up and stretched. 'But whatever the truth of the matter, we are where we are, and we'll be meeting the CIA tomorrow. Have you thought what we're going to say?'

'We can hardly tell them the truth,' I said. 'They'll think we're mad.'

'Agreed. Yet I reckon we should tell them all we know about the Soviet plot for a nuclear Cuba. But first, I need to put you right on the details, so we can give them a consistent story. As I said, your memory let you down. You were too eager to show off on TV.'

'Believe me, it wasn't like that. I'd no intention of showing off. I was put under unreasonable pressure by the interviewer.'

'Okay, fella, but let's get a few things straight, shall we? President Kennedy was unaware of the installation of nuclear missiles on the island until mid-October of 1962. So when you blurted it out in late June, even the Russians must have been shocked. I bet many of the top brass in the Soviet military had no idea of the plan, but once you'd leaked it, it would make sense for the Kremlin to go for broke. I guess they've got the missiles and warheads ready, and ships lined up to transport them to Cuba, where they're frantically building the launch sites, months ahead of their original schedule.'

'Sounds scary.'

'And who's to blame for that? All it took was a two-minute gaff on British TV to trigger a frenzied escalation, one that has the potential to blow up in a matter of weeks.'

'Hell, Simon! You're making me feel extremely guilty. What have I started?'

'Don't be too hard on yourself. There's a simple solution. All we need to do is keep our nerve, and our leaders need to keep their nerve, too. If they do that, things will turn out just fine. Trust me.'

'Maybe, but you haven't said how you came to be here, with me. I reckon it's time for you to come clean. What do the CIA want from *you*?'

'I guess I don't have your presence of mind, Roger. On that first Sunday in June when I "arrived" in 1962, I was scared out of my wits – very nearly went insane. I fled my parents' home and for six whole weeks hid out in the forests of Virginia. I went down as a missing person. The police were involved, there were search parties, appeals for witnesses. My parents were distraught. Eventually I was in such a bad way, physically and mentally, that I staggered into a small town and got picked up by an ambulance. I spent four weeks in hospital and another week under the care of a psychiatric clinic, but while I was there, I came across a London newspaper and read about you, and what you'd said on television. Reading between the lines it occurred to me that I knew even more about the Cuban missile crisis than you did, because I'd been closer to it at the time, and I told a reporter from the *Washington Post* as much. He even wrote a piece about me in the paper. It conflicted with some of the things you'd said, but broadly corroborated your story about the plan to install nukes on the island. I was finally discharged from medical care on July twenty-fifth, less than two weeks ago. Back home, I managed to assume a "normal" life. I even got to drive my precious motor again, the first car I'd owned as a teenager. But the CIA had been taking an interest in me, and hatched a plan to pair me up with this weird guy from England. A few days ago they called to say they wanted me to come to Washington and meet you, and that they would pay my fare, to which I replied, "No fear, I'm coming in my own car. You can pay for the gas!"' He laughed. 'So, there you have it, the reason why we're both here today.'

'That clears up a mystery for me, Simon. I couldn't understand why, if the CIA were so interested, they couldn't interview me back home, *and* why they took so long to organise my trip to Washington. Evidently they were waiting for you to recover sufficiently before they could bring us both together.'

'Right.'

'And, days before I left England, I was told about a mysterious someone I'd be meeting over here. Now I know: you're that someone.'

'Right again, and tomorrow is our big day, the day when they interrogate us and try to get to the bottom of what we know about Cuba.'

'So, what do we tell them? Ought we to compare memories and get the story clear in our minds before we face any questions?'

'That shouldn't be necessary now that I've put you right,' he said. 'We're not felons needing to concoct a story to give each other an alibi. We just tell them the truth as we both know it. Insist that America stands its ground, confident that Khrushchev will back down. You and I know in advance that he'll bottle out, don't we? We've lived through it all before, but the president needs to be convinced. He should give orders to blockade Cuba and be prepared to sink any ships carrying military hardware to the island. We don't need to give in to nuclear blackmail. A nation of peasants is no match for the USA.'

'Is that how you regard the Cubans? As peasants?'

'I'm talking about the Russians.'

'Okay, so they did back down, but wasn't it the case that your president did some sort of deal with Khrushchev to get the missiles removed?'

'That's horseshit!'

'Don't you mean bullshit?'

'Horseshit where I come from. That story was invented much later to sooth Russian pride. When the Iron Curtain finally fell, everyone was keen to get on with our former enemies, to welcome them into the civilised world. But right now, in the sixties, we don't need to do any deals with the commies. Just stand up to them and they'll skulk away.'

'If you say so.'

'I know so. Therefore we tell it straight. Just give the CIA the facts, and hope our message makes it all the way up to the president. We've nothing to hide, nothing to fear. The truth will set us free – as someone important once said.'

He glanced at his watch. 'Anyway, Roger, it's nearly twelve thirty, and luckily for us, there *is* such a thing as a free lunch.'

CHAPTER 22: Misadventure

The afternoon was humid and hot, much hotter than London would have been in August, as we motored toward the centre of Washington DC, with all windows down.

'Sorry, no air-con,' Simon explained, 'but what do you expect in 1962?'

It hadn't occurred to me to expect anything. As for Simon's car, although small by American standards, it was clearly his pride and joy. There was nothing he loved more, it seemed, than to be out on the highway.

'I know there's a lot you want to show me, Simon, but perhaps we could save it for another day? What would suit me best this afternoon is to lie in the shade and chill out.'

'Fair enough. Look, we're approaching Potomac Park. Ideal if you want to hide from the sun.'

He parked up and we began an easy stroll among the trees. 'Pity you weren't here a few months ago when the cherry blossom was out,' he said. But the leafy canopy was all I needed.

'Obviously you know this area well.'

'I should do. I was born barely a hundred miles from here. In fact, my sister and mom were still living nearby in 2010 – and by nearby, I mean less than sixty miles away.'

I glanced over to my left. 'Ah, look at that strip of cool water.'

'You're not about to jump in? Swimming is strictly prohibited.'

'No, I just want to lie on the bank and gaze at it from the shade of a tree.'

'Come on then, over here…'

Simon's voice was fading in and out as he droned on about his great and marvellous country, and before long I was sound asleep. I might have slumbered on into the evening, had he not woken me with a sharp clap of his hands.

'Hey, Roger, don't you know it's nearly six o'clock?'

'Er – are we going back to the hotel now?'

'No! Remember that bar I visited yesterday? Let's go!'

I didn't have much choice in the matter. Soon we were heading out of town on a broad highway, much too fast for my liking, particularly with no seat belts. After half an hour he turned off along a quiet road heading into the countryside.

'Where are you taking me?'

'I told you. To a nice little bar in the middle of nowhere.'

'Ah, I get it. You want to find the girl you met last night.'

'I did happen to mention that I'd be along again this evening. But don't worry, we'll find another chick for you—'

'I've already told you. When it comes to girls, things always go wrong for me. Unbelievably wrong. Catastrophically wrong.'

'Then let me show you how it's done—'

'No, Simon, no! There's no way I can contemplate having a woman in tow right now. If you must know, I've had no fewer than three girls in my life in the past nine weeks. Nancy, Milena and Nicola, and every one turned out badly.'

'I'm not surprised. Three girls in nine weeks sounds positively greedy!'

'It's not how you think. One I ached for, one I fancied, and one I might even have loved…'

I began choking on my own words.

'Okay, fella. There's no need to get all emotional on me. We'll change the subject.'

He braked hard to take a sharp right-hand bend, before skidding across a narrow bridge that led on to a dirt road. 'Nearly there,' he said.

After a couple of minutes I'd regained my composure sufficiently to lay down another marker.

'Let me tell you something else, Simon. I'm not riding back to the hotel in your car after you've been drinking. I'd sooner get a taxi.'

He chuckled. 'I'm very careful in that department. Yesterday I did have a beer, just one, when I arrived at the bar, but after that I stuck to coffee, and was completely sober when I drove back to the Langton.'

'And then there's the supper we'll be missing at the hotel.'

'Don't worry your head about that. I'll get you something to eat at the bar.'

I wasn't happy. This was my first full day in a foreign country, I was here at the invitation of the authorities, and felt that I ought to behave wisely. But here I was, being bossed around by this apparent huckster whom I'd met just hours earlier, with no idea what to expect at Simon's 'bar'. It could have turned out to be a narcotics den for all I knew. Maybe it was the pessimist in me, but I sensed danger, particularly when our destination turned out to be more than an hour's drive from Washington. Eventually the car turned on to a dusty track that ran alongside a small creek.

'Here we are!' he exclaimed, as the bar loomed into view.

I could see a wooden structure standing alongside a handful of other buildings by the water, with a dozen or so cars parked outside. Simon drew up alongside an archetypal American gas-guzzler and, as he turned off his engine, I could hear music.

'This is it!'

'But where the hell have you brought me? Are we safe here?'

'Of course!' he said. 'I've known this place since I was a kid. My dad used to bring me here on summer evenings. It was here that I met Laura and her mom for the first time, when I was nine. They were regulars.'

'Laura?'

'The girl I was with last evening. We've known each other since elementary school. It was awesome that she happened to be around yesterday, just when I turned up.'

'Ah, I get it. Having reached the age of sixty-seven, you suddenly find you're nineteen again, and what's the first thing you think about? Chasing some girl you knew when you were a kid!'

'Not quite the first thing. I had to re-gain my sanity first. But then, having also re-gained my youth, it was only natural to—' He grinned knowingly at me. 'Of course, fella, I know you're far too sensible to obsess over a girl you knew fifty years ago. Far too sensible!'

'No comment.'

'Well? Are you coming?' he said, springing from the car and slamming the driver's door.

The bar turned out to be less of a dump than I'd feared. It was light and airy, with plenty of open windows on that sultry evening. An ageing African-American man was seated at the piano, while a younger white guy picked out a pleasing rhythm on the banjo. At the bar we encountered a young fellow who apparently knew Simon.

'Hi, Steve. This is Roger from England. He's staying with me in Washington for a few days.'

'Hi,' said Steve. 'Enjoying your vacation?'

'I only arrived yesterday.'

'So, Simon's brought you here to view the local talent, eh?'

Simon cut in. 'We're here for a quiet meal tonight.'

'Is that what he tells you? Wait until Laura arrives. She's a cracker. You should have seen him last night.'

Ignoring the banter, Simon turned to me. 'How about some food?'

'I take it we're not going back to the hotel for supper?'

'Definitely not.'

'Then I'll have a steak, well done, if you don't mind.'

'Just what I fancy,' he said.

We moved from the bar to one of the tables, and in due course two large plates loaded with food arrived. Simon kept glancing toward the entrance, no doubt expecting this Laura to appear at any moment.

'Have I made it sufficiently clear that I don't want to get mixed up with girls?'

'Yeah, but you're not much fun, are you?'

'It's alright, Simon. You go ahead and enjoy yourself. Have a little dance or whatever, but make sure you get us back to the hotel before midnight.'

'Why? Will my car turn into a pumpkin?'

I glared at him, stiffened my lips and said, slowly and deliberately, *Think what we're doing tomorrow.*

'Ah, yes,' he said, his face straightening. 'Better be fully awake when we meet the CIA. I'll tone things down this evening.' Then, realising he'd mentioned 'the CIA' rather too loudly, he glanced over his shoulder to see who might have been listening. Steve was lurking nearby. He caught Simon's eye and moved closer.

'Heard the news?'

'What news?'

'Norma Jean – dead.'

'You're joking!'

'No, straight up. Rumoured to be suicide.'

'That's a turn-up for the Kennedys.'

'I'll say!'

Simon glanced in my direction. 'I don't think Roger knows who we're talking about.'

'Marilyn Monroe,' said Steve. '*The* Marilyn Monroe. America's ultimate sex symbol.'

'Yeah,' Simon sighed. 'I used to fantasise about her as a boy. Mind you, it's rumoured that the Kennedys did more than just fantasise. Some people suspect that both Jack and Bobby were having it off with her. She even sang *Happy Birthday* to the president in public a couple of months back.'

He discarded the last fragment of his steak. 'Marilyn dead, that's big news!'

We'd finished eating and there was still no sign of Laura. My head sagged toward the table as I teetered on the edge of sleep. The sounds of the musicians had a distant quality. Eventually Simon's impatient voice woke me with a start.

'I know roughly where Laura lives. Let's see if we can find her.'

'Shouldn't we be getting back to the hotel?'

'It's only nine o'clock.'

'Feels more like 2 a.m. to me.'

I doubted if Simon was feeding me accurate information, but I had little choice other than to get back into his car, thankful that he'd been drinking cola rather than anything stronger. It was practically dark as we set off at speed along the dirt track. When we reached the tarmacked road he headed in the direction of Washington, but after a couple of miles turned off on to a side road that headed across relatively empty countryside.

'This is a shortcut to Laura's place,' he said.

The road was straight but not particularly wide, and we were travelling far too fast for comfort. Crossroads loomed up ahead, and I noticed the lights of a vehicle coming along the road from the left.

'There's another car approaching,' I said.

'Don't worry,' he replied, 'we have right-of-way.'

Simon slowed down a little, but continued heading straight for the crossroads. In the final few yards I was convinced that the other vehicle wasn't going to give way.

'He's not going to stop!' I yelled, something I later regretted, for if Simon hadn't braked hard at that point our momentum would have carried us across the junction, ahead of the vehicle, and a collision would have been avoided. As it happened, we skidded to a halt in the middle of the crossroads, only to be struck squarely by the other car, which was itself skidding toward us as the driver stood on his brake. The impact was sufficient to crumple the left side of our vehicle, which meant that Simon came off worse than I did.

When the noise had died down, I called Simon's name. There was no response. He was slumped over the wheel, unconscious. Someone was getting out of the other vehicle and coming toward us holding a torch.

'You could have killed us!' I spluttered, shocked but unhurt, then noticed that the lone driver appeared to be a boy rather than a man.

'I'm sorry,' he said shakily. 'I guess I wasn't paying enough attention.' An acknowledgement of guilt if ever I heard one.

He shone his torch in Simon's direction. There were no external signs of injury, no blood loss, but his breathing was weak.

'We must get help,' I said, a note of desperation in my voice.

'I'll see if my car is still drivable.'

The front was smashed, and some bits and pieces had spilled on to the road when the boy opened his door, but the engine started and one headlamp was still working. Cautiously he reversed until he was free of the wreckage of Simon's car.

'You must get help,' I said again. 'Can you get to a phone and call an ambulance?'

'I'll do my best. I think I passed one about three miles back.'

'I'll stay with my friend. Do your utmost to get help – *please!*'

He turned his car round and headed back along the road. I knew he might simply do a runner, and regretted that I hadn't made a note of his registration number. I just hoped the kid would keep his promise. With no medical skill I didn't know what to do for Simon, but, remembering how the woman had placed a coat over Nicola to keep her warm, I reached for a jacket on the rear seat and draped it over him.

A torch would have been handy. I could have used it to keep watch over Simon, but also to signal to anyone else who might approach us. Simon's wrecked car was in the middle of the crossroads, and there was a danger that we might be hit by another vehicle in the darkness. I felt in the glove compartment and found what I was looking for. Flashing the torch over the road I spotted the items that had fallen from the other car, and went over to examine them. Among a scattering of papers was an envelope addressed to a Kurt Dreschel, and inside was a letter from a high school, giving the dates of examinations. I stuffed it into my pocket.

After what seemed an age, but was probably less than three-quarters of an hour, I saw headlights in the distance. They were coming our way, apparently at speed, so I stood up with the torch and shone it along the road, directly into the headlight beam. I was ready to jump out of the way at the last moment if necessary, but the ambulance came to a halt a few yards short of the crossroads. With great care the crew eased Simon on to a stretcher.

One of the men asked me if I was okay. 'I don't want to leave the scene while this wreckage is still in the road,' he said. 'Let's see if we can move it to the verge.'

With three of us pushing, Simon's damaged car rolled off the carriageway.

'Right, let's get your friend to hospital. Jump in!'

The doors were slammed shut and we took off at speed. Staggeringly, this was the second time in just over a fortnight that I'd been in the back of an ambulance carrying an injured friend for urgent medical treatment. As the vehicle approached a built-up area the siren sounded, and we swayed first one way, then another, as the driver negotiated the streets on the approach to the hospital. Minutes later I was again sitting in the waiting area of a casualty department, praying that the news, when it came, would be good. It was 11.30 p.m. when we arrived, and time dragged for at least an hour before anyone approached me. At length one of the administrative staff asked for details of my friend's next-of-kin.

'He's not dead is he?'

'No, we think he'll survive.'

I could tell them very little. I knew Simon's name and approximate age, but as for his address, well, it was somewhere in Virginia, within a hundred miles of Washington. As for his parents, I had no idea of their names, other than 'Blake'.

'We'll inform the police right away.' History repeating itself yet again.

I tried to calm my nerves by losing myself in the latest newspapers, of which there was a decent selection lying around the waiting room. The hours dragged by, until at 3 a.m. a member of the medical staff came to me with news of Simon's condition.

'He's suffering from concussion and hasn't regained consciousness, but we don't believe his life is in immediate danger.'

What was I to do? Here I was, in the small hours of the day, in a hospital in some town whose name I didn't know. There was no way Simon and I would be meeting Russell Chalmers at 9:30 a.m. Luckily I'd made a point of copying his number on to a small piece of card and carrying it everywhere, but he would hardly appreciate being woken at three in the morning. Better to wait until after six.

Relative quietness descended on the waiting area and, stretched out across several chairs, I fell asleep, half-expecting the police to arrive at any moment and bring my slumbers to a premature end.

CHAPTER 23: Kurt

I woke to the sounds of personnel arriving for the day shift. It was nearly 7 a.m., and my first thought was to ask about Simon.

'He's in a stable condition, but remains unconscious.'

My second priority was to contact Chalmers. I asked to use the telephone at the desk, and took a deep breath before I spoke.

'Bad news. Simon's been involved in a car crash. He's in intensive care in – er – sorry, I don't even know the name of the hospital.' A member of staff put me right.

'It'll be some hours before I can come over,' Russell said. 'I'll need to speak to colleagues and reschedule the day's events. This is a damned nuisance!'

My inclination was to respond with something defensive, such as, 'It wasn't my idea to go driving late at night', but I held my tongue. Chalmers had reason to be annoyed, but some sympathy for Simon's situation wouldn't have gone amiss. I put the receiver down and wondered how to pass the time until he arrived. It might be afternoon before he'd be able to collect me. At least I wasn't hungry, with last night's steak still lying heavily on my stomach.

Reaching into my pocket I found the envelope that had fallen from the boy's car. On it was the name, 'Kurt Dreschel'. Who was he, I wondered. Perhaps the police had already picked him up, yet it was strange that they still hadn't come to the hospital.

I stared at the address. Dare I try to find the lad? Was I being unwise even to think of it? I wandered on to the hospital forecourt at the beginning of another humid day. Two taxis happened to be parked close by, the drivers leaning against their vehicles, smoking or just relaxing in the morning sunshine. Would they recognise the address? Curiosity got the better of me, and I showed the envelope to the first cabbie.

'Do you know this place?'

'Sure,' he said. 'I can have you there in half an hour.' Then, thinking I wished to engage his services, he began to open the car door for me, while I stepped back, unsure what to do.

'Well?'

Was I going or not? I still hadn't spent a dime of my latest fifty dollars, so I could well afford the trip. *What the heck*, I thought, *I'm going*. Perhaps it would turn out to be a wild goose chase, but it would be an interesting diversion, and I'd nothing else to do for several hours. So I got into the cab.

The address to which I was taken was in a small neighbouring town. The house was one of a neat row of timber-clad properties bordering an area of parkland. I paid the cabbie, but so as not to risk being stranded, asked him to wait while I found out if anyone was at home. There was no doorbell, so I gave a gentle tap with the knocker. No one came. All the curtains were drawn. Perhaps the folks were still in bed. I knocked harder. It was 8:35, hardly an unreasonable hour on a Monday morning. After one more firm hit with the knocker I heard footsteps on the stairs. The door opened just wide enough for the occupant to peep out, and instantly I recognised him as the young driver from the previous night.

'Hello,' I said, putting on a reassuring smile. 'Are you Kurt?'

'Yeah,' was the nervous reply. He didn't recognise me, having only met me in the dark, and in very stressful circumstances.

'I'm Roger. I was the passenger in the other car last night, who asked you to fetch an ambulance.' The door began to close. 'I wanted to thank you for getting help so promptly.'

'Is your friend okay?'

'Er – yes, no problem. He'll be fine.'

A honking sound indicated that the cabbie's patience was exhausted. I waved him off, then turned to Kurt, who was still peering around the partly opened door.

'I'm in big trouble,' he said. 'It was my mom's car, and I don't have a license to drive. I thought you were the police coming to get me.'

'I'd like to help. Have you told your mother about the accident?'

He looked away, his eyes showing the first evidence of tears.

'May I come in?'

Slowly he opened the door, and led me into the living room, where he sat, head in his hands, looking down at the floor.

'Is your mom around?'

He raised his head slightly. 'She died yesterday morning.'

Taken aback, I said, 'Oh dear,' or something equally vacuous.

'She was very poorly near the end, and I was there when she passed away. When I got home from the hospital I took her car out of the garage and drove off, half-intending to kill myself. I thought I might drive off the end of a jetty into a creek, or smash into a tree at high speed.'

'You don't still want to kill yourself, do you?'

'Probably.'

'Can anyone else help? Do you have any brothers or sisters?'

'No.'

'What about your dad?'

His reaction was immediate. I'd said the wrong thing. Anger welled up in his voice. 'My father,' he spluttered, 'as I discovered two days ago… my father is one of six Russians.'

The significance of his words was lost on me, so I said nothing. Surprisingly, in view of the fact that I was a total stranger, he proceeded to enlighten me further, as if these were things he needed to get off his chest. I now know that some of what I was about to hear had been divulged to no one else.

'My mother brought me here from Germany after the war. I was her only child. Life was tough, but she did her best for me. When I started school she trained as a teacher, and we were able to move to a better house, this one. Then a year ago her illness started. She hid it from me at first, but the cancer eventually took over and she had to give up work. The doctors did their best for her, but she lost the fight yesterday.'

'And you don't have any other relations over here?'

'No, and I don't even know of any back in Germany. I'd always assumed my father was a German officer who'd been killed in the war, and my mother let me believe this until two days ago. Then, knowing she was dying, she decided to tell me the truth. I wish she hadn't, but I suppose she thought I had a right to know. If she hadn't told me at that point, I would never have found out.'

I waited, too ignorant of the events of 1945 to anticipate what was coming next.

'My mother's family lived in eastern Germany. As the Red Army advanced they treated the civilian population very badly. They were war criminals like the Nazis. Do you understand? War criminals!' His young eyes flashed with anger. 'Are you hearing this?' he bellowed. 'Stalin's troops were war criminals!'

'Yeah, okay,' I said softly.

'My mother was nineteen. Her parents were already dead. She had an elder sister who killed herself rather than fall into Russian hands. Mom hid in a cellar, but they found her. She was violated by six soldiers. That's why I say one of them was my father. I didn't know any of this until Friday, not long before Mom lost consciousness for the last time. Can you imagine how it feels? I shouldn't be alive. I'm a misfit!'

'Don't talk like that,' I said. 'There's no blame attached to you. You're as innocent as your mother was.'

He was sobbing and unable to speak for several more minutes. I had no business intruding into his grief, and so I sat there feeling hopelessly out of my depth.

'I'd like to help if there's any way I can,' I said. 'You ought not to give up, for your mother's sake. She cared for you all those years, knowing full well how you were conceived. You've already told me she did her best for you. You owe it to her to do your best.'

At that point his rage boiled over. He picked up an ornament and smashed it against the wall, then reverted to sobbing. When he next spoke it took the form of a half-choked yell.

'I detest the Russians! They shot one of our planes down a few days ago. If I were the president, I'd nuke them right away!'

It would have been unwise to argue, so I said nothing until he spoke again.

'Who are you anyway? Your accent, it's strange.'

'I'm English. I arrived over here the day before yesterday. Last night I happened to be out with my friend—'

'And I ruined it for you, didn't I? Now the police will come and lock me away.'

'Look, Kurt, you made a mistake taking your mom's car, but you must call the police and tell them the truth. Explain how you felt. Surely they'll take your state of mind into account.'

'You mean, I'll be banged up for five years instead of ten?'

'You might not be "banged up" at all.'

'I will be if your friend dies.'

'Don't worry. He's going to be okay.'

'Anyway, I don't want to live anymore.'

Was he genuinely suicidal? I wasn't competent to judge, but it was out of a feeling of inadequacy that I said what came next. The words sounded trite even as they emerged from my lips.

'You may be hating yourself right now, but God loves you,' I whispered, remembering what my father used to say.

'What? How can "God" love me?' he said, his anger rising again. 'I shouldn't even exist.'

A response – helpful or not – came to me in a flash.

'Then neither should the rest of us, since armies have always done that kind of thing. We've probably all got a rapist in our history if we go back far enough.'

Perhaps philosophy wasn't what he most needed at that moment, but I waffled on.

'And in any case, you are still you, wherever you came from.'

He shrugged and put his head in his hands once more.

'I want to help you, Kurt,' I said. 'Don't give up hope. You've had over twelve hours to kill yourself, so I'm guessing you're not really intent on doing that.'

He reverted from anger to weeping once more. 'I don't know. I'm a total mess.'

I began to think of practicalities. 'Look, I'm only here for a short while, then I'll be going back to England. Do you have a friend who might be able to help? A school pal perhaps? Someone who will stick by you?'

'There's Gerry, he's my best buddy at school. We've known each other since we were five.'

'Then let's give him a call, talk things over—', but before we could pursue that possibility there was the sound of an automobile outside, and moments later someone was hammering on the front door. Kurt glanced at me apprehensively.

'Go on,' I said.

As he opened the door I heard the voice of a police officer. 'Kurt Dreschel?'

'Yes.'

'May we come in?'

'Yes, sir.' He led the two uniformed officers into the living room. They stared at me as though mildly surprised to find someone else in the house. One of them was about to address some words in my direction, when the other launched forcefully into Kurt.

'Can you tell me where you were at nine-thirty last night?'

'I was driving my mother's car.'

'So, where's the vehicle now?'

'It's in the garage.'

'Do you have the key?'

Kurt reached across to a shelf and picked up a bunch of keys. 'It's this one, sir.' The other officer said, 'I'll take a look,' and headed out of the room.

'We're investigating a hit-and-run incident,' said the first man. 'There's a guy in a coma in the county hospital.'

'Coma?' echoed Kurt. He caught my eye. I looked away and turned to the officer.

'Kurt's had a bad couple of days.'

'So has the guy in the hospital,' he retorted, but then seemed to realise what he'd just heard, an English voice. He turned to me. 'Who are you?'

'My name is Parnham. Roger Parnham.'

'Parnham! I heard that name on our radio only a few minutes ago. An alert to be on the look-out for someone by that name. There's a state-wide search under way. What the hell are you doing here?'

'Trying to help Kurt. Some terrible things have come his way. You need to hear the whole story.'

'We'll get the whole story, alright,' said the officer. He turned to Kurt. 'Tell me more about last night.'

'I crashed the car,' he said, managing to remain cool despite the cop's aggressive manner. 'I shouldn't have. I'm sorry.'

The officer turned back to me. 'Were you with him?'

'No, I was in the other car.'

'The other car? The one that was hit?'

'Yes.'

'Then you're a key witness.'

I was about to enlighten him further when his colleague returned from the garage. 'The vehicle's clearly been in an accident.'

'Call HQ,' said the first officer. 'Tell them we've found the hit-and-run driver, *and* the English kid, the one they're looking for. Two for the price of one. Not bad, eh?'

I was about to register a protest at being called a 'kid', but the officer got in first.

'Right, you guys, you're coming with us.' He turned to Kurt. 'I want all your house keys and the car key. Someone will be coming to take the vehicle away. If there are any personal items you'd like to have with you, you'd better get them now.'

'I want to help you, Kurt,' I said. 'Is there anything I can do?'

'Here's Gerry's phone number,' he said, handing me a scrap of paper. 'You could call him and explain what's happened. I'd feel less alone if he could keep in touch.'

'I'll do my best.'

By the time Kurt had assembled a few items, the second officer had returned from the squad car.

'Another vehicle will be coming to collect the English kid,' he said. 'We're to wait here until it arrives.' He turned to me. 'You'll be taken back to the Langton Hotel in Washington.'

Neither of the cops appeared to be aware of the fame, or notoriety, that Simon had claimed was attached to me in the States.

'We'll need to get a statement from him,' said his colleague. He turned to me. 'You can start telling us more right now.'

He insisted the four of us sit down, which we did for around twenty minutes while we awaited the arrival of the second car. I gave the officers my account of the previous evening's events in a way that was as sympathetic towards Kurt as I could reasonably make it, without actually lying. It wasn't a formal statement, I didn't have to sign anything, and we'd hardly finished when two more cops entered the room. My escort had arrived.

'Don't give up hope,' I said to Kurt as he was led away to one car, I to the other.

The second vehicle was manned by a plain clothes officer and a uniformed driver. On the journey back to Washington the plain clothes guy began to lay into me. He didn't seem to have any idea of CIA involvement, and apparently thought that I was connected with the diplomatic service, perhaps even the British ambassador's son. In any case he was quite clear about one thing. I wasn't supposed to be roaming the American countryside as if I was a tourist. Earlier that morning he'd been sent to the hospital to pick me up, only to find out that I'd disappeared without trace. It was some time later when he learnt that I'd been found at Kurt's home. He didn't seem too pleased about his 'wasted time'.

'When we get you back to the Langton you're to stay there, and not leave the hotel under any circumstances. Is that clear?'

At that point I said, for no good reason, 'I'm a British citizen.'

'So? That doesn't give you the right to go wandering around our country, getting involved in stuff that's none of your business.'

I was beginning to regret being an eighteen-year-old, and a young-looking one at that. I didn't feel I'd been at fault in any of the previous twenty-four hours' events, but to people like this officer I was just a 'kid'.

When the car reached the Langton the officer escorted me inside. He checked with the staff that they knew who I was, and again warned me not to leave the building. In due course someone from 'the authorities' would be coming to see me, he said. Closeted in the hotel, I would be out of harm's way.

Or would I?

CHAPTER 24: Brian and Sally

'Are you looking for Simon?'

It was shortly after midday when I reached the second floor corridor of the Langton, and, glancing beyond my own room, spotted someone standing outside Room 211, with knuckles poised to rap on the door.

'Why, yes,' he said, adjusting his spectacles to get a clearer view of the stranger who had posed the question. 'You know him?'

'Sort of.'

'Do you happen to know if he's in the hotel right now?'

'I know he's definitely not.'

'Damn! I need to see him urgently.'

'I might be able to tell you more if I knew who you were.'

'Er – I'm Brian Collins, a friend.'

He stepped forward to shake my hand, and in so doing tried to bring himself up to my height, failing by at least five inches, so I found myself looking at his thinning grey hair rather than his eyes – which I later noticed were a matching shade of grey.

'You're English, aren't you?'

Having had little experience of American accents, I didn't know quite where to place his, but guessed it belonged somewhere to the north of Washington.

'That's right. It's my first time in the US. I don't know Simon well; we met only a couple of days ago. We just happen to be staying in the same hotel.'

'A coincidence?'

'Why do you ask?'

He adjusted his glasses again. 'I seem to recognise your face. Aren't you the guy who made those allegations on British TV about Russian involvement in Cuba?'

'I think you've got me mixed up with someone else.'

He ignored what I said.

'Meeting you is just amazing! It's too much of a coincidence that the two of you are in the same city, let alone in the same hotel. Something big must be afoot.'

'I wouldn't know.'

'Don't tell me you haven't talked to Simon about it.'

'About what?'

I began to unlock my door, with the intention of slipping inside and keeping him out.

'Anyway, where's Simon?' he went on. 'Is something wrong?'

'Unfortunately, yes. I don't know if I should be telling you this, but last night he was involved in a car crash. He's in hospital, possibly still unconscious, and the police are involved.'

'Good Lord! Tell me—'

His voice faded abruptly as we became aware of other guests approaching along the corridor. I could have used this as an excuse to get away from him, but his concern for Simon appeared to be genuine and in a moment of weakness I opened my door and let him squeeze in. Seeing only one chair in the room, he offered to remain standing, but I beckoned him to sit down while I squatted on the bed.

'Okay, Brian. I can call you that, can't I? You haven't told me why you're here – why you were at Simon's door.'

He loosened his tie. 'I'm a reporter for the *Washington Post*.'

'Stop right there! Journalists are a no-go area for me.'

'Why? You are Roger Parnham, aren't you? *The* Roger Parnham.'

'I'm not at liberty to say.'

He grinned. 'What's all the secrecy about?'

'Look, Brian, you've no idea what trauma I've been through recently. No idea at all.'

'I do know about your brush with the Soviets. I have a copy of the London *Daily Express* sent to my office every day. That's how I recognised you.'

'That's not half of it, believe me. But you're not coming clean with me, are you? What's your involvement with Simon?'

'I've nothing to hide, so I'll tell you. I covered his strange disappearance a few weeks ago. It meant next to nothing originally, but when days turned into weeks it became a major story in Virginia.

When he came out of hiding I tracked him down in hospital and we struck up a close friendship. I don't know if you're aware of this, but he's had some kind of mental breakdown; imagines he's visited the future, poor fellow. There must be a scientific term for it. I've been trying to persuade him to have ongoing psychiatric help, but when we spoke a few days ago he still wasn't keen. However, he did tell me he'd be staying at this hotel over the weekend, so it seemed a good opportunity to catch up with him. But now you tell me there's been a road accident! How unlucky can he get?'

'Alright, Brian, you've guessed who I am. But I'm not sure I should be talking to journalists at all.'

'Why not? Is it *verboten*?'

'No, but over the past few weeks I've got tangled up in too many affairs that I've lived to regret. In fact, I'm a walking disaster. The main thing for me now is to keep out of trouble, and you'll do well to steer clear of me if you know what's good for you.'

'Hey, you don't need to be scared of me. I know what you mean about "affairs".'

'Okay, Brian. Allow me to do a bit of psychoanalysis on you. I've encountered enough reporters to work out what's going on in that tiny mind of yours. You've had a virtual monopoly on Simon's story, and now you see your chance to be the first American to interview this weirdo from England. And I guess you're going to report what's happened so far today, whether I agree to talk to you or not.'

He smiled. 'Ah, but I can go one better. You see, after I'd published my most recent piece about Simon, a national TV network got in touch. They wanted the chance to interview him, too. In fact, they were hoping to do so today, and knowing that Simon was staying here, I came to negotiate with him on their behalf. Of course, what you've told me changes all that.'

'It certainly does. I don't think he'll be making any television appearances for some time.'

Even as I spoke, I guessed what was coming next.

'But they'd be even keener to obtain an interview with you.'

'No, Brian, no! I'm under strict instructions not to set foot outside this hotel.'

'You won't need to. The TV crew have already arranged to come here to film the interview. They've even booked the conference room.

All that was needed was Simon's agreement. So suppose they meet you instead?'

'I don't think that's something I ought to be doing.'

'Why not? Have you sworn an oath of secrecy?'

'No. I've been told very little.' I reduced my voice to a whisper. 'I know I shouldn't be telling you this, but the CIA were supposed to be collecting both of us this morning, to begin some sort of investigation into our unexplained ideas, but obviously that's been put on hold.'

He was about to press me further, but I had other priorities. 'Do me a favour, Brian, I'm starving. It's lunchtime, and I haven't had a bite to eat since yesterday evening.'

'Okay. You sort your stomach out while I phone Sally.'

'Who?'

'Sally Toms. She's the TV reporter who was coming here to interview Simon. I'm going to tell her I've found you instead.'

'So, you had it all pre-arranged, even without Simon's knowledge?'

'I was pretty sure he'd agree to an interview. It's long overdue. I'm surprised no one else has bagged him.'

'So you think they'll want to "bag" me instead, these friends of yours?'

'Sally's a respected television journalist,' he insisted.

'Look, Brian, as I've already said, I'm not sure this is something I should get involved in.'

'But this is the land of the free,' he grinned. 'Whatever is not expressly forbidden is permitted.'

In the dining hall, while devouring what was left of lunch, I weighed up the situation. Supposing I agreed to speak to this Sally person: some strict ground rules would need to be settled in advance. Not so much as the slightest mention of the CIA, nor indeed of the British Security Service. And the hotel where I was staying mustn't be identified either. In fact, I would prefer the city to remain anonymous as well. Come to think of it, in view of the enemies I'd made back home, I'd want her to pretend she was interviewing me in England, so my trip to the States could remain secret. With these provisos, I *might* be willing to give an interview. Particularly if money was involved.

Brian reappeared as I was finishing my meal. 'The TV crew will be arriving in half an hour.'

'Remember I haven't agreed to anything,' I said, and began to outline the terms under which I might be willing to speak to Sally Toms. He tried to assure me that my concerns would be met. But could I trust what he said?

Sally arrived with a film crew of three. An energetic thirty-something blonde, barely five feet tall, she sported thick scarlet lipstick, fingernails like claws, and spectacles as loud as her Kentucky voice. Brian greeted her as she breezed into the hotel.

'Come and meet our English guest,' I heard him say.

She shook my hand, but before she could utter a word I pointed along the corridor. 'Let's go to the conference room right away.'

'Then you're agreeing to the interview?'

'We need to get a few things clear first. As far as the TV audience is concerned, we're in London. The only American voice to be heard will be yours. If you mention a date, it was yesterday, allowing time for the film to be flown across the Atlantic for broadcast here. And finally, there's the small matter of a fee.'

'You are the real Roger Parnham, aren't you?'

'I don't know any unreal ones.'

'Then I reckon CBS would agree to a thousand dollars.'

'Make it two.'

'I can't guarantee that right now, but I don't see why not.'

The film crew began setting up their equipment. I didn't suppose they had video recorders in 1962. There would be real film rolling inside the camera. Black and white, of course.

'Right, what are we going to talk about?' she said. 'You'll be addressing an American audience, so you'd better get some facts about Cuba clear in your mind.'

She knew her stuff, a consummate professional, so I listened attentively.

'I don't know if you remember, but when Fidel Castro's revolutionaries took over the island three years ago, our government was quick – perhaps too quick – to recognise the new regime. In fact, Castro made a goodwill tour of the US soon after. Imagine that! But it all went sour when he declared himself to be a Marxist, abolished elections, and started nationalising American-owned companies. It was then that the CIA began plotting his downfall in earnest, and when Jack Kennedy became president last year they expected to have his full support for an invasion of the island by a force of Cuban exiles. The Bay of Pigs: an utter disaster! But it was then that the Russians saw their chance. They awarded Castro the Lenin Peace Prize and drew him deeper into their orbit, and that's where he is today. Oh, and I didn't mention, earlier this year Castro was excommunicated by the Pope.'

'That must have been a blow,' muttered Brian, who was overhearing our conversation.

'Anyway,' Sally continued, 'the President didn't waste much time in advising US citizens to start building fallout shelters in readiness for a nuclear attack. Not from Cuba, of course, but from Moscow. And now, Roger, you've raised the tension to boiling point with your allegation of nukes less than a hundred miles from our shores. So bear these things in mind when you decide how to answer my questions.'

'Okay,' I said, 'but one other point. It's unbelievably sweaty in here, and it'll be even worse when they switch those big lamps on. What about some ventilation?'

One of her colleagues went over to a window and began to open it.

'Only an inch or two,' she said, 'because of the traffic noise.'

Brian offered to fetch an iced drink. 'Thanks, buddy,' I said.

I sat in a padded chair, my shirt open at the neck, and sleeves rolled up. The heat didn't seem to bother Sally. She sat in a similar chair close by, scribbling a few notes to guide her through the interview.

'Right, let's go,' she said, as the film crew signalled they were ready.

'Welcome to London,' she told her audience, 'where I have with me eighteen-year-old Roger Parnham. On June twenty-fifth this year he appeared on British television and declared that the Soviets were installing nuclear missiles in Cuba.' She turned to me. 'But you've never revealed the name of your Russian informant, have you?'

'Why should I?'

'Did you travel to eastern Europe to meet him?'

'Who said it's a him?'

'You mean it's a woman?'

'I didn't say that.'

'Still, I understand there's been an attempt on your life, right here in the street.'

'That's true, which implies that someone knows what I said is correct.'

'You realise the US government are trying to confirm if your allegations are true, using aerial reconnaissance?'

'Yes, but it's difficult. They're looking for concrete structures which might be the foundations for medium-range launch pads.'

This may have sounded knowledgeable, but what Sally didn't know was that I was making most of it up on the spot. I was even surprising myself and finding it amusing, an easy way to earn a couple of thousand bucks. The idea of having an Eastern Bloc informant was particularly comical.

'So, suppose you're correct,' said Sally. 'What should America do about it?

'Well, from your point of view it's got to be stopped. Let's think how you might do that.'

I concocted an argument based on snippets I'd read in American newspapers in the hospital waiting room. It gave me a mild sense of fun, playing with ideas I'd picked up a few hours earlier.

'You could launch a direct invasion of the island from the sea, but it would have to be on a massive scale, costing many lives on both sides. And the Russians wouldn't stand idly by. They'd move to support their ally. Result: world war. *Or*, you could try to destroy the missile bases from the air by direct bombing, but that wouldn't be easy either. It might take many attempts and cause thousands of casualties on the ground, including Soviet technicians. And it would be sure to provoke a Russian response, not necessarily over here, but in Europe. It would give them an excuse to invade West Berlin, and things could easily escalate out of control, again leading to all-out war.

'I think your best bet, to begin with at least, would be to impose a naval blockade of Cuba, preventing the approach of any ships from the communist bloc. You'd have to put it in place early enough to prevent the nukes themselves ever arriving on the island – and again, things could turn very nasty, since a blockade could, in itself, be construed as an act of war.'

'So, which option would you recommend?

'I'm no military strategist,' I said, almost pompously, 'but I think a naval blockade would carry the lowest risk, coupled with the greatest chance of success. Yet for such a plan to be credible, you'd have to be prepared to attack Soviet ships on the high seas, an approach that would be fraught with danger.'

'So, Mr Parnham, if you could send a message to our president right now, what would it be?'

I looked directly at the camera. 'Well, Mr President, sir,' I said, 'it's a tough call, but I suggest you put that blockade in place as soon as possible, to starve the missile programme of resources. That way the nukes could never be deployed. Insist that the Soviet supply ships turn around. Show Khrushchev your resolve and he'll back down.' I had Simon's assurance of that. 'Don't give in to nuclear blackmail.' Simon's words echoed around my skull. 'Stand firm, sir. *No deals.*'

Sally addressed her TV audience. 'Well, folks, you heard it here first, on CBS. The next big thing in—'

There was loud smashing sound as the conference room door was kicked open and an enraged figure burst in.

'What the hell's going on in here?'

Chairs and tables were flung to one side as he headed to where we were sitting.

'You damned fool!' he yelled at me.

I was dumbstruck. I'd never witnessed the full might of Russell's temper before. He was a force to be reckoned with. The Lone Ranger had nothing on him when it came to blind fury.

'Who are you?' screamed Sally. 'What gives you the right—'

He yelled back, and started to manhandle her. One of the camera crew moved forward, and sensing an opportunity for a moment of heroism, took a swing at Chalmers.

'Not so fast, you ignorant jerk—'

Chalmers picked him up bodily and flung him across the room, where, fortuitously, he landed on a well-upholstered sofa.

'Send for the cops, someone!' yelled Sally.

Chalmers was now turning his attention on the equipment, knocking over microphones and trying to force open the camera in order to expose the film and ruin it. The guy who'd attacked him moments earlier staggered across the room, grabbed a wooden stand and whacked Russell across the head. He fell to the floor, out cold.

Sally shouted to another of her colleagues. 'Quick, grab the camera and get out of here, fast. Make sure the film gets to the studio safely. I want the interview shown nationwide tomorrow evening.'

She turned to me. 'Thanks, Roger, that was great. You'll be hearing from the company in two or three days. Oh, and where's Brian?'

Poor Brian was hiding behind a display board. He emerged timidly and stared down at Chalmers, who was still unconscious.

'Think carefully before you report any of this in the *Washington Post*,' Sally warned him. 'Now, I reckon we should make ourselves scarce before the police arrive.'

That seemed a good idea to me. Hurrying out through the doorway I glanced back and thought I saw Chalmers beginning to stir. I shouted goodbye to Sally and Brian, headed upstairs, dived into my room, locked the door, and wedged the chair hard up against it.

CHAPTER 25: Newspapers and News

'Were the cops here last night?' I asked the man on reception as I made my way to breakfast.

'No, but an ambulance crew was. They carried a guy out of the conference room on a stretcher.'

I let my eyes wander, pretending to be unconcerned. 'There's something else I wanted to ask. Do you have the *Washington Post* delivered here?'

'Yes, sir. Three copies each weekday, and four at weekends. You'll find newspapers in the rack behind you.' He pointed across to the far wall.

From then on it would become my habit to grab the *Post* each morning on my way to the dining hall. Quickly scanning that day's edition I could find no mention of an altercation at the Langton Hotel, and interestingly, not a single article attributed to a Brian Collins. Was he a genuine *Post* reporter?

After breakfast I wandered the first floor of the hotel, and found three lounge areas equipped with television, each tuned to one of the three major networks, NBC, CBS and ABC. From now on I'd be paying more attention to the news, with CBS my channel of choice, as it was the service piped to the *non-smoking* lounge. And, if Sally had her way, it would be screening my interview that very evening. The broadcasting schedule indicated that the national news bulletin would be on at 7:15 p.m., so I would aim to be there by seven.

The rest of the day had a certain emptiness about it. What was I supposed to be doing? The CIA had brought me here for reasons best known to themselves, but Chalmers had been my only contact with the outfit since I'd arrived in the US, and now he was wherever the ambulance crew had taken him. No one else, from any organisation, had attempted to contact me. Still, I was staying in a half-decent hotel, the food was plentiful and reasonably good, laundry was included, and it wasn't costing me a penny. There was an abundance of reading matter: newspapers, magazines and a small collection of books. I didn't need to be bored. My weekend had been packed with enough action to last a month.

I took my evening meal early so as to be in the TV lounge for seven o'clock. Local news came on first, followed by the main bulletin at a quarter past. Then, at seven thirty, 'In a change to our normal schedule, Sally Toms brings you an interview with—'

I became acutely self-conscious. There were about twenty other guests in the lounge and they would be sure to recognise me as the guy being interviewed. I got up and walked smartly to the door, glancing back to see what was coming next. Peering over my shoulder I could see shots of the conference room and Sally beginning her introduction. It was my cue to beat a hasty retreat to my room.

As I sat in the chair with my feet on the bed, wondering if Chalmers might be watching the interview from a hospital bed somewhere – and having a heart attack at what he was seeing – I remembered a solemn promise I'd made. I'd told Kurt I would try to contact his friend Gerry. Where had I put the phone number? It was still in the inside pocket of my jacket. I reckoned there would be just enough time to get to the pay phone in the foyer and make the call before the interview was over.

'Gerry's away at summer camp,' said a female voice. 'He'll be home on August seventeen.'

'When he gets back, please tell him a friend of Kurt's was trying to contact him, and I'll call again later.'

That was all I could do.

The best way to avoid the eyes of other guests at breakfast time was to eat early, as early as it became available, which was seven o'clock. Thus I set my alarm for six-thirty. Grabbing Wednesday's edition of the *Washington Post* from the rack, I could already see the banner headline: 'NO DEALS, Mr PRESIDENT'. I found a corner table in the dining hall, sat with my back to the few other guests who were there, and devoured my cereal, eggs, bacon, beans, toast and coffee as fast as I could without choking. Before leaving I concealed a couple of small cakes inside my jacket, then headed back to my room, where I spread the paper out on the bed and read every word of the front page. My TV appearance was causing a stir right across America. The interview had been brief, allowing every word to be repeated in print. Inside the paper the political columnists were airing their views. Some appeared to be knowledgeable on matters of military strategy, while others preferred to speculate wildly in order to disguise their ignorance. But no one at the *Post* had questioned the assumption that the interview had taken place in London. In fact, the film was scheduled to be screened on BBC television the next day, so I could imagine my foreign embassy 'friends' in Britain renewing their efforts to find me over there. Good luck with that.

There was one moment of excitement the following day. A letter arrived from CBS, with a form to sign and return. They would be sending a cheque for twelve hundred dollars, my fee for the interview. Not quite the two thousand I'd suggested to Sally, but still a substantial sum to add to my steadily growing fortune – although I'd no idea how I would pay it into my account in Nottingham.

Days passed. We were now deep into August, and still no one from the authorities had been in touch. Yet my hotel bill was continuing to be paid, perhaps by default. Meanwhile, the worst aspect of my existence was the fact that I was being kept under a kind of house-arrest, while an inviting city beckoned beyond the windows. I wondered if I might dare to sneak out, and whether anyone would notice if I did. It was tempting. And there were other baffling questions. Why hadn't the police visited me to obtain a formal statement about the circumstances of the crash that had landed Simon in hospital? And what was Simon's condition? He might have died for all I knew.

It was not until August the 18th, fully two weeks after my arrival in America, that some of these questions began to be answered. Late that morning there came a knock on my door. It was Chalmers at last, still physically formidable, but strangely diminished in energy and self-assurance.

'How are you, Roger?'

'I'm fine, but I could ask you the same.'

'I'm okay,' he said, 'considering I've spent a week in hospital, and several more days recuperating at home.'

'A week in hospital? Why?'

'Haven't you heard? It was a head injury. Quite nasty. I sustained it here at the hotel – in the conference room, I think. Something must have fallen on my head. I don't remember much about it, but I seem to recall that you were there with a blonde woman and some guys with a camera. Yes, that's right, and I got real mad. Sorry!'

Wow, I thought, a knock on the head has worked wonders for Russell's personality!

He stroked his crown cautiously. 'However, I've come to tell you about someone else who's still in hospital. We've received word that Simon is now out of the coma, sitting up in bed, and beginning to talk freely.'

'That's excellent news.'

'Isn't it just? I wonder if you'd like to come with me to visit him?'

'Of course! It would be great to see Simon again. Besides, I haven't set foot outside this wretched hotel for over a week.'

'Okay,' he said, 'I'll pick you up in the morning.' Then, 'Huh, let's go down to the bar. I'm only just getting back into the swing of things.'

At the bar, Chalmers confined himself to fruit juices. It was as if I was speaking to a different guy from the one who'd met me at New York airport. Subdued, he was none the less clued up on the gathering international storm.

'Did you see the news this morning, Roger?'

News? How could I have missed it? But, in view of his altered personality, I was relaxed enough to tease him a little. Did he mean the news that East German guards had started to shoot people who tried to flee to the West over the Berlin Wall? Or that there had been an attempt on the life of President de Gaulle? Or even the reports that Saudi Arabia might be about to abolish slavery?

'No, fella, I'm talking about your favourite subject: Cuba. Last night Adlai Stevenson, our ambassador at the UN, had an almighty ding-dong with the Soviet representative. He spoke about the grave situation developing on the island. Of course, the Russians responded by categorically denying everything. Stevenson was as good as calling them liars. Which, of course, they are.'

'Sounds highly dangerous.'

'That's putting it mildly.'

He downed the last of his grapefruit juice. 'Anyway, what time shall I pick you up in the morning? Shall we say ten o'clock?'

This was the new Russell, negotiating rather than barking orders. Not ranting over my TV appearance as I might have expected. Not even mentioning it.

'Okay, see you tomorrow at ten,' I said, and returned to my room, where I reflected on the international drama now unfolding. Simon had been right. As a consequence of my original television interview, events were moving at an accelerated pace. The confrontation at the UN had happened in *August*, weeks ahead of what I remembered from the 'original' 1962. Things could get out of hand all too quickly. I only hoped that Simon was also right about how the story would end.

CHAPTER 26: Warburton

It was an hour's journey to the hospital where Simon was being treated. Chalmers seemed more confident now, and quite relaxed as he drove along the highway, making occasional light-hearted comments – about the weather, about his favourite films, about the price of avocados – until we were on the final approach to the hospital. Then his mood changed. In fact, everything changed as a result of what we saw. The police were out in force, their vehicles blocking the hospital entrance. Whatever they were up to, Chalmers had received no prior notification. He parked the car, and with a 'wait here', jumped out, leaving me to watch and wonder. I saw him approach one of the officers and begin an animated discussion before the two of them disappeared into the building. There wasn't much I could do but sit and wait, glad that the car was parked in the shade. Half an hour went by before Russell returned, grim-faced.

'Simon's gone!'

'Gone?'

'Disappeared, sometime between five and seven this morning. They're confident he's no longer in the hospital.'

'He discharged himself?'

'No chance. He wasn't in a fit state. It was all he could do to sit up. He must have been wheeled out of the place, and no one so much as noticed.'

My immediate thought was CCTV, but this was 1962.

'So, he's been taken? Abducted?'

'We must assume so. Probably on a trolley, or in a wheelchair. Someone could do it, you know. Simply dress up in nursing gear. Yet there was supposed to be a twenty-four hour guard in place. Someone has serious questions to answer. It's all so damned stupid!'

Chalmers seemed to be regaining his old assertiveness, if not his former temper.

'But why?' I said. Even as I asked the question, I was formulating my own answer. It had a familiar ring about it. Simon had been saying some provocative things. Perhaps just the one piece in the *Washington Post* had done it for him, when he'd revealed even more than I had about Soviet involvement in Cuba. As a result, the CIA had brought him to Washington, and Brian had sniffed him out. Brian in turn had informed the TV company, and they'd been planning an interview. Someone else must have been taking notice – someone who also would dearly like to speak to Simon. Who might that be? I couldn't be sure, but I had my suspicions, and even more sinister was the thought that there might be at least one double agent within the CIA itself.

'The cops are trying frantically to find witnesses,' he went on. 'The FBI have been called in, and they've put out a nationwide alert. He's got to be found, for his own sake. He still needs medical care. And beyond that...'

Yes, I knew. Beyond that, there were the political and military implications. Whoever had taken Simon wasn't doing research into road traffic accidents.

'You realise there's no question of you staying at the Langton any longer. We were about to move you in any case, well out of the reach of journalists and TV crews, but now it's even more imperative. Under duress, Simon might reveal what he knows about you, and that could put your safety at risk.'

Hell! I thought. *London all over again.*

'I'm taking you back to the hotel for now, and there'll be a police guard on the place until we can get you moved. Okay?'

It had to be okay. I had no choice but to go along with whatever they saw fit to do.

At least two plain-clothes police officers were detailed to watch over me at the Langton. One of them had been assigned the task of breathing very closely down my neck. He had a chair at the corner of the corridor that ran past my room. When I visited the bathroom he lurked outside. When I went to the dining area he too had a meal, sitting separate from me, but with a clear view of my table. The other guy was on watch at the main entrance. I didn't see much of him, nor of a possible third officer lurking at the rear of the hotel.

It was mid-morning on Thursday, August the 23rd, when Chalmers arrived with news. 'We're moving you to Andrews Air Force Base,' he said. 'Secure accommodation has been arranged there.'

'An airfield?' I echoed. 'Where might that be?'

'Barely a dozen miles from here.'

'Do I have to go?'

'I'm afraid you've no alternative. You can't imagine we'd send you back to England now, surely?'

'Well, no, and I wouldn't want to go. It's been suggested that my very existence is 'inconvenient' to someone over there – and in any case, I'd like to know that Simon is okay. Also, there's a lad called Kurt, possibly being held by the police. I'm concerned about him as well. In fact, I've been trying to contact a friend of his—'

'You've been doing *what*? Kurt who?'

'Dreschel.'

'*Madre mia!* That young man is the subject of a serious police investigation. You've no business getting involved!'

Chalmers was back to his old form. Arguing with him was pointless.

A final night at the Langton was followed by transfer in a police car to Andrews Air Force Base. I was expecting some kind of aerodrome, with a few hangers and a dormitory. I was wrong. Andrews was a huge place. Not merely an airfield, but a whole community, with houses, stores, medical facilities – all the infrastructure of a small town – and untold government and military premises on site. I was driven to one of the less accessible parts of the base, to my accommodation in a restricted area. There I was introduced to a Sergeant Dan Warburton of the military police. He was to be in charge of my welfare and security.

Warburton was the sort of character for whom the description larger-than-life was doubtless coined. Flamboyant, eccentric, about fifty and of mixed race, he was a great hulk of a man, yet surprisingly athletic for his weight. He was a guy with 'presence', who liked to be the heart and soul of whatever was going on. I got the impression that

e'd missed his true vocation as a stand-up comedian and had to make
do with amateur performances. Most of his jokes either were, or
bordered on, sexist, racist, or at least non-PC – not that I heard
anyone use that term in 1962 – and one of his specialities was gags
about honeymoon couples. It occurred to me that the wedding night
genre had all but died out by the start of the twenty-first century,
whereas in the early sixties it was still going strong. In those days,
before the Swinging Decade had run its course, the wedding night was
still supposed to be Their First Time, and so provided fertile ground
for the comic imagination, whereas no one thought like that in 2010.

Warburton was a little too fond of laughing at his own jokes, but
his infectious, deep-throated chortle made up for that. I addressed
him as 'Sergeant', while he had an annoying habit of calling me
'laddie'. I had my own small room at the base, and would be having
meals with some of the military personnel. I decided that this wasn't
going to be much fun, even with the resident comedian's gags, and
feared that boredom might soon take over, but I couldn't have been
more mistaken. After settling in over the weekend, the first three days
of the following week brought action in the shape of visits from three
teams of investigators.

On the Monday I was interviewed, at long last, by three officers
from the CIA. Chalmers was one of them, but I wasn't told the names
of the other two. Apparently they'd amassed an abundance of
intelligence data, including numerous aerial photographs,
corroborating my claim that Russian engineers were overseeing the
construction of launch sites for nuclear-armed missiles on the island
of Cuba. They demanded to be told how I'd known about this
programme back in June, fully nine weeks earlier. Who'd tipped me
off? My initial response, that it had been 'mere guesswork' was
dismissed as 'utterly implausible' by Chalmers, with 'a probability of
less than one per cent.'

To say that I was made to feel uncomfortable would be putting it
mildly. This encounter was ten times worse than my interrogation by
'Boyle' and company on June the 30th. At least *they* had accepted that I
was some kind of nutter. As far as these American agents were
concerned I must have been in touch with an informant at the heart
of the Soviet military – someone they would dearly like to speak to

themselves. I could detect a whiff of desperation in their questioning. As for putting forward a theory of parallel universes, I might as well have invoked the existence of leprechauns and hobgoblins. What they wanted were precise details of my contact.

'Just tell us, and we'll leave it at that. Otherwise, expect to see us again in a few days.'

One final remark – which I found hilarious – was advanced by the youngest member of the trio as they were leaving. He'd been 'truly impressed' by how knowledgeable I'd appeared to be in the CBS interview.

The following day brought a visit from two police officers seeking further testimony about Simon's road accident. They extracted a full statement from me. And on Wednesday – *oh, joy* – two members of the British Security Service, apparently based in the US, questioned me about my experiences with Soviet agents in London, tying their investigation to Nicola's murder. One of them was a pompous buffoon by the name of Lawrence, richly endowed with an over-inflated sense of his own importance. Asked if they were any nearer finding the poor girl's killer, he gave an evasive reply, and to make things worse, just as they were leaving he turned to me with a sickly grin.

'Oh, and by the way,' he smirked, 'our colleagues in London have been investigating the Soviet Embassy staff. You may be interested to know that your 'Miriam' is twenty-three, and apparently young boys aren't her forte.' I could have planted my fist down his smug, self-satisfied throat.

The following day I was overtaken with guilt that I hadn't contacted my parents since that July day when I'd phoned them from the London police station. I'd thought of calling them many times since, but those intentions had never been converted into action. Only now did I approach the sergeant with a request to be allowed to phone them.

'Oh, I don't know about that, laddie,' he said. 'I'll have to check with my superior officer.'

Checking didn't take long. Phoning my parents was a no-no. In fact, phoning anyone was a no-no, but I could write to them any time, provided I was willing to allow an intelligence officer sight of the contents. Those were the terms, and if I didn't like them, I knew what I could do. So, I wrote a letter, and trusted Warburton to get it into the post for me.

At Andrews I had full access to the news media. All the major American newspapers were available, as were the national television channels. The potential confrontation between the great powers was beginning to dominate the agenda, while life in other areas went on much as usual. Nelson Mandela had been arrested in South Africa, Martin Luther King jailed in Georgia, and arguments about the circumstances of Marilyn Monroe's death continued unabated. But then, early one morning, Warburton burst into my room wearing a grin that seemed to more than fill his face.

'Hey, laddie,' he said, 'have you heard the one about the politician, the show-girl and the spy?'

I wondered where was he going with this. A threesome was hardly a promising start for a wedding night gag, but I went along with it. 'No, tell me. I could do with a good joke to cheer me up.'

'It's no joke, laddie. It's the latest sensation around the camp. Someone tuned in to the BBC this morning and picked up the news. It's all happening over there.'

'What?'

'A real-life sex story, juicy as you could wish for! One of your newspapers is reporting that the British War Minister, a guy called Profusion or something, has been having an affair with a teenage girl. And if you don't think that's sensational enough, there's more. A Soviet military attaché has been sleeping with the same tart. Now there's a turn-up for the books, eh, laddie?'

Wow! I thought. Andrew Barnet really has been doing his stuff. It's barely twelve weeks since I tipped him off, and he's unearthed enough evidence for the *Express* to dare to go public with it, changing the course of history yet again. And I'm not even there to claim my fee!

'These politicians are all the same,' Warburton said, 'like the Kennedy brothers. Can't keep it in their pants. But it doesn't come much riskier than this one, does it? A member of your government sharing a girl with a Soviet spy. Holy mackerel! They're all at it, you know, these Russians. Their jobs at the embassy are just a cover for espionage, and for one lucky Ivan, that included the bonus of bedding a young – what do you say – popsy? Just think of the opportunities for pillow-talk! What was the minister thinking of?'

'God knows. According to my friend Harry, Russian agents are all over our state security services, even infiltrating the aristocracy. And, by the way, you were pretty close when you used the term, *Ivan*. The naval attaché's surname happens to be Ivanov. Oh, and get it right: the British minister's name is Profumo.'

'But it's not a good look, is it? The man is expected to announce his resignation today, and in the middle of the biggest international crisis since Suez. Holy Moses! The vodka will be flowing in Moscow tonight.'

'Well, Sergeant, I know it's a tall order, but if you could get hold of today's *Daily Express*, I'd be mighty grateful.'

'I'll see what I can do. A copy might arrive here tomorrow, but don't bank on it.'

It was now the 29th of August, and the TV networks were reporting dramatic scenes at the UN Security Council, where Adlai Stevenson was presenting photographic evidence of missile bases in Cuba, and demanding a response from the Soviet Union. That very day, as if to show their defiance, the Russians set off another gigantic nuclear bomb in the Arctic, and the following morning came news that a second US spy plane had been shot down over Cuba, and the pilot killed.

'They've gone too far this time,' said Warburton. 'We'll be bombing the anti-aircraft bases any day now.'

'I reckon you'd do well to keep away from Cuba,' I said.

'For your information, laddie, we have a permanent presence on the island – well, on forty square miles of it. It's called Guantanamo Bay. Naturally, Castro wants us out, reckons it's an illegal occupation, but there's nothing the bugger can do about it. Every year we send him a cheque for the rent, and every year he refuses to bank it, because to do so would be tantamount to acknowledging our right to be there. But guess what? The revolutionaries happened to cash one of our cheques by mistake, and that, as far as the US is concerned, ratifies our lease. Now that, you must admit, is bloody hilarious!' He roared with laughter.

'So, can you trust your president to stand up to the Russians?'

'Our Jack? How would I know? He's already presided over one disaster, the Bay of Pigs. We trained over a thousand Cuban exiles to go home and overthrow Castro. At first Kennedy supported the invasion, then he bottled out. He failed to send vital air support when it was needed, so the poor sods didn't stand a chance. It was all over in less than three days, leaving Castro with hundreds of prisoners as bargaining chips. That's not my idea of strength. If the invasion had succeeded, we wouldn't be in this diabolical mess now, would we?'

I didn't know what to think. I was witnessing a parallel version of history, where events were unfolding some weeks earlier than had been the case in my memory of the 'original' 1962. The Soviets were in a hurry. Things could turn ugly very fast. Nuclear disaster isn't supposed to happen by accident, but could anybody be sure of that? All it takes is a few Castros, Khrushchevs and Kennedys – and their backers – together with a large helping of misjudgement and distrust. When Cuba turned communist the Russians could hardly believe their luck: an ally in the western hemisphere, with the potential to draw more of Latin America into the Marxist camp – and, more immediately, the opportunity to tip the balance of power in the region, by installing doomsday weapons within close range of America. Much of the US could be threatened. Medium range missiles based in Cuba would have the potential to devastate targets as far north as southern Canada. However, as if to put a spanner in the nuclear works, someone in England seemed to know what they were doing, even before they'd done it. There must have been a mole at work in the highest echelons of Russian power. The nuclear armament programme had to be accelerated. Eastern Bloc ships were arriving in Cuba almost daily, and work on the missile systems was proceeding with indecent haste. A deadly race was underway, with no certainty as to who would be the winner. In fact, no one could win, but the whole earth could lose.

Sunday, September the 2nd, brought a dramatic development. There had been rumours from early morning that the president would be making a special statement on radio and television later that day. As the time approached 5 p.m. at Andrews, 2 p.m. on the West Coast, people began to gather around their TV sets. When Mr Kennedy did appear he was in sombre mood. He had a momentous announcement to make; not exactly a declaration of war, but a threat of unilateral action against a foreign power on the high seas, unprecedented in modern peacetime. In view of the unambiguous evidence of the installation of medium range nuclear missiles in Cuba, he was proclaiming a quarantine zone around the island, backed up by a rigorous blockade by US forces. Any Eastern Bloc ship carrying military materials would be stopped, using whatever force was necessary. He accused Khrushchev and company of duplicity, citing their repeated denials of 'what clearly is happening in Cuba'. He advised his fellow Americans to remain calm, stay put and be vigilant. 'Our resolve remains firm,' he said. American forces were now on their highest state of alert.

'Just watch,' said Warburton. 'We blockade Cuba, they blockade West Berlin. They did it before, in 1948.'

The following day brought reports of panic-buying on a massive scale, of food stores emptying and gasoline stations running dry. Late that morning, CBS broadcast an interview with a family in Boston, loading their car ready to flee to relatives in the rural midwest. 'We're not hanging around for the nukes to arrive,' said the mother. I guessed that would be the cue for numerous others to follow suit. Come to think of it, what was I doing at Andrews? An obvious target for a bomb!

In mid-afternoon, the UN Secretary General, U Thant, called on both sides to agree to a cooling off period, to avoid an outbreak of hostilities. Within hours the word from the White House was that the President had rejected U Thant's proposal, because it would leave the suspected nuclear weapons in place. 'We have to know that they are taken out of service,' was the official line.

On Tuesday, September the 4th, the news bulletins were dominated by a single theme. Television channels were giving as much information as they could, including maps purporting to show the positions of Soviet ships approaching the quarantine zone.

'One of them is clearly an oil tanker,' said an 'expert'. 'Is that a legitimate target or not? Its hatches are probably too small to accommodate missiles or nuclear warheads.'

Sergeant Warburton seemed to know more than the TV pundits. 'They say the latest reconnaissance pictures are stunning, laddie. Clear enough to confirm that some SS4s are fully operational, and poised for launch.'

Who could be feeding him this stuff? Surely it was classified information. But now I had to admit it: I was scared, *very* scared. Even if I could have got out of here days ago, what would have been the point? London would be no safer than Washington if the whole thing blew up. I reflected on Simon's advice: 'Just stand up to them and they'll skulk away.' You'd better be right, buddy.

As evening came on I was too wound-up to sleep, and that was probably true of half the US population. The TV channels stayed on all night, and off-duty personnel at Andrews were glued to the screens. By four o'clock on the Wednesday morning tiredness began to get the better of me, and I slouched off to my room, where I was asleep in a matter of minutes.

CHAPTER 27: Consequences

A door slammed nearby, wrenching me from sleep. The morning sun was glinting on my window pane. Sweating profusely I sprang out of bed in a single movement, and grabbed the nearest clothes. A few minutes later I found Warburton putting the finishing touches to his breakfast.

'Hi, laddie! You overslept? I was about to come and get you.'

'Why, any news?'

'Plenty. The eyes of the world are focussed on what's happening off the Florida coast.'

'Have the Russians turned back?'

'Not yet. The convoy isn't showing any signs of stopping. It's sailing straight toward the quarantine zone, with the leading ships expected to cross the line by midday. But our forces are ready.'

'Aren't the two sides talking to each other?' I said. 'Surely some sort of compromise can be worked out.'

'With Khrushchev? I doubt it. If he wanted to negotiate, he'd be turning those ships around right now. And in any case, I seem to remember you giving the president some advice on TV not so long ago. Didn't you tell him, *No deals?*'

'Yeah, but surely he wouldn't take any notice of me! And in any case, I didn't really mean it. I was only…speculating.'

'What? It's a bit late for that now, laddie!' He nodded toward the TV. 'All normal programmes have been cancelled. CBS is covering the story non-stop.'

I glanced at the screen. The camera panned along a busy highway thronged with vehicles of all shapes and sizes.

'These people are as panicky as you are,' chuckled the sergeant. 'See, they're driving off into the desert because they're scared of the Russians.'

'How can you be so flippant? Don't you know what a modern war would do?'

'Don't worry, laddie,' he said. 'There's an air-raid shelter two hundred yards from here. But it's not fallout-proof, so don't forget to take some plastic sheets and sticky tape to seal the gaps.'

I was relieved when he finally went, leaving me to have my breakfast in peace – a kind of peace, guilt-ridden as it was. Could I really have changed the course of history to this extent?

Two hours later Warburton returned, now in a more sombre mood.

'The marines are about to board a Soviet vessel. This is when it starts to get serious.'

I'd no idea how he knew about the boarding party. It hadn't been mentioned on CBS. The commentators had speculated endlessly about such tactics, but Warburton's information was more specific.

'A shooting match could start at any moment,' he said, no longer his usual relaxed self. For the first time I could detect tension in his voice.

'How will we know if the fighting has begun?'

'We'll know alright,' he said. 'For one thing, the president won't want to linger in the White House. You can guarantee there's at least one intercontinental missile permanently targeted on Washington. He'll be brought to this airbase by helicopter. I don't know if you've seen it, but since last year there's been a special plane based here, called Air Force One. Supposedly the president can continue to govern the country from the air if there's a war.'

I remained glued to the television coverage through most of the afternoon. The most dramatic news came soon after three o'clock, when there were reports that a US destroyer had opened fire on one of the Soviet ships. There followed an hour of speculation about what this would mean, before a further report saying that one of the American vessels had been torpedoed. There was desperate talk about the need for de-escalation.

At 4:45 p.m. a siren began to wail. Warburton bellowed from the doorway. 'Follow me, laddie! Quick, run like hell!'

'Run? Where?'

'To the damned shelter, of course!'

Everyone was running. I ran, head down, guided by the concrete wall to my right, with the entrance to the shelter still eighty yards away. Then it happened – a brilliant flash from somewhere over to my left. I was blinded, scorched, and moments later it was as if a huge hand hit me. For a split second I knew I was being flung sideways through the air toward that wall.

CHAPTER 28: Elaine

My bedside telephone rang, waking me with a start. I had to force my eyes open. Morning light was streaming through the thin curtains to my right. I reached for the receiver and fumbled to get it to my ear.

'Hi, Dad! Happy birthday!'

'Huh…what? Oh, hi, Elaine. What time is it?'

'Nine o'clock. You're not still in bed, are you?'

'Er—'

'That must have been one hell of a retirement party last night. I'm sorry I couldn't be there.'

'Retirement? Last night? Oh, yes…I must have had too much to drink.'

'That's not like you, Dad. I had you down as more of a tea drinker.'

'Well, I don't know…it's been a funny sort of night.'

'Anyway, it is your sixty-sixth today, so I was wondering if we could meet up at lunchtime. I'm free from one till two.'

'Er, yes, of course.'

'What about the *Trip?* I know it's your favourite Nottingham pub.'

'The *Trip?* No, not there. What about the *Sal?*'

'The *Old Salutation?* Are you sure you can make it? You don't sound at all well.'

'I'll do my best.'

'Okay, I'll see you at five past one.'

I staggered out of bed and moved over toward the small window. Cautiously parting the curtains, I peered out. My Toyota Corolla was in its usual place, parked on the driveway of my retirement bungalow. I quickly let go of the curtains in case someone out there should spot me, although I didn't quite know why. The folks in the village were excellent neighbours. I just wasn't ready to confront another soul as yet. Turning back toward the bed I caught sight of my face in the mirror on the dressing table. It came as a minor shock to see myself completely bald. My hair had slowly ebbed away over the years, so why was I suddenly missing it now?

I ambled across the hallway and into the kitchen. Dazzling sunlight was reflecting off the stainless sink. Hanging on the wall to my left was a calendar, open at June 2010, and yes, the third, a Thursday, was my birthday. I'd marked it with a large blue B, next to the bold R marking 'retirement' on the previous day. The radio on the window ledge seemed to be inviting me to switch it on. I wished I hadn't. They were discussing a massacre that had happened only yesterday, right here in England. It was headline news, twelve people shot dead by a taxi driver in Cumbria. Derrick Bird had first killed his twin brother before going on a rampage through three communities near the coast. I quickly turned the thing off and returned to the bedroom to sort out some clothes for my trip into Nottingham. Casual-but-smart would be the order of the day. I didn't want to disappoint my daughter by appearing to have let myself go, simply because I no longer had to turn up at the weedkiller factory.

'You've made it, then,' Elaine said as I greeted her outside the pub. 'When I called this morning you sounded as if you were dying. Either that, or you'd just woken from a bad dream.'

'Maybe I had. But don't worry, I'm feeling much better now, although I must admit, waking up today was a very strange experience.'

'I guess that's what retirement does for you, Dad. That sudden relief – or is it emptiness – when you know you won't have to go to work ever again? In either case, I always had the impression that you didn't really enjoy your job; something about the stench of chemicals. You must have been looking forward to today for a long time.'

'You're right, for a very long time. In fact, ever since I was an apprentice.'

'Surely not! Wishing your life away like that.'

'No, I exaggerate. After all, many of the chaps who were apprentices with me are dead now. Maybe it was those very chemicals that killed them – either that, or the tobacco. I guess I'm lucky to still be alive. I just wish I'd done more with my life.' I looked at her with a hopeful smile. 'But thankfully there's still plenty to look forward to, like greeting new arrivals—'

Elaine was the only redhead in the family. I'd been hoping she would have produced a grandchild for me by now, but I'd have to be patient a little longer. I knew that she and Robin aimed to start a family eventually, but for now her career came first.

'Who knows,' she said with a wry smile, 'you may be lucky one day.'

We found a secluded corner in the *Old Salutation*. The bar was quiet, and in little more than five minutes we were comparing our drinks, a long-standing ritual.

'Your verdict?'

'Disappointing,' she said. 'Seven at best.'

'Blame me. I chose the pub.'

Elaine was cradling the cup in her hands and studiously inhaling the aroma. A self-appointed connoisseur of coffee, she'd developed a habit of grading her caffeine experiences on a scale of one to ten. Eight was quite good, nine exceptional. Nothing had yet achieved ten. That pinnacle was held in reserve for the notionally perfect coffee, if such a thing could exist.

'Definitely a seven,' she confirmed. 'Typical of pubs. Why don't they invest in decent beans?' She stirred in an extra sugar. 'Anyway, is the cider up to scratch? I noticed you asked for a whole pint today. I've only ever known you drink halves.'

'The cider? Well, it is my birthday.' I took a sip. 'It's perfect. So, how's the estate agency doing?'

'Still struggling, I'm afraid. The full effects of the 2008 crash haven't worked their way through the system yet. Even now, house prices are well below the peak they reached two years ago. No chance of a bonus this Christmas.'

'Then you should divert your attention elsewhere. How about writing *A Guide to the Coffees of Great Britain: where to discover the finest on offer*? It could be a bestseller.'

She ignored my suggestion and reached into her bag to pull out a small parcel. 'Anyway, Dad, here's your present.'

By its size and weight I guessed what it was.

'Well, aren't you going to open it?'

'Let me hazard a guess,' I teased. 'It's not about gardening is it?'

'No! Credit me with a little more originality than that. It's by an American professor who has a new take on twentieth century wars. I know you love history, so here's your chance to read an alternative one.'

'An alternative history? I'm intrigued.' I began to slide the book out of its wrapping. The title read, *World War and Cold War: a new perspective*, and below it, the author's name: Dr Kurt Dreschel.

'Crikey, Elaine! What the—'

'You don't mean you've already read it?'

'No.'

'Then why the shocked look?'

'Oh, it's nothing, but thanks, darling. You can't begin to imagine how mesmerised I am by that title. In fact, I'd love to meet the author and discuss his theory with him.'

'Then you're in luck. He's currently on a lecture tour of Britain to promote his book, and I happen to know he's at Nottingham University this very evening. A couple of days ago he was featured in an article in the *Evening Post*, which prompted me to buy the book. Other than that, I know nothing about him.'

'Listen, I absolutely must be at tonight's lecture. Any idea what time?'

'Let me check.' She took out her phone. 'Here it is. He'll be speaking at seven o'clock, in the Trent Building.'

'Right, I'll be there.'

Suddenly I thought of something else. 'Oh, and while you're on that new-fangled device, could you look up a name for me? Do a search for *Chapman Pincher*.'

'That's an unusual name. There can't be many of those... Yes, here he is. It says he was known as "The Lone Wolf of Fleet Street", and worked to uncover Russian spies in the British Secret Service. He even believed that the Director General of MI5, Sir Roger Hollis, was an agent of the Soviet Union. And *wow*! It gets worse. He suspected the Labour Prime Minister, Harold Wilson, of being one as well.'

'Is Pincher still alive?'

'Let me see…yes, he's now in his nineties. Why, have you met him?'

I ignored the question. 'And while you're still on the internet, would you mind looking up another name? *Edgar Lustgarten.*'

A few more flicks of those nimble fingers and she'd found what I wanted.

'Lustgarten? One-time president of the Oxford Union, he was a barrister, crime writer, and hosted numerous TV programmes in the fifties and sixties – serious ones by the sound of them. Died in 1978.'

She put the phone down. 'Why the sudden interest in these men? I can't imagine that someone who's spent all his working life in chemical factories would have crossed paths with many people like them.'

I chuckled. 'Is that what you think of me? Little more than a peasant? Listen, young lady, don't talk your old dad down. Just because you've made it as an estate agent – and by your own admission, a struggling one – you've no idea what I got up to in the sixties, when these characters were in their prime.'

'Well, whatever it was, it's all behind you now.'

'Yeah, and I'm glad it is.'

I glanced around. The bar was now crowded with people on their lunch break. 'Aren't these places so much more pleasant now that smoking has been outlawed?'

'The smoking ban?' she said, looking surprised. 'It came into force three years ago. It's taken for granted now. Keep up, Dad.'

Elaine downed the remainder of her coffee. 'So tell me, how are you planning to spend your retirement?'

'In brief, by keeping out of trouble and enjoying each day as it comes.' I stared into my half-empty cider glass, uncertain whether to drink the rest. 'But first, I aim to be at that lecture this evening.'

CHAPTER 29: Confrontation and Conciliation

I made my way to the Highfields campus well in advance of seven o'clock. It was a pleasant place to wander on a summer's evening. After pausing to watch the waterfowl on the lake I ambled up to the Trent Building and took my seat in the lecture room. I feared Dr Dreschel might be disappointed with the turnout, as there were only thirty or forty of us in the audience. The first thing I noticed when he entered the room was that he was nearly as bald as I was. He gave us all a friendly smile and began his lecture, delivering it entirely without notes or audiovisuals. To describe it as spellbinding might be a slight exaggeration, but it was one of the best talks I'd heard in a long time.

His thesis was as follows. The two greatest threats to Western democracy in the first half of the twentieth century were national socialism and Soviet communism. Although they were sworn enemies of each other, they had much in common. Both were totalitarian in nature, subordinating the rights of the individual to the interests of the state, using whatever brutality they deemed necessary to enforce their will. The free nations of western Europe and North America had nothing to gain by allying with Stalin and waging war on Hitler, since the Fuhrer's great ambition was to expand eastwards and obliterate Bolshevism. It would have been better for the world if the Nazis had been allowed to attack Russia unhindered. Huge loss of life would have been incurred on both sides – which happened in World War Two, anyway – but it would have resulted in two tyrannical regimes wearing each other down, a fitting spectacle from the democratic West's point of view. The Germans probably would have been able to take Moscow and form a government there, but controlling such a vast country would have drained their resources. Nazism would have been fatally weakened and Bolshevism marginalised. As it was, the alliance of the free nations with the USSR meant that Stalin was able to overrun most of eastern Europe as the Nazis retreated, sowing the seeds for the grim Cold War that lasted for over forty years. An overall lose-lose situation for the Western democracies.

At the end of his talk Dreschel opened up the meeting for questions. Immediately a young woman at the back rose to her feet and screamed, 'Holocaust denier!'

'Sit down! Be quiet!' was the general reaction of the audience, but her tirade continued.

'I've studied your published works, Dr Dreschel. You've been methodical in documenting Stalin's supposed atrocities, but you've had relatively little to say about the savagery of Hitler's regime. From the massacre of Polish officers in the Katyn forest to the final assault by the Red Army on Berlin, you've concocted a misleading account of brutality by "Britain's ally in the war" – but do you even recognise the existence of the Nazi extermination camps?'

For a moment the professor's composure looked to be in doubt. The room fell silent as people awaited his response.

'I've never denied the reality of the Nazis' final solution,' he said, calmly, 'and I categorically reject the notion that I've ever "concocted" anything. I've always been "methodical" in my work as a historian – but I'm frequently accused of bias by witless communist sympathisers like you!'

At this the woman screamed an obscenity and stormed from the room, followed by two or three others who'd been sitting near her on the back row. Dreschel held his nerve and fielded a variety of questions for over half an hour. By then it had become obvious how much he detested the Russians. Perhaps that was the principal motivation for his 'alternative history' thesis. Eventually the rest of the audience drifted away, but I remained, my principal business yet to be done.

Dreschel squinted at his watch, gathered a few papers into his case, and made for the exit.

'Excuse me, professor—'

He didn't even turn to see who was addressing him. 'I'm sorry,' he said, 'I must be on my way. My train leaves within the hour.'

He was already through the doorway and heading along the corridor. I would have to intercept him in the next few moments, or the opportunity would be lost. I knew that a polite, 'I'd like to ask you a few more questions' wouldn't be sufficient to arrest his progress. I'd have to be a little more confrontational, even outrageous, if I was to stand any chance of making the contact I desired.

'It was interesting to hear your views on Soviet history,' I said, breathlessly, 'because the truth is, you're half-Russian yourself, aren't you?'

Without slowing his pace he glanced in my direction and curled his lip dismissively. Very well, I would have to be even more provocative.

'And you would never have known the truth, had your mother not told you shortly before she died.'

That did the trick. He stopped abruptly, and for the first time that evening the professor was speechless. He glanced both ways along the corridor, which was now almost empty, before whispering between gritted teeth, 'I'm sorry, say that again.'

'Before your mother died in 1962, she told you that you had a Russian father.'

I was fully prepared for him to take a swing at me, and was poised to dodge a flying fist, but, rather than provoking aggression, my words induced a state of profound shock.

'How can you possibly know that?'

'Then you agree I was right.'

'What is this? Blackmail?'

'No, sir. I'd like to think that I'm your friend.'

'Friend? Is this some kind of sick joke? Who are you, anyway?'

'Roger Parnham, retired industrial chemist.' I held out my hand toward him, but he shrank back.

'That explains nothing. No one, but *no one,* can possibly know what took place between my mother and I in those last days…unless that hospital ward was bugged. Yes, it must have been. But that was nearly fifty years ago. How has the recording surfaced now?' He glared accusingly at me. 'This is a leftist plot to discredit me, isn't it?'

'No, nothing of the kind,' I said, 'but may I suggest we go somewhere else to talk? Somewhere more comfortable than this corridor. What about the union bar?'

'But I need to call a taxi. My train leaves for Birmingham in fifty minutes' time.'

'I can give you a lift to the station if you like.'

He looked uneasy. 'This is a trick, isn't it? I bet you're not acting alone. There's no way I'm getting into a car with you. Heaven knows where I might end up.'

I did my best to assure him that this wasn't a conspiracy, and that I had no accomplices or malicious intentions. Also, that any information about his past would remain confidential. 'And no,' I said, 'there aren't any hidden recording devices in my car.'

'Very well,' he said, somewhat reluctantly.

His willingness to go along with my suggestion was chiefly down to his need to understand how an obscure English guy could *know the unknowable*. It was the greatest jolt of his life, second only to the original disclosure of how he'd been conceived.

When we reached my car, Dreschel insisted on sitting in the driving seat, so that no one could drive it away against his will.

'What do you know about my mother's final words to me?' he said. 'And how in God's name did you find out?'

'I'm sorry, Dr Dreschel, but I have to confess to a selfish motivation. I know it means stirring up painful memories, but this is the best chance I have of checking out the reality of something that happened to me recently. I can only say that the way I found out these things is extraordinary, but it certainly didn't involve secret microphones. Neither was I in the hospital. I've never been to the place.'

'Then how did you—?'

'I'm not at all sure myself, but let's say, I suspect information can travel through time in ways as yet unknown to science.'

'You're doing yourself no favours,' he said, 'peddling New Age nonsense like that!'

'I'm sorry if it sounds implausible, but it would be remarkable if our species knew everything about the nature of time, especially when it comes to the imponderables of consciousness and death.'

Dreschel was too unnerved to want to argue. I knew I risked causing him further anguish with my continued probing, but this was too good an opportunity to miss.

'You lost your mother to cancer when you were seventeen, didn't you? But before she passed away she told you how she'd been attacked by Russian soldiers in 1945.'

He rested his forehead on the steering wheel and looked down at the floor.

'How did you react to that revelation?'

'I was devastated,' he said. 'Almost suicidal.'

'So you went home, saw your mother's car in the garage, and decided to take it for a spin.'

'You seem to know everything, Mr Parnham.'

'Actually, I don't. This is precisely where my knowledge runs out. Would you be willing to tell me what happened on that drive?'

'I might as well, since you appear to know everything else. I was acting irresponsibly, of course, and I'm only glad that I didn't hurt anyone. It was getting dark as I tore along the country road, and when I approached the bend I was going far too fast to retain control. Swerving to avoid an oncoming car, I skidded into a creek, where I would have drowned, if the guy in the other vehicle hadn't dived in and dragged me clear.'

'Do you know who it was who saved your life?'

'He was a young fellow called Simon.'

'Simon! Not Simon Blake?'

'You *do* know everything!'

'No, that was just a lucky guess, a kind of coincidence,' I said. 'But did Simon ever tell you why he was out driving that night?'

'I seem to recall he was on his way to meet a childhood sweetheart.'

'That doesn't surprise me.'

'Ah! It's becoming clear to me now,' Dreschel said. 'You've been in contact with Blake. He's your source of information, isn't he?'

'No, it isn't like that at all. In a sense, I've never met Simon, and he certainly doesn't know me. But tell me, are you still in touch with him?'

'Hardly. We haven't met for years. He moved to the west coast. And in any case, I don't rub shoulders with many multi-millionaires. The last thing I heard was that he had serious heart trouble. He might be dead for all I know.'

'But, if you don't mind me saying so, from those traumatic beginnings you've done pretty well for yourself, haven't you? A respected authority on European history.'

'That was largely down to the help of friends. With my mother gone, I had no one in the world, no relatives whatsoever outside of Germany at least, but the family of a school buddy took me under their wing until I went off to university.'

'Your friend, was his name Gerry?'

'There you go again, Mr Parnham. You'll have me believing in telepathy before you're done! Yes, it was Gerald Grant, and we're still the best of friends. I'll always be indebted to his parents.'

'Tell me, Kurt – if you don't mind me calling you that – can you remember anything else from 1962?'

'That's a ridiculous question, if I may say so. Assuming you're familiar with my work, you already know the answer. I've published numerous papers on what became known as the Cuban Missile Crisis.'

'Then you'll know how the situation was defused.'

'I certainly do, and I was quite sure of the truth long before the American public became aware of it.'

'The truth?'

'That's right. In the prevailing folk myth, a courageous young president faced up to Nikita Khrushchev, and the Soviet leader was the first to blink. Kennedy called his bluff, a risky strategy, and won, and so became the hero of the free world.'

'You say *myth*?'

'Yes, because it wasn't like that at all. Early on I suspected that the two leaders had reached some sort of compromise. Khrushchev would remove his rockets from Cuba on the understanding that Kennedy did likewise with similar weapons threatening the Soviet Union. You see, the Americans had their own nuclear missiles based in Turkey, close to the border with the USSR. It was a close-run thing of course, but as the Soviet supply ships approached Cuba, contacts between the superpowers allowed an understanding to be reached. I couldn't prove it for a long time, and it suited the US administration to let people believe the Russians had bottled out in the face of American resolve. In fact, when Bobby Kennedy, one of the key players, wrote his own account of the crisis, he implied there was no offer to withdraw the Jupiter missiles. It wasn't until the Cold War was over that the American side officially admitted that JFK had done a deal with Khrushchev. Without that *deal*, that willingness to compromise, who knows what might have happened!'

'Yeah, who knows?' I echoed.

'And within months of that confrontation, the famous "hotline" was established between the White House and the Kremlin, in the hope that the world could never come as close to disaster again. So, Khrushchev had a bad press in the West for many years, as the heartless bogey man, but I'm convinced he didn't want a war. He *never* wanted one. It was he who famously said something like, "In the next war the survivors will envy the dead". I reckon he was just as honourable a man as Kennedy, but happened to come to power in a country with a tradition of despotism rather than democracy.'

I was struck dumb for a moment. Was I hearing this from Dreschel's own lips? Khrushchev the virtuous, from the arch-Russophobe? Amazing! Of course, I reflected, he was speaking of Khrushchev *in comparison with* Kennedy. His remarks might imply a higher-than-expected appraisal of the Russian, or, equally probable, a lower one of JFK.

'Remember,' Dreschel continued, 'it was Khrushchev who first pointed out the nakedness of the emperor, when he stood up before the Communist Party Congress in 1956 and denounced Stalin as a tyrant. Stalin, arguably the greatest mass-murderer in history.'

There was no doubting the contempt in his voice as he uttered that last statement.

'Oh, I don't know,' I said, 'he's up against some pretty stiff competition.'

Dreschel glanced at his watch. 'I really do need to catch that train.' He shuffled out of the driving seat. 'I'll let you drive me to the station.' I felt honoured.

'Look, Roger,' he said as we sped into Nottingham, 'we must keep in touch. Email me when you get home.' And later, as I dropped him on the station forecourt, he issued an invitation. 'You must come to see me in Boston some day. Ever been to the States?'

'Hmm...yes and no.'

'I'm guessing that's a typical response from you,' he chuckled, and turned as if to go, but with a final backward glance, asked, 'What are your plans for the future?'

'Well, I've only just retired,' I said, 'but already I've had enough excitement to last me a lifetime. I guess from now on I'll do my best to keep out of trouble, and resist the urge to meddle in matters I don't understand.'

'I'm sure that's a good strategy,' he said, then smiled, waved goodbye, and disappeared into the station.

ACKNOWLEDGEMENTS

would like to thank Rosemary Kind, of Alfie Dog Limited, for her
encouragement and invaluable advice and support through the process
of preparing this work for publication.

Thanks are also owed to my dear friend Neville Seabridge, and to my
niece, Enid Instone Brewer, for reading through the story in its late
stages and making important suggestions as to how the text could be
improved.

I also thank my son-in-law, Matthew Byrne, for valuable legal advice
connected with the publication of this book.

Finally I would like to thank my granddaughter, Ellie Robinson MBE,
who, through her own passion for writing, unwittingly prompted me
to re-draft the original version of this story in January 2021. Without
that stimulus, I very much doubt if *No Deals, Mr President* would ever
have appeared in print.

Printed in Great Britain
by Amazon